1st Edition

J. N. Chaney
Copyrighted Material

This novel is a work of fiction. Names, characters, places, and incidents are either products of the author's imagination or used fictitiously. Any resemblance to actual events, locales, or persons, living, dead, or undead, is entirely coincidental.

www.jnchaney.com

THE VERNAL MEMORY

BOOK 4 IN THE VARIANT SAGA

J.N. CHANEY

For Rob,

A human.

BOOKS BY J.N. CHANEY

The Variant Saga:

The Amber Project

Transient Echoes

Hope Everlasting

The Vernal Memory

Renegade Star Series:

Renegade Star

Renegade Atlas

Renegade Moon

Renegade Lost

Renegade Fleet

Renegade Earth

Standalone Books:

Their Solitary Way

The Other Side of Nowhere

CONNECT WITH J.N. CHANEY

Join the conversation and get updates in the Facebook group called "JN Chaney's Renegade Readers." This is a hotspot where readers come together and share their lives and interests, discuss the series, and speak directly to J.N. Chaney and his co-authors.

https://www.facebook.com/groups/jnchaneyreaders/

He also post updates, official art, and other awesome stuff on his website and you can also follow him on Instagram, Facebook, and Twitter.

For email updates about new releases, as well as exclusive promotions, visit his website and enter your email address.

https://www.jnchaney.com/variant-saga-subscribe

Enjoying the series? Help others discover the *Variant Saga* by leaving a review on Amazon.

CONTENTS

ACKNOWLEDGMENTS

I'd like to extend my appreciation and love to all the people who made this series possible. First, to my family, whose supportive words have continued to help drive me forward. To Sarah, who has been a constant inspiration to me as I have delved more and more into this mad world. Next, to James, Boyce, Geoff, Dustin, Nick, Heather, Dylan, Josh, Leslye, Brad, Steven, Vickie, Travis, Stephanie, Jessica, Jennifer, Valerie, and all the many people who have helped me along the way. To my beta readers, who have proven useful and encouraging throughout this entire series. Finally, to Rob, a true friend and one of the most talented people I know, whose council and advice has helped forge the finer points of this tale, and for whom this book's dedication is deservedly given.

I could not ask for better people to have with me on this

great journey, and while we may not always talk, know your actions have made an impact on this work and my life. It is only because of you that these pages exist, and it is because of you that others will follow.

PART I

There can be no tyrants
where there are no slaves.
–Jose Rizal

A good deal of tyranny
Goes by the name of protection.
– Crystal Eastman

PROLOGUE

IN THE MIDDLE OF A RAGING SEA, a lone ship slipped between the towering waves. The strong winds raged, and thunder cackled in the night, taunting the boat with its ferocity.

"It is a good night to be at sea!" cried the captain of the *Waveguard*, beating his chest to the song of the storm. The rain blew hard into his face. "Tonight we are alive!"

This was a ship known in many harbors, for none had such a crew. Its captain, a legendary wavemaster, had traveled most of the known world, seeing more than most men could dream. Yet here, amidst this wild and natural chaos, he was truly in his element.

"Shall we circle back, sir?" called Sederin, a newer member of the crew. He'd joined several months ago, but had only made it through a few storms, and none so fierce as this.

"Do not be fooled by this tempest!" shouted Hux, staring out into the storm. "She means us no harm."

"Yes, sir!" answered Sederin, a confident smile on his face. It was the look of a man who had complete faith in his leader.

"Have the others head into the cabin," ordered Hux. "Tell them to secure our passengers. Stay on deck until everyone is clear."

"What about you?" asked Sederin.

"I'll join them soon," he bellowed, turning back towards the sea.

The crew scrambled to leave, having secured the storm sails and cargo. They'd ride out the remaining winds safely from within.

Hux would follow soon, but not yet. He was made for this, born and bred in saltwater waves.

He took a deep breath of the thick air, and smiled.

The *Waveguard* had recently passed through the border of Everlasting, a forbidden kingdom on the other side of the great wall, probably to no good end. Probably to death.

It was the realm of the gods, the host of the great Eye, the golden city on the hill. No place in all the world was more mysterious or dangerous. One of the last uncharted frontiers. For these reasons and more, few men had dared to venture here, to the land beyond the walls. The world would call him a fool for this, a witless man of senseless delusion and risk.

Hux grinned a wild, mad smile as thunder echoed against the horizon's edge, and he let loose a mighty bellow of a laugh. Let them mock him for daring to live. Let them call him a fool!

He would see the gods, themselves, and rest his spear upon their necks. Let the deities of Everlasting come and try to stop him. Let them greet him at the gates.

With all his strength and spirit, he would resist them.

For Hux was a wavemaster of the sea, which meant he could not be ruled. Not by any man alive, nor god on Heaven's throne.

Rain beat against his face, and he sat atop the bow, fighting heavy winds. Despite his lust for adventure, Hux still had a mission, a reason for his destination—to rescue Terry, a friend and ally, who'd been stolen to the other side of the wall, seized by some monstrous creature.

A Guardian of Everlasting, protector of the gods…or so the legends had said.

But Hux was, in his own view, a real seeker of truth, not so eager to believe in fairytales. He would sail and see with his own eyes. He would fight.

"Captain!" called someone from the cabin door.

Hux turned at the voice and saw a broad-chested man waving at him. It was Ludo, a farmer, and one of the *Waveguard's* newest passengers. "Aye!" responded Hux, leaping down.

"One of your crew has fallen. They require assistance," said Ludo.

"How bad is it?" asked Hux, entering the door with him.

"Ysa says he will live. It's only a few cuts."

"If it isn't bad, why did you call for me?" asked Hux.

"Because you were sitting out in a storm like a madman, you fool," said Ludo. "Something had to be done about it."

Hux laughed. "Aye, I am a fool, I suppose. I signed up for this mission of yours, didn't I?"

"An action I do not take lightly," said Ludo, looking him in the eye.

"You asked me to help you rescue an innocent man…a *good* man, I should add. I couldn't turn you down," said Hux.

The ship jerked, and they each held the rail for a moment. "Regardless, I thank you, sir," said Ludo, standing straight.

"None of that!" laughed Hux, slapping the farmer's back. "Not from a man who fought a Guardian and lived. You call me by the name my mother gave me."

They entered the lower deck, which was filled with cots and benches, crewmates scattered throughout. Ysa, Ludo's wife and a former priestess of the Eye, sat with a stack of bandages, tending to the injured crewman. She was a quiet woman, but deadly, gifted with enough power in her to rival a small army. Hux didn't know a man alive who could kill a woman like that.

The ship lurched and Hux grabbed one of the nearby pillars. Ludo stumbled, catching himself on a bench. "Watch the storm," laughed Hux.

"I don't know how you do this," admitted Ludo.

"It's easy. You just need to train your legs to love the sea," said the wavemaster.

The outer door swung open, and Sederin came inside. "Captain!"

"What kept you?" asked Hux.

"Sir, there's something in the water. I saw it not far from us. Some sort of object coming out of the sea!"

"Wind and rocks, that's all," said Hux. "The waves rise and fall…create illusions in a storm like this."

"It wasn't a rock, Captain. It moved on its own, and there was some kind of light."

"A light?" asked Hux.

"Green, like nothing I've ever seen," said Sederin.

"Show me," ordered Hux.

"You're going back out there?" asked Ludo.

"Only for a moment. Stay here and watch the others," answered the captain. He followed Sederin, stopping a few times whenever the storm tossed the ship. A shower of hard rain hit them as soon as they opened the door.

Sederin grabbed hold of the railing to steady himself, then pointed starboard. "It was over there!"

Hux saw nothing, but he knew better than to jump to conclusions. He scanned the horizon, observing the roaring waves of the black sea, letting his eyes adjust to the storm, staring through the chaos.

Beneath the surface of the darkened sea, a glimmer appeared, growing brighter. It lifted higher, becoming clearer, before finally breaching.

Surrounding it, a large body rose from the roiling waves, standing far above the ship's mast. Towering over everything, steady in the heavy winds, the monster raised its tentacled arms high into the sky. Its daunting green eye shone on the distant cliff near the shore, scanning to the left and right, as though it were looking for something. "What in the world is that?" balked Hux.

"Is it a Guardian?" asked Sederin.

Ludo stood behind the captain. "It's not like the others. This one is different."

"We need to turn the ship around," said Sederin. "There's still time to flee!"

"Won't it see us?" asked Ludo.

"Quiet down," said Hux, lifting his arm to silence them. "We're anchored now, and there's space between us. The storm is too strong to risk a move."

"But staying could be suicide," said Sederin.

"Quiet yourself, boy," ordered Hux, keeping his eyes on the lurking fiend in the water. "You'll give us away."

The Guardian twisted its glowing green eye to the north-east, the opposite direction of Hux's ship, and then paused. It lingered there a moment before slipping back into the storming sea, submerging completely.

Sederin opened his mouth to say something, but Hux motioned his hand to quiet him.

The sky lit up, roaring a thunderclap so loud it shook their chests. The cackle startled the other men, but the seasoned captain would not be moved. He could sense the coming threat. He could feel the waters shift. "Nobody move," he whispered to the other two.

"What is it?" asked Ludo.

The planks of the ship shuddered with the slightest of movement. The others might interpret it as part of the storm, but such was not the case. The water beneath the boat had been displaced. "The monster is moving below, passing to the other side. Remain completely still."

"Beneath us?" Sederin's eyes widened.

"Still your feet," Hux whispered, to which his crewman obliged.

Seconds later, an emerald beam of light rose from the nearby waves, piercing the clouds. The Guardian revealed itself once more.

Sederin took a step back, nearly collapsing, when Hux grabbed him by the shoulder, keeping him still. The three men stood motionless, staring into the breadth of the goliath, insects before a god.

The Guardian's green eye swept across the waters and onto the beach, darting between the trees. It waited there a moment, then plunged into the waters from which it came, tossing the ship and forcing Sederin and Ludo to the deck floor, while Hux caught himself on the railing.

Hux let out a hand to Ludo, who took it. "Easy," said the captain.

"It didn't see us," said Ludo.

Sederin got to his feet, a look of both wonder and panic across his face.

"I'd wager it's looking for something," said Hux.

"It completely ignored us," said Ludo. "I've never seen such a thing."

Hux nodded. The beast had left their vessel alone and untouched. Either the Guardian had not seen them or it was more concerned with something else. "Perhaps it thinks us unworthy of its time. We are but men, after all."

"What sort of world have we come to?" asked Ludo, staring where the Guardian had gone.

"You asked me to take you to the realm of the gods," Hux told him. "I should say, we've finally arrived."

1

Ortego Outpost File Logs
Play Audio File 1287
Recorded: March 21, 2351

***HARPER**: The second delivery should be leaving Central tomorrow afternoon. We had to wait for the storm to pass through here before proceeding, hence the delay.*

***CURIE**: There's no helping it. We couldn't afford to lose the cargo.*

***HARPER**: You're not wrong about that. Those injections take time to produce, so it'll be at least a week before we have another out your way.*

***CURIE**: I understand. I'll make certain everyone gets their assigned dose. They're all pretty excited about it.*

***HARPER**: Are you sure they understand what you're asking them to do?*

***CURIE**: I'm planning another briefing as soon as the supplies arrives, but I think we're all on the same page.*

***HARPER**: Just make sure you remind them about the limitations. This isn't a permanent solution to Variant, but it's close.*

***CURIE**: I'll make them take notes if I have to. Don't worry.*

***HARPER**: Good. With any luck, these inoculations might be the last step in finding an actual cure to Variant.*

***CURIE**: Do you think we're really that close?*

***HARPER**: If you'd asked me a year ago, I would have said there was no chance. However, after everything we've seen, I'm staying optimistic.*

End Audio File

Garden Headquarters
March 21, 2351

SOMEWHERE UNDERGROUND, deep beneath the streets of Everlasting, Terry sat with his back against the wall. He watched in silence from the corner of a claustrophobic room as a dozen rebels unloaded armfuls of stolen weapons. It was not the first time such a thing had occurred in the few weeks since his arrival, nor would it be the last.

"Trouble?" asked a female voice. He turned to see the armored soldier Jinel Den standing over him, her rifle firm against her chest.

"What?" He blinked.

"You look troubled," she told him. "Or are you nervous about the mission? Don't worry. I'll be fine." She laughed.

"I should go with you," he said, eyeing the rifle. "That way, maybe you could avoid a full-on firefight."

"We already talked about that, remember? You're staying out of the enemy's sights."

"I'm faster and stronger than all of your soldiers. I could get in there and do what you need without being seen. You wouldn't have to—"

"You're too valuable to risk like that. I can't have you getting caught. It's not worth it."

He pressed his lips together in frustration. She was right, of course. If the Leadership dissected him, found the key to his strength, they'd start engineering their own hybrids. It wouldn't take long for them to create an army and wipe out all of Garden's resistance.

But he also hated the idea of both sides slaughtering each other. It all felt so pointless.

One of the other rebels called for Jinel from across the room. She waved at them. "Time for me to go," she said, glancing at Terry.

"I just want to help," he muttered.

"And you will," she assured him. "I'll find something you can do. Something important."

He watched her join the rest of her team and leave. The bustling interior of the base suddenly grew much quieter as the two dozen soldiers disappeared into the hall toward the exit. In their place, a few analysts worked quietly in the corner, waving their hands against an invisible display only they could see. Even here in this underground bunker, Everlasting's advanced technology was abundant.

"How's the floor?" came a woman's voice. It was Lena Sol, standing a few feet away, smiling down at him. "Isn't it cold?"

He gave her a wry smile. "Should you be walking around with a hole in your chest?"

"I'm feeling much better now, thank you." She sat down next to him, wincing a bit.

"Liar."

"What about you? How are you feeling?"

He shrugged. "I'd rather not be here, stuck in the ground."

"You must be eager to see your friends again."

"Yeah," he whispered, staring at the floor.

She frowned. "It isn't going to be a simple thing, getting you to them. Everlasting's monitoring systems have the entire domeguard under scrutiny. Even an insect would have a hard time slipping through."

"We'll find a way. Every day, Jinel and her people try to break the system. Maybe today they'll get lucky and succeed."

Lena gave a slow nod. "Perhaps."

"You don't seem very confident."

"The system is secure. Without proper credentials, penetration is impossible."

"I take it you don't have any."

"Not personally. After my inquiry into the database, my access credentials have been expunged."

"You're sure about that?"

"Jinel Din has already checked."

"That's too bad. Garden could have used the help," said Terry.

"I suppose so."

"You suppose?" he echoed.

"I apologize. Of course, I find it unfortunate."

"No, please, say what you wanted to say," said Terry. "What's on your mind?"

She hesitated, but went on. "I only mean that, if you'll pardon my candor, we know so very little about this organization. There is much to learn about their goals and ambitions. We only have the information Jinel Din has seen fit to share, which admittedly sounds very encouraging, but—"

"You don't trust her?"

"I do, but her testimonial is only one of many. I would like very much to question the other members of Garden before coming to any definitive conclusion. I would certainly prefer to believe they are working for the benefit of Everlasting, but at the same time we have witnessed their violence firsthand. It leaves me…uncomfortable."

"Fighting is like that," said Terry.

"I suppose you understand better than I do."

He wanted to tell her she was wrong, that no one really understood the point of war, but decided to leave it alone.

"I was glad to see you heal so quickly. I have to admit I'm a little jealous." She glanced at her shoulder.

"I'm sorry you got dragged into all this."

"Don't be," she assured him. "I might complain, but I find all of this quite stimulating."

"How's that?" he asked.

"Finally knowing the truth about the Leadership," she said. "Or part of the truth, I suppose. There might be more to come. There might be less."

"The truth?"

"The Leadership tried to tell everyone Garden didn't exist. They actually went so far as to claim Jinel Din had been killed rather than admit she joined the rebellion. I wanted to believe they had their reasons, but the more I talk to the people here, the more I question the Leadership's motives."

"I'm sure you'll find your answers eventually."

"I am certain you are correct," she answered, giving him a faint smile.

Terry wished he had the right words for her, but he couldn't pretend to imagine what she was going through. "How about we get something to eat?" he finally asked.

He pushed himself up, then let out a hand to her. She took it, biting her lip from the pain in her shoulder. "Thank you."

"Jinel told me they confiscated more of that fruit you like. What's it called?"

"Jesotni. The miracle fruit. Is that the one you mean?"

"That's the stuff," he said.

Her face brightened immediately. "Oh, how wonderful."

"I figured you'd like the sound of that."

"They're back!" called one of the sentries guarding the outer door. He gripped the handle and turned it clockwise.

Jinel Din and her team piled into the base as quickly as their feet could carry them. Blood covered most of their uniforms. Two of the soldiers carried a body between them—a man Terry recognized as Kaelin Thad, whom he had met only a few days ago. From what Terry could remember, the boy was only about sixteen years old.

Kaelin moaned in pain, his eyes covered in a cloth, soaked in his own blood. "They're coming!" yelled the boy, flailing his head and arms while his friends tried to keep him steady. "They're coming to kill us all!"

"Quiet him down!" ordered Jinel to one of the medics. "Give him something to make him sleep. Hurry!"

An older man ran to the boy's side. "Hold his arm out," he said.

Terry watched as Kaelin went limp a few seconds after the injection.

"What happened to him?" asked Terry.

Jinel shook her head. "Ambushed."

The doctor removed the rag from the young soldier's face, examining the wounds. "Get him to the regeneration unit immediately."

"Will you be able to fix the damage?" asked Jinel.

The doctor cleared his throat. "The machine can only regrow so much. It cannot replicate entire organs."

"Keep me informed, please," said Jinel.

"Of course," responded the doctor. "Though, he may need a transplant. His left eye is completely gone."

The other soldiers took the incapacitated boy away.

"The hell was wrong with his face?" asked Terry.

"A grenade exploded," explained Jinel.

Lena was standing a few meters behind Terry. "Might I ask what the purpose of your mission was?"

Jinel cocked her brow. "I don't think so, Analyst."

"You still don't trust her?" asked Terry.

"No, I don't," the soldier said, rather frankly. "She's only been here a few weeks. Besides, you need to earn that kind of trust."

Lena raised a finger. "If you'd allow me to—"

"I don't have time for a debate," said Jinel. "Kaelin needs looking after. Excuse me."

They watched her leave into the hall toward the medical bay. "Don't worry," Terry said when they were alone. "She'll come around."

"Perhaps so," said Lena in a defeated tone.

"Hey, come on. You wanna take a walk with me around the halls?"

She smiled at the invitation. "Yes, please."

The afternoon dragged while they waited for news on the wounded soldier. Terry hadn't spent much time with Kaelin, but he'd seen him around. Hopefully the doctor could do something about the pain.

Terry and Lena had volunteered to assist in cleaning and organizing the pantry. Mostly, they did it to keep themselves occupied. Aside from watching the occasional assault team come and go, Garden was a little dull. Officers like Jinel, when they were around, spent much of their time planning and handing out orders. Since neither Terry nor Lena could leave or participate in any of the missions or projects, they were left in the base to carry out inconsequential tasks. Terry had complained about this a few days ago, citing boredom and a willingness to participate, but Jinel simply said it wasn't time. "I am working on something for you," she kept telling him. "A few more days. I promise."

Those days had passed now, and Terry wanted answers. How long was he supposed to stay in this underground cage before they let him do something? How long before they let him in on whatever it was they were doing? *Maybe they never will,* he thought, not for the first time.

"What are you thinking?" he heard Lena ask him.

"Nothing, sorry," he muttered, snapping out of it.

Lena smiled at him. "I don't believe you."

He scratched the side of his jaw. "I was just wondering how long we need to stay down here before they start telling us their plan."

"I suspect it will be some time, given our outsider status."

"I hope you're wrong," he said, and he let out a yawn.

"Are you tired?" asked Lena.

"Annoyed, mostly" he admitted. "And drained, I guess. Frustrated."

She said nothing as he headed to his bunk—a box of a room that he suspected used to be a closet. After closing the door, he sat with his back against the wall and shut his eyes, letting his mind drift to another world—the one inside his head.

Suddenly, he was sitting in a field, feeling the soft winds of a familiar valley. Ludo's farm stood in the distance, the light from the two suns reflecting off its windows. This was so much better than the cold underground of Garden, with its lifeless Spartan design. Terry hated living in a hole. Ever since he first walked out of the ground as a child and saw the light of the true sky with his own eyes, he never wanted to go back. He never wanted to be trapped again.

At least in here, deep inside his own mind, he would always be free. He'd always have this sky.

Terry's door opened in the early hours of the morning, forcing him awake. "Get up," said Jinel Din, clad in her armor, standing in the archway. "There is something we must discuss."

"What is it?" he asked, wiping the grime from his eyes.

"An important matter which cannot wait." She tossed him a fresh shirt. "I'll be in the conference room when you're ready."

She left him alone to gather himself. He glanced at a small device on his table, which told the time of day. It was still before the first sunrise. What could she possibly want from him so suddenly, and at this hour? *Maybe it's about John and Mei,* he thought, trying to be optimistic.

Despite knowing he shouldn't, Terry rushed through the halls with anticipation. He rounded the corner to the conference room door. When he arrived, he tapped gently on the door.

"Enter," said a muffled voice.

As Terry cracked the door open, he noticed Jinel Din sitting at the far end of the table. Two others sat in the adjacent chairs —Morgan Thur and Vivia June, two of Garden's most prominent commanders. Morgan, a stout woman with broad shoulders and thick arms, boasted her rifle on the table, gently tapping its butt with her thumb. Vivia, who was far less physically intimidating than her companions, had a thoughtful, serious look in her eyes.

"A bit small, isn't he?" asked Morgan.

Terry looked at Jinel. "What is this about?"

"Welcome," said Vivia June. "Terry, is it?"

"It is," he answered.

"Look at his ears," said Morgan.

"Round, like the other humans," said Vivia.

Terry cocked his brow. "What do you know about humans?"

"Not as much as I'd like to," said Morgan, glancing at her weapon.

"Everyone, please stay on point," said Jinel. "This isn't why I called this meeting."

"Apologies," said Vivia.

"So, what is this about?" asked Terry.

Jinel cleared her throat. "You'll remember I mentioned I was working on something you could help me with. This is it."

"Does it have something to do with my people?"

"Not quite, I'm sorry to say. We're still trying to figure out a way to contact the other humans, but I could use your help with something else, if you're willing."

"I'm not killing anyone for you," said Terry.

Jinel nodded. "That's good, because that's the last thing I want."

"Since when are you about nonviolence?" asked Terry.

"None of us wants to kill anyone," said Vivia.

"We only do it because we must," Jinel agreed.

Terry said nothing.

"Sit, please," she went on.

He did as she asked, minding the hard stare coming from the other two women. "I can't promise anything until after I hear the plan."

"Of course," said Jinel. She turned to Vivia. "Go ahead."

"You'll recall your encounter with the sentry unit near the border wall," said the woman.

An image of a mechanical beast flashed before his eyes. Metallic, strong, and with swords for arms, it stood as high as a building. He'd watched it kill a priestess with a single blow. "You mean the Guardian."

Vivia glanced at the others, a clueless expression on her face. "Is that what the natives call them?"

"If memory serves, they think of them as gods," recalled Jinel.

"Not gods," corrected Terry. "More like monsters."

"Oh, that's right. They think *we're* the gods," said Jinel.

"In any case," continued Vivia. "You managed to disable one by yourself. A remarkable and *uncommon* feat."

"Uncommon?" asked Terry.

Morgan Thur laughed. "She means it's never been done."

"Right," said Vivia. "In any case, there remains some curiosity on the nature of this accomplishment. We have the recording, so we've seen the battle ourselves. It's—"

"The recording?" asked Terry.

Jinel nodded. "We have a plant inside the Tower of the Cartographers. That's how I knew where to find you when you were taken."

"Do you have a lot of moles inside Everlasting?" asked Terry.

"We have enough," said Jinel. "Let's leave it at that, shall we?"

Vivia leaned forward. "Terry, I have a few questions I need you to answer about your encounter."

"Which part?"

"The weapon you used. Can you tell us about it?"

"You mean the sword?"

She nodded.

"A friend of mine gave it to me as a gift," he said, thinking of Plead. "Why?"

"Was it made of a certain material? Something unique, perhaps?"

"Sure," he answered.

"Can you be more specific?"

"Plead said it came from overseas. A place called Tharosa, I think."

"Tharosa? You mean the northern country in the mountains?" asked Vivia.

"Right. He said the smiths who made it came from somewhere else and settled there." He tried to remember the details. "I think they were called Carthonons?"

"*Carthinians*," corrected Vivia. "They were exiled from Lexine. I don't know if there are any left, though."

"We'll have to check the database," said Jinel.

"That's if the records are even up to date," interjected Vivia. "Our contact at the Citadel still hasn't responded to—"

"Vivia!" snapped Jinel. "Please, contain yourself."

"Apologies." The strategist stiffened.

"You can't reach your contact?" asked Terry.

Jinel glared at Vivia. No doubt, the two would have words later. "Don't worry about that. They're late sometimes. It's to be expected."

"If you can't contact them, what are you going to do?" he asked.

"The database can be accessed in other ways. It'll just take longer. Don't worry."

"Why not ask Lena for help? She must know a thing or two."

"Lena Sol has yet to prove herself loyal to Garden. We cannot afford to give her access to the network without knowing her true character. I'm sure you understand, but steps must be taken for everyone's safety. If it takes longer to achieve our goals, so be it."

"But—"

Morgan Thur slammed her fist on the table, startling everyone in the room. "Enough of this," bellowed the general. "My men are waiting for me. Hurry and get on with it, Jinel Din. He told you where he got the sword, so let's end this meeting and be done with it."

"Hold on, what's all this about, really?" asked Terry. "You drag me in here, reference some footage you watched of me fighting, and then drill me about a sword I no longer have."

"Wasn't it clear?" asked Vivia.

"Wasn't *what* clear?" asked Terry.

"The Leadership's sentries are a serious threat to Garden," explained Jinel. "We called this meeting because we need a way to stop them. Your sword seems like a possible solution."

"You don't have weapons that are better than a piece of metal?" asked Terry.

"Most of Everlasting's weaponry consists of ancient technology which predates the Cataclysm. The sentries…or Guardians, if you prefer the term…are from that era as well."

"And according to our sources," continued Vivia June. "The Leadership can no longer reproduce these sentry units."

"They can't make any other Guardians?" asked Terry.

"Indeed. You see, the sentries were originally constructed

with a certain metal alloy—an exceptionally rare and nearly unbreakable material known as orinchalium." Vivia raised her finger towards Terry. "The very same used to craft your sword, in fact."

Terry pictured the weapon he wielded against the titan Guardian. He could still recall the grip between his fingers. The pressure he felt when he stabbed the monster. The scream of the man inside its chest.

"If you haven't deduced it by now, the only type of material capable of breaking the sentry's shell is the same metal with which it was built," said Vivia. "The only problem is that no one knows where to find it. Even Everlasting hasn't been able to locate a proper source."

"How's that possible?" asked Terry.

"It's one of the rarest materials on the planet. Everlasting is a powerful nation, but there are limits to its reach. The Rosenthal Satellite can only scan so much of the planet, particularly below the surface. Even if there was orinchalium beneath our very feet, we would have no way of finding out."

"We know the southern tribes have shards of it, largely taken from ancient ruins and wreckage," explained Vivia. "However, a handful of daggers would hardly accommodate our needs. We need more."

"Much more," added Jinel.

Terry thought about his fight with Zika and the other priestess. "Even if it's not a lot, that's gotta be better than nothing."

Vivia shook her head. "We have no way of tracking each and every shard the natives have in their possession, nor do we have the time for such an undertaking. Unlike the Leadership, we have no satellite uplink or floating citadel to guide us in our search. For that matter, we do not have the paralyzing toxin to subdue the natives, should they resist our requests. Only the Leadership has access to that."

Jinel sighed. "Besides, a few dozen knives would hardly be enough. We need the source."

"What would you build with all of that?" asked Terry.

Morgan raised her hefty rifle. "Bullets," she said with some eagerness. "Fastest way to shut them down."

Her tone was unsettling, but he ignored it. "So, what's your plan? Attack Tharosa and hope they have the metal?"

"We would never wage war against anyone but the Leadership," insisted Vivia. "What kind of organization do you think this is?"

"Since you don't talk to me about what you're doing, I don't really know, now do I?" he asked.

They dismissed him, and he returned to his room to rest. Maybe these people were on the right side of this war, but they sure didn't act like it sometimes. There was a hunger here for vengeance, for blood. He didn't blame them for that, but as long as they kept him in the dark, there wasn't much he could do to help them.

2

Ortego Outpost File Logs
Play Audio File 1301
Recorded: March 21, 2351

MITCHELL: *Based on the research notes acquired by Doctor Curie from Simon Landis's team in Central, I am certain the inoculations will prove successful. Having been a student of Doctor Archer's work, it seems fitting Landis should be the one to develop a proper deterrent to the Variant gas. Compared to the rest of his peers in the genetics department, he is certainly the least useless of the lot, though perhaps a bit self-indulgent, having named the drug after himself in a shallow attempt at immortality.*

Regardless, the inoculation remains only a temporary fix, so more work will be needed soon if it is to act as a true and long-lasting treatment.

Currently, the medication will allow the user to breathe the atmosphere for approximately eight days without hindrance, requiring periodic renewals every six to seven days to maintain immunization. I find this to be most impressive, but it is only a step forward, not a solution. Landis explains in his notes that the process has been refined to the furthest possible extent, lending his doubts to the notion of any future adjustments.

For this reason, Curie has suggested we continue on with Landis's work ourselves, searching for whatever gaps he may have overlooked in his own research up to this point. No doubt, Landis will reject the idea outright, claiming perfection, but he would do well to read his history carefully.

Innovation often requires more than a single perspective if it is to achieve its true goal. We build our future on the backs of yesterday's giants. It is the only way humanity knows how to move forward.

It is the only way in which we can survive.

End Audio File

Central
March 21, 2351

SERGEANT JOHNATHAN FINN stood at attention inside the office of Colonel Avery Ross, the head of the military and one of the most powerful people in all of Central. He'd been called here for a single reason: to discuss the current situation in Everlasting, an advanced city on the planet of Kant, and how it could potentially affect the future safety of the rest of humanity.

"At ease, Sergeant," acknowledged Ross. She motioned for him to take a seat, so he did.

Another man was standing to John's side. Captain Thistle,

his direct supervisor and former team leader. "We've already covered the basics. Let's hear what you think, Finn. What's the assessment?" he asked, taking a seat next to John.

"It's rough over there, but things are easing down. The Leadership's got those rebels on the run, last I heard."

"That's Garden, right?" asked Ross.

He nodded. "They pop up and attack, but disappear before the military can move in on them. Their tactics make it hard to predict where they'll go next, but the city has been wired with surveillance cameras, and the Leadership has stationed soldiers everywhere. It seems like every attack Garden makes, it only gets less effective."

"Terrorists," muttered Thistle, almost in disgust.

"Maybe, but we don't know the situation. It wasn't that long ago that we had our own little insurrection, if you'll recall, Captain," explained Ross.

"That was different," said Thistle.

Ross took a moment before she continued. "I wouldn't be so quick to condemn them. Not yet, anyway."

"Ma'am?" asked John.

"Terrorists never think their cause is unjust. It's all a matter of perspective. George Washington fought against a government he believed to be tyrannical and wrong. He attacked the enemy at night on Christmas Eve, slaughtering them like cattle in their sleep, and it was hailed as a great victory by the American people. Had you asked the English, they might have told you otherwise. They might have said that what he did was cruel and cowardly, since it was customary for each side to set down their arms on this holiday. If the American rebellion had failed, the history books would likely have called Washington a traitor. But as we know, that's not how it went, and Washington became a great figure in history. You see my point. It's all about perspective. Maybe Garden is the same as Washington. Maybe they have a cause worth fighting for. For all we know, there's something else going on inside that city. Something corrupt."

"You think the Leadership is hiding the truth?" asked John.

"You've been there. What's your opinion?" she asked.

It was a tough question to answer. John had met with the Leadership several times, but had learned so little about them. The only real friend he'd made during his time in Everlasting had been Lena Sol, one of the city's analysts, but she'd all but disappeared a few weeks ago. The last he heard, she was promoted and transferred outside the city. "I honestly don't know," he finally admitted. "They kept us pretty isolated when we were there, except during the attack. Even then, none of us could speak the language."

"That shouldn't be much of a problem now that we have a few of their translators," said Ross.

"Not enough for everyone, but it's been useful," said John.

"The Science Division is working on their own. We should have something ready in a month or two. I'm sorry." She sighed. "I know that's not helpful, Sergeant."

"No, please, I appreciate it," said John, giving her a bright smile. It wasn't Ross's fault that these things took time, so he wouldn't bother getting upset. He'd deal with the situation as it unfolded. The translators he already had at his disposal would have to do.

Besides, Mei and Sophie were already working on learning the alien language on their own. It might be slower than using a device, but it was still progress.

"Before you leave for Kant, there's one last thing," began Ross.

He paused. "Is something wrong?"

She held up a hand. "Nothing like that. I just need you to understand something."

He looked at Thistle, who gave him a knowing nod. "Of course, ma'am."

"The situation placed before us is unprecedented, so I would caution you as we move forward. Assisting Everlasting with their medical research is the primary mission here. If it can be avoided, you must do your best to abstain from any confrontation with one of these foreign organizations. That means both the Leadership and Garden. Of course, the future is never entirely predictable, so I will expect you to use your own judgement. If a situation arises in which you have no other choice, then do what you must. Your job, as always, is to ensure the safety and security of Central and all its people. At the end of the day, nothing else matters."

Ortego Outpost
March 22, 2351

John stood patiently before the portal, waiting for the latest shipment from Central to be moved into place. It was the second one today, actually, and came with several crates of inoculations for the Variant gas. Additionally, it contained a great deal of provisions, extra CHUs, and even a few special requests from various personnel, making for one of the largest orders since this mission began.

It was also long overdue. The Science Division's disorganization after the loss of their director had resulted in a strange power gap. Unlike the political revolution which took place within the ranks of the military, back when Colonel Ross managed to replaced Colonel Bishop, no one was around to do the same for Doctor Tremaine. Instead, the board took control.

As Mei had explained it, the board wasn't very organized and liked to avoid making decisions whenever possible. Without someone to oversee the flow of responsibility, the board let most of the power trickle down to the department heads. This allowed Mei to handle her team as she saw fit, but it also meant she wouldn't receive the added assistance from Central that she so desperately needed. Not at first, anyway.

Another woman by the name of Doctor Breslin Harper managed to step in at just the right time and do what needed to be done. She didn't become the new director, by any means, nor did she seem to want the title, but she did manage to get things moving again. Harper was the reason Mei's team grew in size, and she also opened communications between the military and the Science Division. This allowed the two branches to better develop and coordinate their operations on the other side of the portal, saving both John and Mei a bit of work. It made things significantly easier for everyone involved, but perhaps more importantly, it meant that somebody in the Science Division actually gave a damn about what Mei was trying to do. For so long, John had watched her work and toil to near exhaustion, all without any thanks or appreciation. It was good to know someone in Central had her back for a change.

"We're all loaded up, sir," said Meridy, a member of John's squad.

"Sounds good," replied John. He stepped next to the crates, which were resting on a large transport platform. Two flippies stood idle in front of the cargo, waiting to proceed through the portal. They would handle all the heavy lifting in the tunnels.

"Fire it up!" called Meridy to one of the scientists. A man named Arthur.

John was still acquainting himself with all the new people under Mei's supervision. He hadn't spent much time on this side of the portal since the influx of personnel, but he planned on learning all their names in time. Sure, it wasn't something he had to do, necessarily, but John had always found value in connecting with people and getting to know them. *It's like mom always used to say,* he thought. *You can never have enough friends.*

The portal came alive at once, swirling into a cloud of chaotic darkness. Seconds later, it slowed and faded. Now John stood before a door, brought forth out of nothing. Like Alice and the looking glass, he peered through it and into another world. Another universe.

"Time to go," he said, and in response the flippies began to move. They passed through the rift and into Kant, and John soon followed.

On the other side, Mickey and Track waited to greet them. "Welcome back!" shouted Mickey.

"Sorry to keep you boys waiting," said John.

The portal closed once everyone was on the other side. Meridy disembarked from the ramp and proceeded to guide the flippies to the outer hall, and then he gave Zoe permission to take over. She would handle the little robots now, remotely controlling them from the camp outside.

A few of Mei's people worked diligently on some of the nearby consoles. John greeted them before continuing.

He walked into the hall with Mickey and Track at his side. "We're heading back to Everlasting, along with this shipment," said John.

"Another trip to the big city? You spoil us, boss," said Mickey.

Track groaned. "Can we walk this time? That ship of theirs makes me sick."

Mickey scoffed. "You're crazy. Did you already forget about the monsters? Those ain't no razorbacks or gophers out there, you know."

"I'm not stupid," said Track. "I wouldn't go alone."

Mickey laughed. "It'd be suicide if you did! Right, boss?"

"Sure," said John, nodding slightly. The thought stuck with him as they went, and he couldn't help but wonder about the dangers of the jungle. As they made their way along the ancient corridors, John began to think about Terry. A picture of his friend, bloodied and torn, buried in the mud of this foreign place, forced its way to the forefront of his mind. *No, stop it,* he thought, shaking the feeling away. Dwelling in those fears would accomplish nothing. That wasn't how John did things.

Terry wasn't dead, he told himself. Not until he found a body. Not until he turned this planet over on its head. He would remain optimistic, the same as he always had.

Bravo Gate Point
March 22, 2351

"STAY STILL and this shouldn't hurt," said Mei, holding a needle between her fingers.

"Are you sure?" asked Mickey, a frightened look in his eyes. He wore a breathing apparatus over his nose and mouth, a soon-to-be relic of technology, should the inoculations prove effective. "What if something happens? How do you know it'll work?"

"Relax," said Track, standing near his terrified friend. "Doctor Curie knows what she's doing. Ain't that right, Doc?"

Mei looked her patient in the eye. "Trust me. I wouldn't give you something dangerous. The inoculation is designed to be harmless. Regardless of its effectiveness, it will pass through your body in little more than a week."

Mickey slowly nodded. "O-Okay."

Mei pressed the needle into the soldier's arm, injecting the liquid while keeping pressure on him. "There," she said, pulling it out and dabbing the puncture with a piece of cloth.

"I guess it wasn't so bad," muttered Mickey, staring at his arm.

"You're such a baby," said Track, smacking his friend on the shoulder. "I'm next, yeah?"

"Have a seat," said Mei. Each of the soldiers were set to receive the inoculation by the day's end. Barring any unforeseen side effects, the dose would provide them the ability to breathe the Variant gas, ultimately replacing the need for an external machine. Instead, their lungs would now be capable of filtering the gas directly, nullifying its toxicity completely. It wasn't a permanent solution, since the inoculation would only be good for a week, but it was a massive leap in the right direction.

Mei opened a small black box, which had six doses enclosed in it. She placed the empty needle inside and took out another.

Track grinned and presented his arm to her. "Can't wait to taste some of that air."

Mei remembered the moment she took her first breath of Variant, back when she was thrown into that awful chamber. She also recalled the second she stepped out of the Sling and onto the Surface, tasting pure Variant for the first time. She and her friends had spent their whole lives in Central, never fully understanding what awaited them up there, never knowing what was missing. That first breath was like a rush of life, filling her lungs with something new, and for the first time in her life, she felt fully alive. She felt like herself.

Mickey and Track would probably not experience any of

this. They weren't genetically engineered to process Variant in the same way that she was, so it was unlikely that any strong changes would occur. No enhanced reflexes, eyesight, or strength. Nothing to make them into super soldiers, but that was fine. Simply being able to breathe freely without the use of a device was its own reward.

"Here you go," said Mei as she injected Track with the needle.

"When can we take the breathers off?" asked Mickey, referring to the device on his mouth that kept him from suffocating.

"An hour, at least," explained Mei.

He frowned. "Aw, man. That's so long."

"Deal with it," said a familiar voice from behind Mei. A man she knew so well.

"Boss, you come to check up on us?" asked Mickey.

John placed his hand on Mei's shoulder as he stepped beside her. He looked at her and smiled. "I gotta make sure my boys are squared up. Who else is left?"

"I've taken care of everyone except Short and Hughes," said Mei.

Track motioned toward one of the CHUs. "Pretty sure they're in there."

"Guess we'll have to bring it to them," said John.

With the case of inoculations under her arm, Mei got to her feet. "You'd think they would want to get this done as quickly as possible."

"Pretty sure those two have other things on their mind." He gave her a wry smile.

"You think?" she asked.

He started walking. "Let's find out."

The camp bustled with activity, thanks to the new arrivals from Central. Doctor Harper managed to convince the board to expand the size of Mei's team from a mere four to a full twenty. This allowed the Ortego outpost to stay fully manned without taking away from her mission on Kant. Even better, it allowed her to bring Sophie and Tabata to the new location, much to their delight.

The new additions were surprisingly useful, too. Having them around let her accomplish more without straining herself with the minutiae. Looking back, Mei never realized how overworked she'd been during her time at the Ortego outpost. All those late nights and long hours seemed to blend together like a dream. Still, she wouldn't trade those months for anything. Bart, Zoe, Sophie, Travis, and even Tabata had become like family, each of them pushing the rest to succeed. Each believing in the dream.

When they arrived at the CHU, John gave three knocks on the door. "Open up!"

Mei could hear some hurried shuffling coming from the other side. "Ouch!" said a woman's voice, trying to whisper, but failing.

The door cracked open enough to reveal a set of hazel eyes. "Sergeant Finn," said Short, totally surprised. She had a blanket wrapped around her. "What're you doing here?"

"You missed your injection," he answered, nodding to Mei. "What's the hold up? You doing something in there?"

"No, I just fell asleep," she said, quickly.

John raised his brow. "Don't suppose you know where Hughes is, do you?"

Short's eyes flickered away from the door. "No, I haven't seen him."

"That's too bad. We've looked everywhere. Might have to send the boys out to look for him. I sure hope he's not dead." He glanced at Mei and winked. "Right?"

"It's true," said Mei.

Metal clanged from somewhere inside the CHU. "Dammit!" snapped a voice.

John grinned. "What's that in there? Got yourself a visitor, Short?"

The soldier squirmed. "No, it's, uh…" She frowned. "Oh, fine." She opened the door, revealing a man in the back corner of the CHU, his face covered with a shirt. He seemed to be struggling to get it on.

"Hey, it's Hughes," said John. "Short, did you know he was back here?"

She grimaced, closing her eyes. "Oh, God. Oh, God."

"Boss, is that you?" asked Hughes, trapped by his clothes. He finally managed to twist the shirt in the right direction, yanking it down.

"Sure is. Good to see you aren't dead after all."

"Heh," said Hughes, scratching the back of his head. "We're in trouble, huh?"

"I'm sorry, Sarge. I was gonna tell you. I swear!" insisted Short. "We meant to stop. It just got out of control."

John smiled. "What do you think, Mei? What should I do?"

She opened the box and took out one of the needles. "I say you cut their rations and separate them," she said, trying to sound casual. "Maybe send them home for further discipline."

"Wait, you're taking our food?" A look of terror fell over Hughes's face.

"Who cares about rations!" barked Short, eying her accomplice. "I can't get court-marshalled!"

John laughed. "Relax, you clowns. Nobody's going back home. We're just messing with you."

Hughes blinked. "Huh?"

"We both already knew about your little scandal weeks ago," said Mei. She took Short's arm and wiped a cloth to sterilize the skin. "John's just messing with you."

"But why didn't you say anything?" asked Short.

Mei inserted the needle into the woman's arm. She barely flinched.

"Been planning to bust you for a while, but didn't get around to it until today. I wanted to catch you in the act, too. It's more fun that way." He grinned.

"So you don't care?" asked Hughes.

"Depends. Are you both staying in this relationship?" asked John.

The two glanced at each other, speechless.

"It seems like they haven't had the big talk yet," said Mei. She put the needle back in the box and retrieved a second one.

"Here's the deal, and then you can talk it over—if you wanna keep this going, fine, but you can't be partners. I'll reassign Short to be Meridy's spotter. If you break off the romance, you can stay a team. That's the deal. Sound good?"

"Yeah," said Hughes, nodding slightly.

Mei took his arm and proceeded to give him the injection. "Good luck," she said.

John and Mei left the couple behind to discuss their potential future together, then headed straight to the supply CHU to store the inoculation box. As soon as the door closed, John laughed so much that his cheeks turned red.

"Did you enjoy yourself?" asked Mei. She couldn't help but smile. His laughter was infectious.

"Are you kidding?" he asked, wheezing. "I've been waiting to do that ever since we heard them that night in Everlasting!"

"You're crazy," she said, placing the box in one of the larger crates. "Why'd you let them off so easily? Isn't it a big deal to fraternize when you're in the same unit?"

There was a short pause, and then she felt his hand touch her shoulder. It slid gently down her arm. A moment later, he kissed her neck. She smiled and turned around to embrace him.

John leaned in and gave her a deep kiss, hard and full, holding her for a long time.

When they finally released, she saw him smiling, looking into her eyes with that intimate expression.

"What was that for?" she asked, her voice slightly above a whisper.

"Just a reminder," he said as his eyes flicked from one part of her face to the other, studying it.

"Of what?" she asked.

"We grew up together. We were teammates together. I can't fault someone for falling for their best friend. It happened to me."

"You're such a softy," she said, teasing, but kissed him anyway.

He smiled. "It's what you love about me."

After the Blacks had been inoculated, it was time to check their adaptability. Everyone lined up and, under careful observation from several of Mei's team, removed their breathers and attempted to take their first breath of Variant air.

Most of the soldiers were able to do this without issue, although Mickey seemed to struggle a bit more, due to some anxiety. "Just open your mouth and breathe," said Track, who had already taken the plunge.

Mickey stood with his breather off, holding his breath, somewhat terrified.

"I promise, it's easy," said his friend. "Look. In, out. In, out. You got this."

Mickey nodded a bit reluctantly. Closing his eyes, he cracked his mouth and took in a fast, deep breath, then immediately started coughing.

"What are you doing!" cried Track. "You were supposed to do it slow!"

Mickey continued to cough until he was blue in the face with tears in his eyes. "I didn't...mean to...ugh...it stings...!"

Mei watched this with some curiosity. "Are you okay?" she asked, knowing the answer before he could give it. Her reports indicated a 99% conversion rate, so for anyone to have a negative reaction to the drug would be rare.

Before Mickey could answer, Mei felt a tap on her arm. "Ma'am, if I could steal your attention for just a moment," said Sophie Mitchell, her longtime assistant and friend. "Inoculations have been distributed to the science team as requested."

"Are there any signs of rejection?" asked Mei.

"None," responded Sophie, almost disappointedly.

"Were you hoping for different results?" asked Mei, noticing the girl's tone.

"Some variety in reaction would have made for better data, I suppose," said Sophie, but then shook her head. "However, today was a success. I have yet to witness any negative reactions." She glanced at Mickey, who was now breathing normally, despite still looking terrified. "Even that one seems to have adjusted."

"We'll have everyone keep their breathers on their person for the foreseeable future," added Mei. "Just to be safe."

Sophie nodded. "Wise decision, ma'am. How long do you think it will take them to perfect the treatment?"

"You mean, make it permanent?" asked Mei.

"Quite so," said the assistant.

"I can't begin to guess. To be completely honest with you, I'm still surprised we made it this far, but maybe that's only because I haven't had the opportunity to sit down and analyze the drugs yet."

"When were you hoping to get started?"

"Tonight, actually. I need to learn everything I can about it before I leave for Everlasting."

"That gives us five days, I believe," said Sophie.

"Four," corrected Mei. "The Leadership asked us to arrive a day earlier. Apparently, there's a ceremony they wish us to attend."

"Then we haven't much time to spare. That is, if you'll allow me to help."

"Allow?" asked Mei, somewhat surprised. "Like that's ever stopped you before."

3

Ortego Outpost File Logs
Play Audio File 1339
Recorded: March 23, 2351

MITCHELL: *Regarding Lanrix, otherwise known as compound NX-20299-91, our initial analysis shows everything to be as it is described in Landis's notes. The drug allows the user to breathe normally when immersed in Variant, but its effects begin to degrade after a week, requiring periodic boosters.*

As expected, a solution was not evident upon our initial examination, but Doctor Curie remains optimistic. The fault, she says, is in the source of the data. Landis's research used several batches of cells from multiple humans and hybrids to achieve this end result, but he never examined anyone or anything from Kant. This was an understandable oversight, since our team did not discover Kant until Landis's work was in its final testing phase.

The difference between the purity of Variant on Earth and that of Kant is small, but still important to the native population's development. Thus, these native organisms are more adapted to the gas and could assist in discovering a better method of adaptability. However, this also means they are even further genetically removed from humans than, say, a kitoboro.

Regardless, this has provided Doctor Curie and I with a place to begin our work. Having already mapped several genetic sequences of Kant's animal population, we should be able to discover whatever is missing. We shall finish what Landis began.

End Audio File

Garden Headquarters
March 23, 2351

After weeks of living in the underground Garden bunker, Terry had developed a daily ritual. His morning routine was typical—wake up, groom himself, get dressed, and then get breakfast. He typically met Lena in the dining room at around this time. She'd quickly grown to be a close friend, and the two spent most of their time together. As outsiders to this place, they'd formed an early connection. Today, however, when it was time to meet for their morning meal, Lena was nowhere to be found.

Maybe something came up with Jinel, he thought as he ate his food alone. *Maybe she finally asked for Lena's help.*

After breakfast, Terry walked around the facility, which he would normally have done with Lena. They would discuss whatever activities they overheard from the other soldiers—anything they learned about what was happening outside. Sometimes she might ask him questions about Earth, which he was happy to answer, and he would do the same with her about Everlasting. She was one of the most intelligent people he'd ever met, always ready to talk about anything and everything, driven by a natural curiosity. By comparison, he was far simpler, though she never seemed bored by his stories. On the contrary, she seemed to take great joy from them.

Terry eventually made his way to the analytics room. This was where Garden analysts performed the bulk of their hacking, though they only had a handful of terminals at their disposal. To his surprise, he found Lena sitting there as well, quietly observing the technicians from the far back wall. "Hey," he said when he saw her.

"Good morning," she answered, but without the typical smile he was so used to seeing.

"I missed you at breakfast." He sat next to her, and together they watched the analysts.

"I apologize. I should have gone, but the thought of eating unsettled me," she said.

"You felt sick?" he asked.

"Perhaps." Her voice trailed with the word, growing distant.

He wasn't' sure what to say. Something was bothering her,

he could clearly tell, but the necessary words escaped him. If only he could understand—

"They have me again," said one of the analysts, waving his hand at the empty space above him. Each of them were using implants, so only they could see what they were doing. Lena had explained this to Terry a few weeks ago, but he still found it difficult to imagine.

"If they get too close, cut your connection. Follow procedure," said one of the others.

"Dropping the link," said the first analyst.

"Hold on. We might be able to—"

"I can't wait any longer. I have to drop."

Lena leaned a little forward, focused on the analysts, an intensity in her eyes.

"We lost it," muttered the second analyst.

"Apologies," said the first. "There was nothing I could do."

The other analyst sighed. "Try again. We have to find a way through."

Terry nudged Lena. "You know what they're doing?" he asked.

She nodded. "It would appear they're attempting to break into one of Everlasting's security nodes."

"Is that hard?"

"It depends on the level of security. The city's network is open to most citizens, so access is simple enough, but the Leadership uses several layers of encryption for each of its departments, all with their own unique validation checks. In other words, there is no universal access code. The system is compartmentalized."

"Did they do that because of Garden?" he asked.

"Not originally, but it would explain the recent network upgrades. I oversaw and participated in several of those, but we were never told the reasons. It makes sense in hindsight, however, that Garden would be the cause of such widespread changes."

One of the analysts threw his arms up in frustration, shaking his head. "We've tried this six times and nothing. I need a break."

"Keep going," said one of the others. "Jinel Din needs the data. You heard what she said."

Terry glanced at Lena. "Can't you do something?"

"I've been forbidden from engaging in such tasks," she reminded him.

"Even if you know you can do something?"

Lena said nothing.

Terry scoffed. He got up and went to the other analysts. Specifically, the only one he recognized. A man named Hob. "Hey, sorry to interrupt. Geno Hob, right?"

The man flinched, surprised to see him. He'd apparently been too engaged in his work to notice Terry and Lena sitting in the back of the room, watching. "Oh, yes. Hello. Did you need me for something?"

Terry shook his head. "I just wanted to ask, are you trying to get into a network? That girl over there knows how. She can help you."

Hob looked at Lena, curiously. "What?"

"She's a former analyst. She knows what to do," explained Terry.

"We are all former analysts."

"But the thing you're trying to break into, she helped build parts of it. She might be able to help you out."

They all turned around to see the girl on the floor. Hob raised his brow. "Why haven't I seen her before? Is she assigned to a different station?"

"She's only been here a few weeks. They haven't given her a job yet. Now, are you going to let her help you?"

"Are you certain you can get inside?" Hob asked her. "This isn't the main network."

"Which is it?" asked Lena.

The analysts exchanged glances. "The Master at Arms' personal account."

Lena blinked. "Master Lao? He has at least seventeen levels of security safeguarding his files."

"We are aware. Does that mean you can't do it?"

She approached them. "My implant ID is 77-4201-3LS. Patch me in, please."

"Very well," said Hob. He moved out of her way, allowing her to take his place at the terminal. His eyes dilated for a moment as he stood motionless. "There," he finally said, coming back. "You've been granted level-3 access."

She nodded. "Understood."

Terry watched from a few steps behind her as she proceeded to touch the air, making motions and performing unseen tasks that were exclusive to her own eyes. One of the other analysts stiffened as he stared at the space in front of him. "She's upgraded her account to level-8," he exclaimed in disbelief.

"Is that a big deal?" asked Terry.

"The most anyone here has had is level-5," said the analyst. "Only those closest with the Leadership are given this level of access."

Lena gave no response. She simply continued her work, moving through the network in some unseen digital world. This was her area of expertise, Terry knew. This was Lena Sol in her element, the same as any warrior using the weapon of their choice. It was clear from the expressions on everyone's face that, at least in this place, Lena Sol was without an equal.

After a few minutes, Lena sat up. Her eyes went back to normal and she relaxed. "The files have been delivered to your basket. I deleted the footprints as well."

"You're done already?" asked Terry.

"Remarkable!" shouted Hob.

"What is?" came a voice from the doorway. Terry turned to see Jinel Din watching the situation. She looked rather annoyed.

"This woman," answered Hob. "She was able to access the network and—"

"What?" snapped Jinel. "You gave her access to a terminal?"

"O-Of course," said Hob, who was quickly realizing his mistake.

"Calm down. Lena just helped you out. She did in two minutes what your people couldn't do all morning," said Terry.

"What did she do, precisely?" asked Jinel.

"The data you requested from Master Lao. We have it now, thanks to this woman," said Hob.

Jinel stared at Lena. "Is that so?"

"Given enough time, I'm sure you could have managed it. All I did was exploit an issue I found several months ago, but never had the chance to repair. There are several files that perform security checks when accessed. When a very specific series of these files is opened in rapid succession, it sends a series of checks to the account, sometimes resulting in a full reset. When this happens, the account level is randomized to anything between level-1 and level-15. I simply performed the necessary steps to replicate this until it provided the necessary results."

"You mean you exploited a glitch?" asked Terry, thinking he understood.

She nodded. "I had to do this five times before it worked properly, but once I had the appropriate access, the rest was simple."

"Impressive. I had no idea such a flaw existed," said Hob.

Jinel examined Lena with a look of reservation. It was clear she didn't trust her, even now, but she couldn't deny what Lena had done. "I need to talk with the analysts privately. Please, excuse us."

"I was only trying to help," said Lena before turning to leave.

As she reached the door, however, Jinel spoke again. "Analyst Sol."

Lena froze near the door. Terry could feel her heart racing.

"Thank you for the work," Jinel said, clearing her throat.

Lena smiled at the words, opening her mouth to say something in return.

"But if you do it again, I'll have you confined. Is that understood?"

Lena stiffened. "Of course," she answered, quickly.

"Good. Now, enjoy the rest of your day."

Bravo Gate Point
March 24, 2351

"I NEED A FAVOR," said Mei. She stood before John in the woods, having tracked him down in the middle of the afternoon, not bothering to call ahead.

He wasn't surprised, knowing firsthand how determined she could be once an idea crawled its way inside her head. She'd stop everything to see it done. No food, no sleep. Nothing until the job was finished and she found the answer she needed. By the look on her face, John could tell this was one of those moments. "Just give me the word."

"I need the DNA of a native. Someone born on this planet who can breathe Variant," she explained.

"Does this have something to do with the inoculations?" he asked.

She nodded. "I'm trying to make the effects permanent. We've been examining native animal DNA, but there's something missing. It's too foreign, but I think if we can find a humanoid, it could bring us over the line. We might solve it."

"Are you asking me to kidnap one of them?"

"Of course not," she said, appalled. "You don't have to do anything. Master Gel has some native blood on file in the Citadel. I just need you to help me get it."

"You could've led with that," he said, half-grinning.

She gave him a gentle pat on the arm. "Let's not dwell on the past."

He winked at her, then tapped his ear to radio the team. "Alright boys, let's pack it up and head home. Double time it to my position. Over."

"Thanks," said Mei. "What are you doing out here anyway?"

"I told you back in the lab before I left. You didn't hear me?"

"I don't remember that. Maybe I was distracted."

"You'd make a terrible soldier. Your situational awareness is awful." He laughed. "We're out here because someone reported movement, but it seems like it was only an animal. Brooks found a nest a little while ago."

"Anything we've seen before?" she asked.

"Another one of those bulletproof rhinos," he said, tapping his chin. "Something like that. Want me to bring it in?"

She considered this for a second, but shook her head. "We have other priorities for now."

"Right, your new mission," he said, wrapping his arm around her. "When do we leave?"

Garden Headquarters
March 24, 2351

TERRY WAS ALONE in his room, sitting with his back against the wall, completely still. He sat in the position he used to meditate, the optimal form for clearing one's mind of all outside thoughts and stimuli, the very same he'd used to explore the world inside his head. It also allowed him to focus his energy and his mind, heightening his senses and magnifying his reach. That was precisely what he was doing right now.

In a room on the other side of Garden, far removed from where he sat, two voices spoke of plans and war.

"I suggest you let the analyst continue," said one, which Terry recognized as Vivia June.

"Lena Sol is too close to the Leadership," said the other, who could only be Jinel Din.

"She's provided us with unparalleled access to the Master at Arms' files. Our people are good, but this would have taken weeks without her."

"We have no idea if she can be trusted yet," said Jinel.

"How else would you test her, then? She's no warrior. She

has no aptitude for combat. By giving us this information, she's effectively betrayed the Leadership."

"It could be a ruse," suggested Jinel.

"I'm not suggesting we lose our caution, but allowing her to assist the other analysts would certainly be useful. Besides, you know how close she is with Terry. I'm sure he would appreciate it."

"Maybe, but—"

Several loud thuds, like knocks, echoed through the room. Terry nearly flinched at the sound.

"What is it?" said Jinel.

The door opened. "I'm sorry to interrupt," came a man's voice. It sounded like Hob.

"Go ahead. We're listening," said Vivia.

"We've intercepted a message from Master Lao. There's to be a special ceremony in the Hall of the Leadership. Several key members will be in attendance. I have the time and names right here."

"Is this verified?" asked Jinel.

"It seems so. The transmission has the Master at Arms' signature."

"What should we do?" asked Vivia. "The meeting is happening tomorrow. That's too short notice to organize an assault."

"I'll take care of it," said Jinel.

"How?"

"Precision," she answered. "We'll keep the team small… take out who we can."

"Wait a moment. What other information do we have?" asked Vivia.

"Not much," admitted Hob. "We still don't have access to the other departments, which has kept our reach somewhat limited."

"It's good enough," said Jinel.

"But the cost could be significant if something goes wrong," explained Vivia.

"Don't speak to me of cost. If we believe there is a chance to cripple them, we have no choice but to take it. Hob, keep your analysts on this and let me know of further developments. Vivia and I will begin preparations."

"Understood," said Hob.

Terry felt pressure on him. Something on his shoulder. It tugged him away from the conversation, pulling him back to his room.

Terry opened his eyes. There was a woman before him, lurking over his bed. "I apologize for interrupting, but you weren't moving."

He blinked several times before he realized it was Lena. "Sorry," he mumbled.

"Were you…were you at your farm again?" she asked, some uncertainty in her voice. This wasn't the first time Lena had walked in on him like this. That was when he'd explained meditation to her. She didn't fully understand, which had surprised him since she was from Kant, but she'd done her best and shown respect. He wondered if this was how Ludo felt in the beginning, introducing someone to a new way of thinking. A new way of living.

"Not this time," he told her, getting to his feet. "I was listening to something on the other side of the base."

"What did you hear?" she asked.

"Jinel and Vivia. They're planning an assault on the Leadership."

"When?"

"Sometime tomorrow. They got news of a meeting. Some kind of ceremony. Hob told them about it."

"I-I see. He must have gotten it with the access I gave them." Her voice drifted, and her eyes fell to the floor. Was this guilt he was seeing? Did she think she was responsible?

"Are you okay?" he asked.

"It's nothing," she said, simply.

"Whatever they do, it's their choice. You didn't do anything wrong."

"Maybe, but…but if they die, it's because…"

He put his hand on her arm, then hugged her. To his surprise, he could feel her trembling. "You can't dwell on that. You were trying to help, but it's up to them how they choose to use it. That's how it is with people."

The floor shook as several troops marched through the hall outside his door. He only squeezed her closer. "They make their own lives. You have to make yours, too."

Mei was in the process of packing her bag. Just a few clothes and supplies to last the next few days in Everlasting. She had only meant to stay an afternoon, but Gel had asked for an extension. Apparently, he wanted to introduce her to the genetics team that would be assisting with all future research. There would also be some sort of ceremony.

She didn't care much for any of that. The sooner she returned to work, the better. "You're responsible while I'm away. Don't let the team slack off," she told her assistant, who stood near the door.

"You don't need to worry, ma'am," said Sophie. "I'll continue working until you return."

"I know you will," said Mei, and it was true. If anyone could be as obsessive about their work as Mei, it was Sophie. In all the time she'd known her, the girl had yet to disappoint.

As Mei finished, the CHU flat opened and Zoe stuck her head inside. "Ma'am, are you still here? Oh, there you are."

"Excuse me," said Bart, who was apparently behind her.

The two stepped into the CHU, rushing to Mei's side. "We thought we missed you," said Zoe.

"Still here," said Mei. "Are you two going to be okay?"

"We're not children," said Bart. "Well, maybe Zoe is."

"It's like you want me to smack you," returned Zoe. Before he could answer, she continued. "Are you sure you have to go yourself, ma'am? Short told me about what happened the last time they were there. It might be safer if you stayed behind and let Sergeant Finn handle it."

"I appreciate your concern, Zoe, but I'm fine. I'm actually not as fragile as I look," said Mei.

"See? I told you she wouldn't listen," said Bart.

Zoe frowned. "I'm just worried, that's all."

"Don't be," said Mei, letting her arms out, embracing the girl. "I'll be back in two days. You can always call if you need me."

"Or if we don't," added Zoe.

"Keep your head down," said Bart.

The Red Door waited in the field near the camp. When Mei arrived, John and his team were already strapped and ready to go. "Sorry to keep you," she said, climbing inside.

"Better late than never," joked Mickey.

John beamed a smile at Mei as she took a seat next to him. The cabin was completely full of personnel, mostly John's team. Mickey, Track, John, Hughes, and Short, each one fully armed and loaded, made for a powerful escort. Brooks' squad would stay behind to protect the rest of Mei's team as they continued their research during the next few days.

Mei was certain the trip would prove invaluable to her research. The native blood sample she went to retrieve almost certainly held the key to unlocking a permanent solution to prolonging the Lanrix drug.

But that didn't mean she wanted to take the trip. No, Everlasting was in a state of disarray right now. The terrorist organization Garden continued its weekly assaults on the city without reservation. Master Gel had assured her during their latest correspondence that the situation was under control, at least for now, and that their building would be protected.

Still, she remained cautious.

John nudged her arm. "Hey, you alright?"

She nudged him back. "Don't you worry about me."

"Wouldn't think of it," he said, grinning.

The engine suddenly whirled to life, vibrating the floor beneath Mei's feet. It lasted for a few short seconds before the stabilizers kicked in. "Looks like it's go time!" shouted Short.

"Great," moaned Track.

Mei stared out the window towards the camp. Sophie stood near the CHU that housed their lab, along with Zoe and Bart, and together they waved farewell. The ship began to lift off from the field, rising high into the clear sky. Mei kept watching the camp until it was gone.

4

Ortego Outpost File Logs
Play Audio File 1387
Recorded: March 25, 2351

MITCHELL: *As is often the case, I have lost myself to my work. It has been days since I had a proper night's rest, though not for lack of opportunity. I've chosen repeatedly to stay in the lab to work, to sequence strand after strand in search of a solution. The experience is simultaneously exhilarating and maddening, putting me in conflict with myself. Is this what Doctor Archer felt like when he was on the edge of his great answer? Did he ever falter…or did the addiction set in and drive him to the end?*

Passion is a powerful drug, I have found. When such a feeling overcomes someone, they may go without food or sleep, perhaps growing ill in the process. The basic requirements become chores, slight hindrances to the goal. They eat and sleep to live, but they live to find the answer.

With Doctor Curie in Everlasting during the next few days, the bulk of the work must fall to me. I'm not complaining, of course, but without Curie here to ground me, I worry the obsession could be problematic.

End Audio File

Garden Headquarters
March 25, 2351

Terry and Lena stood in the conference room before both Jinel Din and Vivia June. The two had summoned them here to discuss a proposition. "Thanks to you, Analyst Sol, we were able to uncover essential strategic information," began Jinel. "It is for this reason that we offer you the chance to continue your work with us."

Lena looked at Terry, almost surprised. "You're offering me a position?"

"To retrieve further information from the network, the same as you have already," explained Vivia. "Your credentials provided us with access to Master Lao's department, but the others remain impenetrable. We would like you to break them."

"I see," said Lena, growing quiet as she contemplated the proposal.

"You must decide quickly," said Jinel.

"What's the rush?" asked Terry.

"I'm leaving soon and I would like to get this finished before I do."

"Another mission?" he asked.

"That's right. In fact, it's because of Analyst Sol's work that this is happening."

Terry was surprised to hear her speak so candidly about it. He already knew the details of her plan, but she didn't know that. The fact she felt comfortable talking about it, however broadly, felt like a step forward. "Good luck."

She nodded. "We are about to strike a serious blow to the Leadership. Previously, I've made my reservations on allowing you to stay well known, but after these recent events, I believe you can be trusted. Prove me wrong, however, and there won't be another chance."

Lena paused to answer, and at first it seemed like simple contemplation, though Terry knew this was not the case. He could hear her heartbeat racing, feel her pulse as it quickened. She was truly nervous now, but her face didn't show it. "If I do this, I ask only one thing of you."

Jinel raised her brow. "Oh?"

"You've said before that you plan on helping Terry return to his people. Were you sincere in that promise?"

"I was and continue to be," said the commander, glancing at the boy from Earth.

"Then on the day you fulfill that agreement, I would like to join him," she said, looking quickly at Terry. "Is that okay?"

He smiled. "Of course it is."

"It may take some time, but we'll see it done. Do we have an agreement, Analyst Sol?" asked Jinel.

"We do," answered Lena.

Terry watched as Lena received her own workstation in the analytics section. Jinel explained a few things about how Garden's security took precedence, so she should avoid any unnecessary risks when it came to snooping around the network. Lena responded with nods and smiles.

Once ready, Lena took her seat and began acclimating herself with the equipment.

As Jinel began to leave, Terry raised a hand to get her attention. "If all of this was for her, why did you want me here?"

"Wasn't it obvious?" asked the commander.

He shook his head.

"She's your friend and I knew you wanted it."

"Oh," he said.

"That's not the only reason. I also wanted you to see how we reward people. If you stick around and keep helping us, you could go far in Garden."

"I can't do much if you don't offer anything."

"I know, and I'll have something for you when I return."

"From your mission."

"Yes. I won't be gone long."

She left him there alone, and moments later he could hear her yelling orders in the distance.

The assault on the Leadership was about to begin.

Hall of the Leadership
March 25, 2351

Mei sat with her people, waiting for the ceremony to begin. Today, the city would pay tribute to the people they lost on the day that Garden attacked. Gel had insisted she attend. Once it was over, he'd assist her in obtaining the genetic sample she needed. Mei didn't mind attending this sort of thing, but she couldn't help but feel delayed. She had a great deal of work to accomplish, after all, meaning every minute spent sitting here was another minute lost.

Master Trin raised his arm to signal he was about to speak. "Today we gather in remembrance of that fateful day. The day in which our lives were forever changed. The day when—"

John groaned next to her.

"Buck up," she whispered.

He frowned. "It's so boring, though."

She leaned on his arm and felt him relax. Together, they watched Trin continue his speech.

"The Leadership has ensured our city's future once again. I am thankful for the efforts of my fellow Masters, particularly our Master at Arms for staying vigilant in his effort to keep our streets secured."

Mei wasn't surprised that the Leadership had taken all of the credit, but it would have been nice to hear them comment on John and his team, especially since they were sitting right here and listening to all of this. She wondered if John cared, though. He'd never been big on recognition or personal validation. Besides, the Leadership had thanked them all in a private meeting a few weeks ago. Maybe that was enough for him.

She felt John suddenly flinch and rise a little in his seat. "What is it?" she asked.

He was slow to respond. "I thought I heard something, but…" he paused. "No. Nevermind."

"You're sure?" she asked.

He nodded, smiling, then nuzzled her head with his nose. She relaxed and squeezed his arm, letting her eyes wander around the room. John was a soldier, so he was always on high alert, she reminded herself. He was constantly searching for danger.

He turned to look somewhere to the left side of the auditorium, his eyes lingering on one of the doors. John's senses were far more acute than Mei's, not because she didn't have the natural inclination, but because she'd spent less time honing them. While Mei spent the bulk of her days in a lab, sequencing DNA and solving complex problems, John's time in the field had pushed his Variant abilities to their absolute limit. That wasn't to say Mei couldn't spot something coming down the road six kilometers away or hear a whisper in another room, but John could filter the rest of the noise out. He could listen for a single voice in a crowded room of hundreds.

He was never caught off guard.

John stood up, his gaze steady on the doors. "There's someone coming. They're—"

The entrance doors shattered in a spray of metal and

smoke, deafening the crowd. For several moments, Mei could hear nothing. The pressure from the blast hit and for a second it was like she was in someone else's body. Everything was different.

Her heartbeat was so strong, she could feel it. Every breath she took was quicker and lighter. It was harder to breathe, like no matter how much she tried, she couldn't grasp the air. It felt like her organs retracted and shifted, almost like she was falling in free-fall, but worse. All of this in only a moment.

And her eyes hurt. It felt like she had two fingers tapping against them, pushing them deeper into her skull.

"What the shit?!" snapped Short, shielding her ears and face. The words bled through the haze, and Mei blinked.

"What's it look like?" asked Hughes.

A figure, dressed in a full suit of thin, charcoal armor, stepped into the room, unfurling an automatic weapon the length of his arm, taking aim at the stage.

John didn't know what to do. If only he had his rifle, he might be able to shoot this asshole terrorist where he stood. If only the Leadership had allowed him to keep it. No matter. He'd have to do this the old-fashioned way.

He jumped down the seats and started toward this new enemy. The rest of the Blacks followed far behind, trying to keep up.

Despite his speed, however, John couldn't stop a bullet from hitting its target. Several members of the Leadership fell to the floor in a moment's breath. By the time he reached the terrorist, hitting him with what must have felt like the full force of a bull, several of the Leadership were already dead.

John gripped the weapon, still in the man's hands, and struck him in the neck, knocking him to the floor. As he did, the weapon flew free, sliding across the auditorium. Mickey swooped in to pick it up.

Taking the stranger by the throat, John pinned him down. "We good?" asked John. "Someone check the Leadership and see if they're okay!"

A shot fired from somewhere in the back of the auditorium. John looked to see another armored individual, perched on an elevated platform, reloading the gun. Master Lao, who had already been shot, was struggling to get off the stage, blood all over him, when the assailant fired again, striking him in the chest. He collapsed onto the floor.

"Mickey!" shouted John.

Mickey took aim at the assassin and started firing his newly acquired weapon, but the terrorist was already moving, heading out the upper stairwell.

If John hurried, he could cut them off at the exit. They just had to get out of this auditorium and make it to the lobby. They could—

A bullet flew through the nearby exit, hitting Hughes in the chest. He yelped, diving to the floor, and rolling.

"Contact front!" cried Short.

Being the only one with a weapon, Mickey returned fire. On the other side of the doorway, a few enemy soldiers had taken cover, sending a barrage of firepower at the Blacks.

"Get out of their line of sight!" ordered John, gripping the enemy soldier's neck. "You're coming with me!"

But before John could move his new prisoner, a bullet blew struck the man's head. His mask shattered and his face poured onto the stone-tiled floor. The man hung heavy in John's hand.

He let the body go, stepping back, stunned.

At the same time, Mickey was shot in the stomach. He screamed, collapsing, with blood pooling out of him. He rolled to the side and continued to return fire. John shook his head, trying to snap himself out it. "Mickey, toss it!" He let out his hand.

Mickey threw the rifle to him.

With a slow, deep breath, John focused, aiming through the opening at the oncoming fighters. He could see two of them lodged behind a small desk, using it for cover.

Gripping the gun, he fired.

One. Two. Three. Squeeze.

The bullet blew through the piece of office furniture, and someone screamed on the other side.

One. Two. Three. Squeeze.

A body hit the floor.

He waited, aimed and ready, but there was no movement. He listened, concentrating, but heard nothing. Was that all of them?

Hughes lay near him, hand over his chest wound. "We good, boss?" he asked.

Track ran over to Mickey and opened his pack. He took out a clump of QuickHeal and placed it in the wound to stop the bleeding "He's okay. H-He's good. You're good, Mick."

Mickey squeezed his friend's hand. "Easy, Track. I ain't going nowhere. Bullet went clean through."

Track nodded. "Right, right. Yeah."

Short went to the edge of the doorway, peering through what remained of the smoke. "Looks clear."

"We need to evac," said John.

"Not sure that's gonna happen," said Short. "The Leadership's down. I'm thinking it'll be hard for us to get out of here."

"You might be right. Mei, are any of them still alive?" John turned to look at the stage behind him. "Mei?"

No answer.

He couldn't see her anywhere. "Mei?"

"Where'd she go?" asked Short.

John ran to the edge of the stage. It was covered in blood. None of the fallen Masters were moving. He scanned the stadium seats across the auditorium, but didn't see her. "Mei!" he shouted. "Say something if you hear me!"

Nothing.

He felt a panic in his chest. His heart raced faster and faster, even more than it had in battle. Where was she? Why didn't she answer? Could they have taken her? It wasn't like her to run, not even under fire. What was going on? What was—

No, no, no. He couldn't breathe. He couldn't see. He

couldn't think. This wasn't happening. It had to be a dream. None of this was real. It couldn't be.

"Mei!" John screamed, his voice cracking as it boomed through the auditorium. "Mei, where are you!!!"

Garden Headquarters
March 25, 2351

Lena Sol sat behind the uplink console, sorting through files and images hidden deep within the archives of Everlasting's network. She gathered some helpful information which was certain to please Jinel Din and Vivia June. Then she began her real work: searching for Johnathan Finn and the other humans.

Having procured several aliases during her last session, she now had access to the Rosenthal Satellite's recordings and image database. She couldn't directly control the satellite like she could if she were inside the Citadel, because that was a closed system. But the images and feeds were stored on the network itself in order to be further analyzed, which meant she could sneak a glance after the fact.

Lena sorted through by type, cataloguing and saving any unusual sightings or strange occurrences beyond the city's walls. This included tribal conflicts, incoming and departing air traffic from Everlasting, and especially human activity near the portal site. Not surprisingly, the Rosenthal Satellite had been set to monitor the camp as often as possible, recording movement, layout, personnel changes, and so on. Many of the images and recordings had notes attached, detailing any changes taking place, such as the recent increase to personnel. Apparently, Doctor Curie's team had tripled over the last few weeks—something the Leadership seemed to be concerned about.

An alert from the Citadel. Another batch of files from the Rosenthal Satellite.

Lena scanned through them, swiping her hand to sort the newly downloaded files. Over two hundred images from across the eastern side of the continent, most of which pertained to activity around the border. Nothing too unusual, except—

Except for the part where an unknown ship had sailed behind the ocean wall.

Lena examined the craft as it appeared. A foreign ship from Tharosa, judging by the elaborate designs. A trading vessel, perhaps? What could it be doing here? There were no villages within the outer walls, no reason to risk life and limb to sail to such a place. What could they be after?

The images tracked the path the vessel had taken as it made its way through Everlasting's territory over the course of several days. The ship eventually settled near the shore, anchoring itself inside a crescent rock formation, where it had stayed until—

Well, Lena had no idea. The latest timestamp indicated the image was from this morning. She wouldn't be able to see anything more until the Citadel released another batch of files to the network, which could take some time.

She decided to look a bit closer. Maybe there was something

on the surface of the ship to indicate what exactly it was doing there.

The crew, which seemed to consist of a dozen or more individuals, shuffled around the deck through the various images, often moving to and from the cabin interior. Most looked typical of sailors, dressed to fit the sea and its weathered occupations.

All except for two, which Lena found somewhat out of place. The first was a broad chested man with long, braided hair. Next to him, a bald individual with blue tattoos. A woman. Yes, a priestess, in fact. Could it be—

Lena sorted through the pictures until she found one where the man's face was more visible. *There*, she thought, pausing on the image.

She focused and zoomed in on the stranger's face. *It is*, she thought at once. *It's him!*

It was the same tribesman who'd been with Terry during his time in the little house near the wall, back when Lena had first found him. *Ludo*, Terry had called him. A monk and farmer. Somehow, this man had found his way through the border and into Everlasting territory.

Had he come looking for Terry? Had he come to seek revenge on the sentries?

I have to tell Terry about this, she thought. *His friend. This entire crew of people. They're in danger if the sentries spot them.*

She started to get up, but stopped. She wouldn't be able to show him the scans, since he didn't have an implant, so she'd have to transfer the files to a display. The analysts had to have a few sitting around here somewhere.

Lena found one on a nearby console, already packed with files. She transferred its contents onto one of the local drives, then added the images and some video feed. *There*, she thought as it finished loading, and left quickly into the hall.

5

Leadership Report 226755.424

Recorded 03.25.884

Subtitled: Retribution

KAI: *How severe was the attack?*

GEL: *Very. It would seem most of the Leadership has fallen. You and I are all that remain. Master Quin is missing, but it is believed he was either slain or taken hostage.*

KAI: *What of the Master at Arms? Tell me he at least survived.*

GEL: *Dead. Everyone is gone.*

KAI: *This is outrageous. Without Master Lao, we cannot hope to—*

GEL: *Rest easy, Master Kai. I have already transferred authority to my department. Law enforcement personnel are standing by.*

KAI: *Already? What do you mean? The line of succession is to fall to someone in the Master at Arms' department.*

GEL: *In such chaotic times, we cannot entrust the full strength of the department to someone who is not a Master. I placed protocols in the system some time ago to self-activate in case of such an event. When the system detected the death of Master Lao, it transferred his authority to Master Trin. However, since both are now deceased, the line of succession has fallen to me.*

KAI: *You? Don't be absurd. If such responsibilities are to be transferred, they should fall to me. My authority is second to none.*

GEL: *Which is why the system has granted you dominion over the remaining departments. Rest assured, I have only taken the Master at Arms' department, along with my own. You have received the breadth of other responsibilities.*

KAI: *I see, so you would control both the Citadel and the armed forces.*

GEL: *While you manage all other operations pertaining to the city and its infrastructure.*

KAI: *Fine, but we should transfer responsibility back to the associated departments as quickly as possible, once new Masters have been assigned.*

GEL: *I agree, certainly. However, I believe I have sufficient evidence to retaliate against the enemy, should we see fit to do so.*

KAI: *You know their location?*

GEL: *One of several, but specifically their primary base of operations. I can have our forces there in—*

KAI: *Do it. Whatever it takes to stomp them out. They must pay for what they've done today.*

GEL: *By our combined will, Master Kai, I shall see it done.*

End Audio File

Garden Headquarters
March 25, 2351

Jinel Din returned from the mission unharmed, along with only a few others. The rest had been completely wiped out. Terry watched as they arrived, shocked at how few returned.

She collapsed on the floor and removed her visor, still out of breath from the fight and subsequent escape.

"What the hell happened out there?" asked Terry, standing over her.

She smirked through heavy breaths. "Killed them," she said, raising her gun to the others. "We killed them all!"

The soldiers cheered.

"Killed who?" he asked, afraid of what the answer might be.

"The Leadership. The Masters. One of my men shot them all down in a single burst. I saw it through his eyes."

"His eyes?"

She tapped the place where the implant was, near the temple. "We all saw it through him. I've never felt so alive, Terry, or so justified."

He said nothing. Part of him wanted to argue that it was murder, but he knew better. This was war, and everything was justified, according to those who waged it, no matter how horrible the atrocity.

"You're wondering about civilians, aren't you," she said, though it wasn't so much a question as an observation.

"And?" he asked.

She leaned against the wall, staring at the ceiling. "No casualties from us. A few soldiers, maybe, but I don't know. As soon as my man fired his weapon, the defense system activated and all our coms went down. Most of the team engaged outside the building, but none of them made it back. I didn't see what else happened, but since only six of us are here, I'm guessing the rest are dead."

"You left with fifteen people," said Terry. "I only count six survivors."

"That's right," she said, nodding. "Sacrifices, each of them. They will not be forgotten."

"What happens now? You took the Masters out, but what about the military? What about the Guardians?"

"That comes next," she said, reaching out her hand to him.

He grabbed it and helped her up.

"For now, we stay quiet and out of sight," she said, patting his shoulder. "There are still a few members of the Leadership in service. Not everyone was there today. They'll be looking for us, but we'll already be gone."

"Gone?"

"We can't stay here. First thing tomorrow, we're leaving and heading to another bunker near the outskirts of the city."

"You think they'll come for you? I thought you people were good at covering your tracks," he said.

"We are, but we didn't have enough time to prepare. It was sloppy, I admit, but the cost was worth it."

"I hope you're right," he said, watching the surviving soldiers disperse into their living quarters. "If this doesn't end soon, you people aren't going to last."

After checking his bedroom and a few other frequently visited spots around the bunker, Lena found Terry sitting alone in the dining area. He had some fruit on his plate, but wasn't eating. The look on his face suggested he was lost in thought, a look she'd grown accustomed to. "I've found you," she said, taking a seat across from him. "I've been searching everywhere."

"Sorry about that," he said, smiling a little.

She thumbed the pad in her hand. Maybe if she showed him this, it would help clear his mind. "I have something for you."

He sat up. "Oh?"

She activated the screen, which already had the picture of the man on the boat loaded and ready, and then placed it in front of him.

He stared curiously at the image for a second before he realized what it was. "What is…" He dropped his mouth. "This is Ludo! Where did you find this? What is he…why is he on a ship?"

"I was browsing through some of the satellite images when I found these. The system flagged them for security purposes."

"Security?" he asked.

"This ship is inside Everlasting's borders. Normally, the sentries would have been summoned to this location once analysts in the Citadel received the feed. However, this has not yet occurred."

"Why not?"

"It could be one of several reasons, but I suspect the recent storm shielded them. The satellite has some difficulty with recognizing anything during such an event. Now that the weather has cleared, however, operations have resumed."

"Does that mean Everlasting will go after them?"

"It is difficult to say. After I left my post to find you, I heard from one of the soldiers that the attack on the Leadership had been a success. Such an event is unprecedented and could very well alter protocol. As it is, they could be found at any moment."

"How far are they from the city?"

"I might be able to find the exact distance, should we require it. However, without a means of leaving the city, I'm afraid contacting them is highly improbable. The domeguard is impenetrable."

Terry stared at the image on the display. "I have to get to them. He's my friend, Lena. I can't let anything happen to him."

"I know, Terry, and I will help you do it," she said. "I promise you, we will find a way."

Terry stared at the image of Ludo. He couldn't believe his eyes.

Sitting there with Lena, he was overcome with both joy and fear. Joy, because it meant his friend was alive and well, or at least appeared to be; fear, because now his friend was in danger, probably because of Terry. That was the only reason Ludo could have come here.

Ysa was with him, Terry quickly noticed, and the ship had to be the *Waveguard*, Hux's vessel. Each of his friends had banded together in the hope of finding him. This much he knew, almost instantly.

"Thank you," he told Lena for the second time.

He'd have to talk to Jinel about this, see if she had a way to reach them. Maybe she knew a way to bring down the city's shield long enough for him to slip through. There had to be a way. He just needed to get to them and—

He paused, hearing something in the distance. Tapping from beyond the outer walls.

He concentrated, listening, and—

A loud scream, followed by gunfire. terry got to his feet, opening his mouth to say something, to warn Lena about—

An explosion shook the walls and floor, shaking him where he stood. Dust fell from the ceiling, and several cries erupted through the facility.

"What was that?" asked Lena, holding the table with both her hands to steady herself.

"We're under attack," he said.

Another boom that shook the foundation. They looked at one another.

"We should go to the tunnels," said Lena, referring to the opposite exit.

More screams coming from the entrance. "I need to see if I can help. You go." He ran to the side of the door. Several people were fleeing down the hall.

"Terry, we must leave together, you—"

"Get there and wait for me," he said, cutting her off. "I promise I'll be there soon."

Lena started to say something, but he didn't give her the chance. Instead, he dashed out of the room and bounded through the hall. He could hear the soldiers engaging up ahead, gunfire breaking loose.

A crowd gathered in the foyer near the outer door, their faces filled with confusion and fear. No one here knew what was going on, only that trouble had come knocking.

Inside the crowd of troops, Terry spotted Vivia June, struggling with a device in her hands as she ran in the opposite direction the crowd. "Hey!" he shouted, forcing his way through the surging mass of people. He grabbed her by the shoulder.

"Who?" she snapped, turning quickly to see him. "Terry?"

"How many of them are there?"

"I don't know. I'm getting out of here. This facility is about to be overrun. Follow me, plea—"

An explosion blew through the outer hall, blasting the doors open and sending everyone to the floor. The flak from the blast flew apart, hitting the other soldiers like bullets, and the room filled with enormous heat, consuming everything.

Terry felt time slow as the flash heat bit into his back, searing his flesh in the brief moment before he could focus his thoughts.

He wrapped his arms around Vivia June, burying her face in his chest as they fell together. The flameless heat melted clothes and nearby supplies, and the stink of charred flesh filled the room in seconds.

"Vivia?" muttered Terry, staring down at the motionless figure beneath him.

Her eyes were closed.

He felt terror as he placed his hand on her chest, then a swell of relief as he found her heartbeat. He turned to the source of the explosion. Several heavily armed men ran through the opening. "There!" yelled one of them. "Everyone inside!"

Terry looked at the unconscious woman in his arms. He could either save her or fight the invaders.

He lifted Vivia in his arms, getting to his feet. The choice was clear.

Two dozen bodies, charred and motionless, littered the room. Terry could sense a few of them still breathing, still clinging to life. Maybe if he was fast enough, he could come back for them.

But he knew, even as he thought it, that there would be no coming back. All of these people were going to die.

TERRY ARRIVED with Vivia at the tunnels, met by a crowd of survivors, including Lena and Jinel Din. It looked like half the population of the base, if not a little more. Maybe about a hundred altogether, which might have been good news if it didn't also mean the other half was missing.

"You're alive!" called Jinel, heading to him. "And you've brought Vivia. I feared the worst."

He carefully placed the unconscious strategist on the tunnel floor. "I'm fine, which is more than I can say for her."

Vivia moved, but didn't wake. She'd been lucky to make it out of there, unlike the rest of those soldiers.

"I suggest waiting before we move," said Lena, checking Vivia's pulse. "This woman needs to rest."

"Where can we go from here?" asked Terry.

"There's another facility, remember?" asked Jinel.

Terry had little interest in heading to another hole in the ground. He had other priorities, like a ship full of friends that could use him. "I'll help you get there," he said. "But then I'm leaving."

Jinel was wearing a breathing mask, and he couldn't make out her reaction. "What do you mean, you're leaving?"

"My friends are looking for me. I need to get to where they are before Everlasting decides to send a couple of Guardians after them."

"I told you already. The other humans can't be reached. They're too far away."

He shook his head. "Not them. I'm talking about someone else."

"Who?"

Lena pulled out the device she'd been carrying with all the pictures on it and presented it to Jinel. The soldier looked it over. "Who is this?" she asked, staring at the screen.

"His name is Ludo and he saved my life," said Terry.

"And he has access to a ship?"

"The *Waveguard* belongs to another friend. A captain from Tharosa named Hux."

Jinel stared quietly at the screen. "Tharosa?"

He nodded. "If they don't get out of there, the Guardians will—"

"Of course," muttered Jinel. "I understand."

Her reaction surprised him. "Can you help me get there?"

"I'll do more than that. I'm going with you."

"What are you talking about? Why would you—"

"If what you've said is true, I'd like to have a word with the man who owns that ship. If he truly is from Tharosa, like you say, then he might be able to help us."

Terry recalled the meeting they'd had about Tharosa. About his sword and the special metal. She didn't have to explain what she meant, because he already knew. "I can't say what Hux will do to help you. He might not care about your war."

"He'll care," she told him. "Because what happens to Everlasting affects the entire world."

Lena raised her finger. "We need to go there now, if you

plan to find them. The images on this device are from this morning. The crew could already be under attack. Moreover, they could have left the area by now."

Jinel gave her agreement. She called analyst Hob from the crowd. The poor man's hands were shaking as he approached. "As we've planned, escort everyone to the northern base. Follow the route that Vivia June and I outlined previously. Do you remember?"

"I do," said Hob.

"I'll return before long, but you must stay out of sight. Seal yourselves inside if you have to. Whatever it takes to stay alive. Above all, protect Garden."

"We will," said the man.

"How do we get to that beach?" asked Terry.

"The tunnels," said Jinel, motioning to the place where they now stood.

"These lead all the way outside? What about the city's shield?"

"The domeguard keeps things out, but it doesn't do a very good job of keeping us inside. There are several exits."

"I thought the Leadership closed all of those," said Lena.

"Only on the surface," explained Jinel. "It's too difficult to update the lower sections. These tunnels, for example."

"Lucky thing," said Terry. "Now we can get outside. I can't wait to leave this city."

Jinel scoffed, then tossed a breathing device to Lena. "Speak for yourself. The rest of us don't do so well outside."

6

Ortego Outpost File Logs

Play Audio File 1405

Recorded: March 25, 2351

MITCHELL: *It seems the worst has happened. After taking a call from Sergeant Finn, I have learned that Doctor Curie has gone missing.*

No, I believe I should say kidnapped. That's the word for what this is. Curie has been stolen from us.

How this could have happened is beyond my understanding. I've been trying to work through it in my head, one step at a time, but the entire ordeal defies belief.

Did Garden know we were working on a drug? How would they possibly have that kind of information? Did they have someone feeding it to them? If so, did they believe Curie could replicate the medication on her own? Without the base formula from Central, such a thing would be impossible, even for her, brilliant as she is.

Which means she will likely be killed.

No, I mustn't think such thoughts. Not if I am to keep my mind about. I need to focus on solving what I can, on finding a solution to the task I was given. Doctor Curie asked me to continue our research on extending the drug's life, so that is what I am going to do.

That, and nothing else.

End Audio File

An Unknown Room
March 26, 2351

MEI OPENED her eyes to a blinding, white haze. She shut them immediately, wincing.

When she tried a second time, she found it easier, but couldn't see much of anything.

No, that wasn't right. She could see shapes, figures, objects. She just couldn't make out the details. The lines were blurred and fuzzy, like she was viewing the world through a pool of water.

Her head throbbed with pain, so much so that it hurt to think. She tried to open her mouth to say something, maybe ask for help, but she couldn't find the words. She groaned.

A voice echoed from somewhere in the room, but it sounded like gibberish.

A small prick in her neck.

No, she tried to say. *Where am I? What's going on?*

But her lips barely moved and the words wouldn't come. Instead, she fell away. Far from the room with the voice. Far from the blurred colors and the watered down world. Far, far away, deeper into the void.

She slept.

Tower of the Cartographer
March 26, 2351

JOHN SAT BEFORE MASTER GEL, not knowing what to do. Not knowing how to fix what had happened, how to get back what was taken.

"I'm certain you must be upset, Sergeant Finn," said the Master Analyst. "But I assure you we are still trying to piece together what happened in that building."

"You have to know *something*," said John.

"Sergeant Finn, you must understand. The city is in disarray. I am doing everything I can to help you, but I find myself overwhelmed. With the loss of the other Masters, the task of managing Everlasting has fallen to a select few. Namely, myself and Master Kai."

"Just point me in the right direction. I can take it from there," said John. He didn't give a damn about the chaos in the city or the workload Gel might have on his desk. All that mattered was finding Mei. Nothing else came close.

"That's the problem, Sergeant. I don't know where to send you. We've searched the location where the enemy fled but found no sign of Doctor Curie. Most have escaped into the tunnels beneath the city, likely to some undisclosed location. I have most of the military out looking for them, but I don't know anything yet."

"Then send me to someone who does!" barked John.

Gel didn't flinch. "There is no such person, Sergeant Finn."

"There's always someone else," said John, getting to his feet. He started for the door.

"I receive intelligence reports every day. Should I find something of value, you'll be the first to know. I understand you must feel overwhelmed, even helpless, but understand the situation. The enemy is scattered and broken. They are desperate. Should you act on your own, they may retaliate against Doctor Curie. Is that what you want?"

He held the door open, squeezing the handle so hard his knuckles went pale from the strain. His anger nearly consumed him. He'd give anything to fix the situation. If only he could go back in time, he'd tell Mei to stay at the camp and wait for him. Anything but this. "I just want to get her back," he finally said.

"I'll make you a deal, Sergeant," said Gel.

"A deal?" John asked.

"Close the door first, if you don't mind."

He did as the head analyst asked.

"What I am about to tell you is highly sensitive, so please

use your discretion. Should it leak, Doctor Curie's life could be in danger. Do you understand?"

John nodded. What was this guy talking about?

"I have a contact working for me who has recently infiltrated Garden. Someone who has begun funneling information to me."

"You've got a spy?" asked John.

Gel nodded. "She has been assisting us with locating Garden for several weeks now."

"If that's true, why didn't you stop the attack?" asked John.

"The information did not arrive in time. It seems the attack on the Leadership was hastily planned, which is clear, given the obvious lack of precautions they've taken. Nonetheless, my contact managed to leak the coordinates of the facility shortly afterwards, which allowed us to respond to precisely."

"Where is this person now? Are they still sending reports?"

"I'm afraid not. Our attack on the enemy stronghold has disrupted the flow of information for the time being. I suspect my informant, much like the rest of the survivors, has fled to another location. I expect to hear from her as soon as she has the capability, however, so I remain optimistic."

John didn't know what to say. A mole inside Garden? If that was true, then they might know something about Mei's condition, even her location. The smart thing to do would be to wait for a message. Information he could use to make an informed decision. That's what Mei would do.

"You must see the benefit of this," continued Gel. "If Doctor Curie truly is being held captive—"

"I get it," interrupted John.

Gel nodded. "Very well, then I trust you will be patient and speak of this to no one. We must handle this delicately if we are to secure a victory and rescue Doctor Curie."

"Fine, okay. Whatever it takes to get her back, but I'm not leaving the city."

"You are welcome to stay in Everlasting as long as you wish, Sergeant Finn," said Gel. "I'll inform you the moment I learn something. However, I do hope you'll have the medical specimen delivered to your research team. I had intended to meet with Doctor Curie to deliver it myself, but—"

"Where is it?" John asked.

"Waiting in one of the laboratories. I can have it brought to you as soon as you're ready for it."

"One of my guys can take it back," said John. He had no intention of going anywhere.

Gel smiled, politely. "As you wish."

John left the office and headed to his room. He didn't do well with sitting around. Better to be out there and on the hunt, not stuck in a bedroom with nothing but his nerves to keep him company. If only he had another alternative, another way to take action.

But instead he had to wait for answers from someone else.

I'm as useless as a child, he thought. *A soldier with no one to fight.*

An Unknown Room

March 26, 2351

Mei woke up, her head spinning and her skin tingling. "Ugh," she managed to groan, licking her chapped lips.

It took a few minutes for her eyes to adjust to the light, but once they did, she found herself sitting up in a chair. A strap stretched across her forehead, locking it in.

Both of her hands were tied to the chair. She couldn't move. Where was she? What was going on?

She could see a cart with some syringes and cloth. Countertops, covered in medical supplies. Was she in a Garden lab?

The scene in the auditorium suddenly flashed in her mind. An intruder in armor slaughtered the entire Leadership on that stage, all while Mei looked on in disbelief.

John had stopped the invader, but not soon enough. The victims had already been claimed, lying in pools of their own blood. Mei had gone to them in an effort to help, but it was no use. The life drained out of them in seconds.

That was when she felt the hand around her mouth, followed by the piece of metal against her neck. An injection to make her sleep, no doubt.

No memory after that. Only the light of this room.

How long had she slept? How far had they taken her?

She tugged on the straps around her wrists, but they were tight and snug. The same was true of all the rest. She wasn't going anywhere.

Mei heard a man's voice coming from somewhere close.

"...human...yes...good blood..." She managed to pick a

few of the alien words out, having studied the language for a few weeks. It wasn't enough to get everything, but it helped. If only she'd learned more when she had the chance.

The only door in the room opened and a man entered. She didn't recognize him, but that was no surprise. Mei had never officially met anyone from Garden before.

He glanced at her as she sat there. "You…awake…"

She said nothing. Better not to let him know she understood anything. Better to play ignorant.

The doctor went to the nearby countertop and grabbed a small device. He thumbed the side of it, turning a switch, and placed it on the tray nearby. "Can you understand me now?"

Oh, good, she thought. *They have a translator.* "Yes."

"Excellent," he said. His lips didn't match the word, which made for an odd visual, like watching a video that isn't synced with the audio. "Can you tell me your name?"

"What is this?" she asked.

"I'm trying to assess your current condition," said the doctor.

She fidgeted beneath the straps. "Why am I tied to a chair?"

"I'm afraid that it is for everyone's safety, including yours. You are to remain where you are for the time being."

"I won't! Now let me out of here! As soon as my people figure out where I am, they'll come for me."

"Unlikely," remarked the doctor, reaching for a small device. A ring of sorts. He touched her temple with it. "Remain still or this will hurt."

She felt a quick shock throughout her body, and suddenly her arms and legs went numb.

A second later, the feeling returned to her limbs, but now she was terrified.

"Fascinating," muttered the scientist.

"Get me out of this thing!" yelled Mei.

He ignored her, pressing the device to her temple a second time. Like before, her muscles went numb immediately, only to thaw a few seconds later.

She struggled beneath the straps. "Why are you doing this?"

"To test your nervous system. Isn't it obvious?" he asked.

She squeezed the arms of the chair until her fingers hurt. "Let me out of here!"

"I suggest you remain calm," said the man. He retrieved another device. A needle this time. "This is going to put you to sleep."

"No, don't!"

But before she could say another word, she felt the metal pierce her skin.

The doctor stepped back, lording over her and watching. "You must be quiet now and rest," he said, smiling calmly. "My name is Fentin, so please remember."

"Fentin," she muttered, her voice fading. "…hate you…"

The edges of her eyes darkened, fading quickly, like entering a tunnel.

She lost her will to struggle, forgot her problems, let go of all the fear. Her will to fight evaporated, and with it, the world.

She faded, drifting into darkness as quickly as she had awoken, lost to a dreamless sleep.

Helpless.

The Tunnels Beneath Everlasting
March 26, 2351

Terry, Jinel, and Lena hurried as they made their way through the tunnels beneath Everlasting. According to Jinel, the Leadership's forces rarely came through these sections, which was why Garden had established a base nearby. The only real problem was the terrain. It was cramped, requiring them to crawl through increasingly narrow passages and channels to get from one section to another. It wasn't difficult, but the hindrance slowed them down significantly. On the surface, it only took half a day to walk the length of the city, but down here the same distance could take days.

Terry moved as fast as he could, assisting the others when the situation called for it. For the most part, Jinel knew the path and had no need of him, but Lena wasn't used to traveling like this. Still, she didn't complain, not even once. All things considered, she'd been exceptionally brave.

By the end of the day, they found the final tunnel, which Jinel said would lead them to the exit. "There's a gate down here that we have to open. They used to have it locked, but we broke it months ago and replaced it with one of our own." She revealed a device she'd had in her pocket. "This is the new key."

"Why lock it at all?" asked Terry.

"It's safer than the alternative. Imagine if a wild animal found its way inside. The domeguard doesn't reach this section of the tunnels, so the gates are all we have."

"I'd be more concerned with the people," he said.

"The natives?" asked Lena.

"Most of them think Everlasting is a holy city. They worship it. There's a whole religion based around this place. If you gave them the chance, some would probably try to come inside."

"More reason to keep it locked," said Jinel.

They found the end of the tunnel and, subsequently, the gate. To Terry's surprise, it was actually invisible. No, not exactly. He could see there was something there, but barely.

"It's hard light," explained Lena.

"What's that?"

"Manipulated photons made to create a solid object. They're largely used in construction as temporary support for larger buildings. I'm actually surprised this one is still in operation."

"Why's that?" he asked.

"It isn't very energy efficient. Not for long term use. The city has had to transition to more traditional material in the last century."

Jinel shrugged. "No one comes down here anymore to fix or replace anything. They're too busy worrying about other things."

"You mean like Garden?" asked Terry.

"Population control. City expansion. The two dozen scientific research outposts they've set up all over the planet. They've been busy."

"She's correct," remarked Lena. "Though, there's more to it."

"There always is," said Jinel. She took the key and showed it to them, ready to activate it. She pointed to her mask. "The air outside is toxic, so make sure your filter is secure."

"Of course," said Lena.

"The filtration system in the tunnels will automatically clean the atmosphere as it enters, but there's no such safety out there. We'll have nothing but our masks to keep us alive. Are you sure you can handle what lies ahead, Lena Sol?"

"I've been in the field before. I'm not afraid."

"Good," said Jinel Din. She tabbed the device in her hand, causing the light to dissipate. "Out into the wild we go."

7

Ortego Outpost File Logs
Play Audio File 1427
Recorded: March 26, 2351

MITCHELL: *I have received word from Sergeant Finn that the genetic material is still being sent from Everlasting. I suppose this is good news, considering recent events, but my thoughts continue to linger on the fate of my mentor. On Doctor Curie.*

Garden has made no demands, which leaves me to believe that they intend to use her, as I suspected. Finn assures me that he is working tirelessly to find her and bring her home, but his words have brought me little comfort.

Nonetheless, I will do everything I can to adequately test the sample. Doctor Curie risked her life for it, so I owe it to her to see this through. The blood may very well contain the solution to the gas, which could result in it saving tens of thousands of lives, now and in the future.

Doctor Curie once told me that humanity would fill the world someday, that together we could change the future. I believed those words, and I believed in her. I still do.

That will never change.

End Audio File

The Woods Outside Everlasting
March 26, 2351

THE AREA beyond the gate was covered in dirt and water, but still immersed in the familiar Everlastian stone and metal architecture. Cracks ran through the foundation, allowing the occasional blade of grass to rise from the earth. The further they walked, the more abundant the fauna became. After a few dozen meters, the landscape had transitioned from one of brown and gray to cerulean blue. The walkways teemed with roots and vines, bushes and flowers, the makings of the natural world. Before Terry knew it, they'd stumbled into an actual forest, surrounded by trees as tall as buildings, overshadowing them so they couldn't see the sky. They had found their way out of the city's underbelly at last, climbed back up into the world and all its dangers.

"Finally," said Jinel, staring at the thickened wood before her.

"Where to next?" asked Terry, looking to Lena for direction.

She retrieved her device, calling up a digital map. "We head east." She motioned to their right. "This way."

"Let's hurry," he said, and together they began to move.

The walls of Everlasting rose high, even taller than the trees of this forest, giving Terry a general idea of his direction. He could also smell salt in the air, far as they were from the sea. If he had to, he could probably find his way to the beach with only his senses to guide him.

Still, the map was more accurate, allowing them to make a straight run for the exact position of Hux's boat, the *Waveguard.* If they kept the pace, the trek might take them a few hours, but there was no telling what fate might befall the crew in the meantime. After all, they had ventured into what was arguably the most dangerous place in all of Kant. Here there were monsters, and they would not take kindly to intruders.

There was no time to waste.

Ludo stood atop the sand of Everlasting's shore. The holy city of the gods lay before him, tucked between the distant forest trees and the violet horizon. It glimmered with the light of the two suns, glowing like an inviting beacon, a pilgrim's destination. Ludo had long dreamed of the sight before him, of standing so close to the City on the Hill. Would he soon be struck down by the gods for defying their will? Would they punish him for his transgressions? He was a mortal man among the divine, and he sensed his sin the moment he pressed his foot into the dirt.

But Terry had been taken from him, his chakka-kin, his family, and he could not let this pass. Whether god or Guardian or priest or common man, Ludo would fight them all to see his friend returned.

Hux had secured the *Waveguard* some distance from the shore, but insisted they wait overnight before heading to the beach. Should any Guardians be in the vicinity, it would be easier to make their escape if everyone was still aboard the ship. As it happened, however, no enemies had come, much to everyone's relief. The following morning, Hux gave permission to Ludo and his wife to take one of the ship's dinghies and make landfall. They were to scout ahead and return with a better understanding of the layout of the land. Given their combat experience and familiarity with the Guardians, it only made sense.

Ludo pulled the tiny rowboat near the edge of the trees, then waved at the crew.

Ysa closed her eyes to listen to the sounds of the forest, which would give them a better sense of danger. "I sense nothing to hinder us," she said, once she was done. Ludo certainly had a talent for meditation, but no one was as proficient as his wife. She remained the greatest of all the priestesses, a stronger warrior than he could ever dream to be. Her chakka ran deep and her soul's wings stretched wide. "Wait," she said, grasping his wrist. "Something comes towards us from the west."

Ludo gripped the hilt of Terry's sword as it sat on his hip, sheathed in a leather scabbard. Should they run into any enemies, he would not hesitate to strike. This blade could cut straight through the skin of a Guardian. All it needed was a strong arm and a sharp eye behind it. Terry had wielded the weapon to its full potential, proving its true worth. Ludo had no such strength, not like his chakka-kin, but he would use the blade as best he could to see this mission through. He would make his friend proud. "How far?" he asked his wife.

"A long walk," she said, listening. "I sense there are three of them."

"Whatever comes, we will be ready."

She nodded. "I know it."

They stepped through the tree line and into the forest's shade.

Terry and the others continued to the east in their efforts to reach the coast. Lena had some trouble with the terrain, so he slowed to help her keep pace.

"I'll take the lead," announced Jinel, and she ran further ahead, her weapon at the ready.

"Sorry to be a hindrance," said Lena. Her voice sounded slightly muffled behind the breathing mask.

"Don't worry about it," Terry assured her. "We'll get there soon."

It was clear Lena wasn't used to exerting herself this way,

especially while wearing so much equipment. "Is it harder with the mask?"

"A bit," she answered, though he could tell her breaths had grown more shallow. The filter on it seemed to limit how much air she could take in.

The thickness of the woods made it hard to tell what lay ahead, even with Terry's enhanced eyes, which were only as good as the available line-of-sight. Now that he thought about it, he couldn't even see Jinel Din through all the foliage and trees. Had she gone so far ahead already? "Hold on a second," he told Lena.

"What's wrong?" she asked, placing her hands on her hips, clearly struggling.

"I just need a minute," he said, then closed his eyes to listen. Far ahead, he heard Jinel's breathing, her footsteps rustling the leaves, touching the bark of a tree and squeezing the butt of her rifle. She wasn't far away.

Good, he could reach her quickly if he had to. No need to worry too—

He paused. There was something else beyond her, another sign of life. An animal, maybe. Two of them, moving in Jinel's direction. They were—

People. Could it be the *Waveguard's* crew? Was it someone else? In either case, they wouldn't know Jinel was a friend. She might overreact and fire at them. Things could go wrong very fast.

"What is it?" asked Lena, who must have seen his expression.

He listened, hesitating, and then he heard a voice. A whisper from far away. "Someone comes," it said. "Prepare yourself."

Terry opened his eyes. "Wait here!"

"Why?" asked Lena.

But he didn't wait to answer, and instead burst into a dash through the woods, avoiding fallen trees and leaping over roots. In a matter of seconds, he was already nearing his target.

Jinel didn't have the luxury of advanced sight, so she wouldn't have the long-range advantage that Terry did. He could get there and stop her from using the gun if he hurried.

The soldier came into view soon, her rifle extended as she stood there, aiming into the forest. She stood in a clearing—a vale within the thick of the woods.

"Hold it!" shouted Terry, arriving from her back.

"I have something up ahead," she said.

"Those might be my friends," he answered, sliding to a stop. "Lower your gun!"

She raised her head from the scope. "It isn't them," she explained.

"Of course it is. I can hear them."

She shook her head. "There's something else. I'm picking up a vessel. No, wait…"

"What are you talking about?"

"It's coming from the sky to the north. I'm tracking now."

That was when he heard it. Engines like a soft roar, gentle and powerful at the same time, growing louder every second. It was faint, but coming fast, heading in this direction. "What the hell is it?"

"It looks like a ship," she answered.

At that moment, Ludo and Ysa appeared from beyond the distant trees. Terry's eyes met theirs, and he could see the shock in their faces.

But before anyone could say a word, a loud hum filled the area, and the ground began to shake. Terry watched beyond the trees as a craft appeared in the distance, heading straight towards them. "Run!" he shouted, pointing to the forest, and the others quickly followed.

Hundreds of leaves scattered into a flurry. The earth rumbled, and Terry felt the ship's vibrations throughout his body.

The vessel flew across the sky, booming overhead and away from them. It soared towards the south, passing the forest and the nearby sea, ignoring them.

Terry let out a short sigh as he watched. "That thing was in a hurry."

A hand touched Terry's shoulder, a reminder of who was there. He turned to see a wide and happy grin. "Terry, I cannot believe it!" exclaimed Ludo.

"I take it this is your friend?" asked Jinel.

Ysa smiled.

Terry embraced them both. "Ludo! Ysa!"

"We came to find you," said the farmer.

"A foolish thing to do," remarked Jinel.

"Brave is the word I would use," said Terry. "Did you have to fight anything?"

"We saw a Guardian in the water during a storm, but nothing happened. It moved on and ignored the ship," said Ludo.

"That's lucky," said Jinel. "You arrived at just the right time. The satellite system couldn't detect you during the thunderstorm."

"Satellite?" asked Ludo, unfamiliar with the word.

"I'll explain later," said Terry. He looked across the vale toward Everlasting. Lena was there, walking slowly between the trees, minding her footing. "I've got another friend to introduce you to. She's just over there."

"It's very nice to meet you," said Lena to the man and woman from beyond the wall. She'd never actually met any of the wild people, but knew their languages and customs about as well as any analyst. Until recently, field work had remained outside of her occupational experience. She'd been content to watch these people from the safety of her terminal, using the Rosenthal Satellite as her personal set of eyes, never getting too close, always watching from afar.

But here she stood here before them, close enough to see their eyes and touch their hands. These distant creatures from beyond the wall had always felt so different, so separate, but now...

Now, they were real. More than images bouncing from one corner of the world to the other.

The large one, Ludo, gave her with a wide grin. He was broad-chested and intimidating, so unlike any of the other men in her city. His skin was rough, not smooth and clean. Is this how all the natives looked?

No, the woman beside him was even more distinct. She looked pristine, almost delicate. Her bald head indicated she was a priestess, blue tattoos on her head and neck. Such things had always felt so archaic and uncivilized, but here, up close, she found them enchanting, like a piece of art in human form. The woman's dark skin glistened in the light. How could someone from the wilds look so beautiful?

"It is good to meet you," said Ludo, offering his hand to her.

She took it, then returned his pleasant smile. "Believe me, the pleasure is mine. Terry speaks highly of you."

The farmer's face grew warm with kindness, relaxing her. For a man so large and intimidating, she could sense his gentleness. His great affection.

"Where's your ship?" asked Terry.

Ludo pointed behind him. "The shore is close. Hux is waiting there for our return."

"Then let's not keep him," muttered Jinel Din, who had been standing silently beside them. She began walking deeper into the woods. "I have something urgent I'd like to discuss with your captain."

STANDING on the deck of the *Waveguard*, Terry felt Hux's heavy arms embrace him, squeezing his chest so tight he couldn't breathe. "Terry, my good friend!" exclaimed the wavemaster.

"Good to see you, too, Hux."

"I wasn't sure we'd find you, Little Traveler. What a gamble it was!"

"I can't believe you came here," said Terry.

"The seas were fierce, but I've never met a storm I couldn't weather," Hux said.

"We witnessed a Guardian in the water. You would not have believed it," said Ludo.

Hux's eyes lit up. "Truly, a mighty beast! It was twice the size of the *Waveguard*. A monster like nothing you've ever seen!"

"You've come a long way just for me. I don't know how to thank you."

"Please, no need for that," said Hux, smacking him on the back. "Now, tell me please, who are these friends you've brought?"

"Jinel Din and Lena Sol," said Terry.

Hux nodded at the two women. "Are they from these lands?"

"We're both from Everlasting," said Jinel.

Ludo's mouth dropped.

"Is it so?" asked Hux.

"It's true," said Terry.

"The city is in turmoil. The Leadership's forces have—"

"You mean to say you come from the Holy City?" asked Ludo, nearly fumbling over his words.

"It isn't holy," said Lena. "We're people, just like you."

Ludo looked at each of them, totally confused. "How can this be? What about the gods? They fly higher than all others, higher than any of us. What of the Guardians? The Priesthood and the Order?"

"I don't know where those things came from, but none of that is Everlasting," said Jinel.

Ysa stood with a quiet look of disbelief on her, and for the first time, Terry realized what was truly happening.

Each had lived their lives under the belief that the gods were real, that Everlasting watched over the whole world and kept them safe. Most of all, however, they had thought their rebellion from the temple a sinful act, a defilement of their beliefs. They'd chosen love instead of faith, burying their guilt beneath all else, forced to live with it.

Here was the truth of the matter, proving all their worries to be for nothing.

If they didn't understand it yet, they soon would.

"Captain Hux," said Jinel Din, staring up at the wavemaster. "I would like to ask a favor of you, if I might."

"A favor? What would someone from Everlasting need from a man like me?"

"Terry tells me you're from Tharosa…that you've traveled most of the world in this ship."

He nodded. "I have seen almost every land there is."

"How long would it take you to sail to Tharosa from here? How great is the distance?"

"Five days, I think, depending on the winds."

"What is this Tharosa like? Is it true they live in the mountains, mining metals and jewels?"

He nodded. "The capital city is built into the rocks. Much of our wealth comes from the mines, but also the trade it creates along the coasts."

"And the metal in that sword," she said, pointing to the weapon on Ludo's hip. The same one Terry had wielded against the titan Guardian along the wall.

"Also from the mines," he answered. "Though, it is far rarer than any other."

"That's good, because I would like you to take me there."

"You wish to go to Tharosa? For what purpose?" asked Hux.

"To save Everlasting and the people who live there," she answered. "To end the war of oppression that threatens to kill us all."

8

Leadership Report 226905.117
Recorded 03.27.884
Subtitled: Update 107

GEL: *What do you know about the vessel departing from the western shore?*

JUNE: *Very little, I'm afraid.*

GEL: *The satellite detected two of our citizens on board the ship. One of them appears to be dressed like a Garden soldier.*

JUNE: *I suspect they are Jinel Din and Lena Sol, but I'm not entirely certain.*

GEL: *Analyst Sol, you say? What gives you that impression?*

JUNE: *The two of them escaped with the rest of us during the attack, but while we fled to a neighboring Garden base, they went elsewhere.*

***GEL**: For what purpose?*

***JUNE**: I'm afraid I don't know, exactly. However, I believe they intended to deliver Terry to his allies from beyond the wall. I suspect the ship you speak of is theirs.*

***GEL**: Why not simply take the boy to his associates and return? Why would Jinel Din and Analyst Sol join them and risk exposure to the gas?*

***JUNE**: What is their current heading? The northern continent?*

***GEL**: An accurate guess, Vivia. They seem to be going to the mining country.*

***JUNE:** There was talk of going after some orinchalium to bolster Garden's arsenal. Terry offered information about the origins of his sword. I would imagine they intend to find more.*

***GEL**: Interesting.*

***JUNE**: Will you pursue them, sir?*

***GEL**: Only after they've attained the orinchalium. We could use that to repair the damaged sentries.*

***JUNE**: An excellent idea, sir.*

***GEL**: Keep me informed. Remember, Vivia June…all is for the good of Everlasting. Do you understand?*

***JUNE**: Yes, sir.*

End Audio File

An Unknown Room

March 27, 2351

"Another one. You won't feel it," said Fentin as he once again injected something into Mei's neck.

She wanted to ask him what he was doing, but her entire body was numb and she couldn't move. She couldn't even close her mouth to keep from drooling.

"There we are," said Fentin.

The blood in her veins, saliva, skin cells, bone marrow, hair follicles. They took little pieces of her every hour of every day, and she could only watch.

Let me out, she wanted to cry. Let me go!

But the words were stuck in her throat, replaced with soft groans. The medication kept the sounds from forming, turned her into a ragdoll. A toy girl for them to poke and prod and tease. She was nothing but an object now.

Her vision fogged and she blinked, although she couldn't feel it—not even as the tears trickled down her cheeks.

Fentin took a cloth and wiped her mouth. "Time to put you away," he said in his native language.

Mei had paid attention during her time in this place, listening and watching, observing the men who came and went. She still didn't know half their language, but she was getting better at it.

Though her body was lost, her mind was not. She could still absorb information. She could watch and learn. No matter what other freedom they took, she still had her mind.

Until they put her back to sleep.

The door opened and a voice called for the doctor to come outside.

"Right now? Very well," he said, placing the medical tool on the table.

Mei watched him head into the hall. The door closed behind him, and she was alone. She could hear a long, low voice like gravel, punctuated briefly by a higher one in response. Was this an argument? New orders? *I need to focus*, she thought, but had little experience honing her abilities. Not like John, who had trained for years to be the best he possibly could. If only she'd spent more time on it, maybe she wouldn't be in this position now.

No, she couldn't think like that. Mei could do this if she wanted…if she focused and called on her Variant strength. *Just do it like John showed you,* she told herself. *Focus and listen.*

She struggled to close her eyes, but slowly managed it. The drugs made it difficult to do much of anything, but at least she had some control. She concentrated on the two voices on the other side of the wall. Two males, one deep and rigid, the other light nervous. The voices grew a bit louder and more pronounced. *Better*, she thought, *but not quite enough.*

She reached with her mind, tried to pull at the sounds. Tried to—

"…report is looking positive…"

The words faded in and out, but she was nearly there. Just a bit more.

"The new tests are done. We're ready for another sample," said one of the voices.

"I'll extract one from her," said the doctor from before. The one who had left the room moments ago.

"Be careful with her. We can't afford to find a replacement specimen."

"She is small, but her body is…" He said a few words she didn't recognize. She still had room to develop her vocabulary, it seemed.

"I trust your judgement. Take as much as you think she can handle, but if she dies, you will be…"

"Very well. Please inform Master Gel that the operation is going smoothly."

Mei's eyes cracked open. Did he just say Gel? Was she hearing this right? No, there was no way that was possible. She must have mistranslated. It wasn't possible, not after everything she'd done for—

The door opened and the scientist entered the lab. He had a worried expression on his face.

Despite knowing she couldn't, Mei tried to move again, tried to do anything. Instead, she only sat there with her mouth open, her entire body numb and useless. She was desperate to understand what she had just heard. Why would Gel have her abducted? Didn't he understand she was trying to help him find a cure for the gas? Was he trying to keep the people from having the cure? Nothing about this made any sense.

The doctor came and sat beside her, picking up a needle and a piece of wet cloth. He dabbed Mei's arm, pausing to smile at her. "Here we go once more," he said, sticking the needle inside and drawing blood. "We have a long day ahead of us."

The Waveguard
March 27, 2351

TERRY WAS glad to be on the sea again after spending so long underground. He found Garden's base to be dimly lit and claustrophobic, especially after spending years in the open country of this beautiful world. The facility had been void of life and color, almost leeching the joy he'd once felt while under the blue leaves of the forests. He hadn't realized how powerful his nostalgia was until the moment he left the tunnels and entered the woods near Everlasting. Now, sitting here with his feet dangling off the side of the boat, he couldn't imagine a life without it.

That wasn't to say he didn't appreciate Jinel Din's help and subsequent protection. He might have died in the lab where she found him, never to breathe the free air for the rest of his days. Thankfully, this had not been the case. With any luck, it never would be.

The sea stretched into the bent horizon, the two suns high above. Their heat hugged his neck and arms, warming him in a way he hadn't felt in weeks. Taking a deep breath of the saltwater air, he exhaled with satisfaction, and smiled. It was good to be back.

The Waveguard would spend a few days at sea while it made its way to Tharosa on the northern continent. Hux had said the acquisition of orinchalium would not be a simple matter, but he assured him it would nonetheless be possible. The wavemaster had many contacts among the more established traders in the region as well as a handful who were, as he called them, of a less savory kind. One way or the other, Garden would have its precious metal.

"Enjoying your thoughts?" asked Lena. Her words pulled him back, and he turned to look at her.

"Just thinking about everything we have to do," he said.

From what little he could see of her face behind the mask, she seemed to be smiling, though he couldn't say for certain. "May I join you?"

"Of course," he answered.

She sat beside him, letting her feet hanging over the side of the boat just like him. For some reason, it surprised him to see her this way. Despite the mask and the equipment, she looked relaxed, like she was enjoying herself. This was a stark contrast to her usual demeanor. Less rigid and more open.

"How do you like it outside the city?" he asked.

"This isn't the first time I've left Everlasting. I used to visit Dr. Curie and Sergeant Finn when I was a liaison to the Leadership. Come to think of it, that wasn't too long ago."

"Were you scared when you first did it?" he asked.

"Terrified," she muttered. "Protocol required us to wear full body environmental suits to minimize any potential exposure, yet I was far more afraid than I am now."

He looked at her hands, which remained uncovered. In fact, aside from her normal clothes and the mask she wore on her face, Lena had nothing to shield her from Variant. "Is it safe for you to be out here?"

"The air doesn't bother me unless I breathe it," she explained. "In all honesty, the suits were unnecessary. We wore them as a precaution, not as a necessity."

"What about the mask?" asked Terry.

"Extremely necessary, I'm afraid. This filters the Variant from the air and allows me to breathe. I'd be lost without it."

"Then, how do you eat?"

"Very carefully," she said, and he thought he caught another smile. "As long as I'm quick about it, I can remove the mask to eat and drink, but it is not a pleasant process."

He sighed. "No wonder you never leave that place."

She dipped her head, looking into the rushing waves along the base of the ship. "It isn't so bad. Things could always be worse."

"Terry!" shouted Ludo. "Come and see this!"

Lena and Terry both turned to the starboard side of the ship to see Ludo holding a large fishing pole. Hux let out a heavy laugh, smacking his chest. "The farmer has become a fisherman!"

"I've caught one!" said Ludo.

Terry got to his feet and went to his friend's side. Lena followed, too. They peered over the side to see the splashing fish as it struggled against the line.

Ludo gripped the wooden pole with both hands, pulling it back and away from the water. "I have it!"

"Hoist it free," said Hux. "Put your back into it!"

Ludo lifted the struggling fish out of the waves and into the air. It was massive in size—roughly as large as his arm. With hardly any effort, Ludo managed to pull the beast onto the deck, flopping it in a pool of seawater.

"Quick, use something to crack its skull. Sederin! Come out and bring me the hammer!" yelled Hux.

Sederin came running a short moment later from within the cabin.

Hux took the tool, cupping the fish by the throat with his other hand, and preparing to strike.

Lena turned away. "I can't watch this."

With a quick, precise strike, Hux brought the struggle to an end. He handed the oversized animal to Sederin, who had to hold it with both arms. "Have this one prepared for tonight's dinner."

"Yes, sir!" said Sederin, leaving with the meat.

Hux grinned. "Such a fine display, my friend. We will eat well tonight!"

"Was it truly necessary to kill it?" asked Lena, her eyes sinking.

Hux chuckled. "Of course. Have you never caught a meal?"

She shook her head. "In Everlasting, we only consume plants and artificial meat."

Hux seemed confused. "What is artificial?"

"It's not real meat," said Terry.

"Not real? But fishing is the way of the sea! Poor Lena, wait until you try our cooking tonight. You won't believe what you've been missing!"

Everlasting
March 27, 2351

John received a call from Master Gel's office in the middle of the afternoon, asking him to report in as soon as possible. He tried to get more information over the communication channel, but the secretary wouldn't clarify. "The Master says the information is rather sensitive and to come at once," said the person on the other end, then they closed the line.

He grabbed his pack and proceeded into the hall, knocking on Short's door. Right away, she opened it, geared and ready to go.

"You get a call just now?" he asked.

"I sure did," she said.

The adjacent door opened and out walked Track. "Oh, I guess everyone's going," he said.

"Let's head out and see what's going on," said John, securing his vest.

The three of them boarded an Egg transport to the Citadel, the floating tower high above Everlasting near the edge of the domeguard. One of the analysts met them on the landing pad and escorted them to Gel's office.

"Wait here," John told Short and Track as they entered

Gel's outer office. "I'll be in and out with info as quick as I can."

"Maybe there's a mission in this," said Track.

"Could be," said John.

As he took a seat before the Master Analyst a few moments later, the man in charge of both the Citadel, as well as the city's military forces, beamed a smile from across the desk. "I hope you are prepared, Sergeant Finn, because I have some very good news for you today."

John felt himself sit up. "Do you have something about Mei?"

"I do," said Gel. "Or rather, I have our next course of action."

Thank God, thought John. "Where is she? What do you know?"

"I've received confirmation that the doctor is behind held somewhere in a Garden facility. My contact assures me that she is safe and unharmed. However, I do not know how long this will last."

"Where?" John demanded to know. "Tell me where they are. We have to get her back before anything happens."

"Please, Sergeant Finn. We must act with precision if we are to secure her safe release. I do not believe her life to be in any immediate danger. Should we act too soon, however, this could change."

John nodded. He couldn't be stupid right now. No rash decisions. "Okay, right. What do we do?"

"It would seem Doctor Curie's location is known only to a

select few within Garden's ranks. This is most likely done in order to prevent such sensitive information from leaking out of their organization. This, of course, makes the task of finding her all the more difficult."

"Then you don't know where she is?" asked John.

"Not yet, but—"

"Why am I here if you don't know anything?" He was beginning to get annoyed.

"Because I believe I know a way to find out," said Master Gel. "But I will require your assistance."

His help? What could Gel be talking about? "Go on."

"One of Garden's top agents has left the city and is attempting to procure a specific resource to use against our forces. I believe this to be a metal known as orinchalium. If secured, Garden could use it to bolster their offensive capabilities, potentially crippling Everlasting's defenses."

"That's awful," said John, taken back by the scope of what Gel had suggested.

"Indeed, Sergeant Finn. But more to the point, this official is also one of the few personnel with intimate knowledge of Doctor Curie's location."

"Then we need to find this person," said John.

"Indeed, and before she returns. Otherwise, she may very well disappear into the underground."

"So, what are you asking me to do?"

"I would like you to accompany a squad of our soldiers on a mission to capture Jinel Din. You have proven yourself to be most adept at combating Garden's forces. With you there to assist us, I believe we may be able to capture her alive."

John considered his offer. He wasn't in a hurry to leave the city, since Mei was currently being held somewhere beneath it, but if this meant finding and bringing her home, he didn't have much of a choice. "Alright. I can do that."

"There are a few caveats," said Gel. "First, Garden is heavily armed and working with a group of natives. We do not know the extent of this partnership, but it remains a danger nonetheless. Be cautious, as many of the warriors and priests have shown exceptional skills in battle. They may not fall easily. Second, and this is critical, you must not kill Jinel Din. We need her alive if we are to ascertain the whereabouts of Doctor Curie. You are to keep her unconscious. She has access to a communications device which will transmit a direct video feed to Garden personnel. If this happens, Doctor Curie's safety will be compromised."

"How am I supposed to knock her out?" asked John.

"We will give you access to our nerve agent, compound AX-12009-B3. You'll recall our forces used it against your—"

"I remember," said John.

"Very good. You are to use the toxin on Jinel Din, then remove the rest of her team as quickly as possible."

"You want me to kill them?" asked John.

"If the prospect bothers you, use the compound," said Gel. "Regardless, the task before you is the same. Secure the target and return her so that we can determine Curie's location and extract her safely. Are you comfortable with what I am asking of you, Sergeant? Do you understand?"

John thumbed the butt of his rifle. "If it means we get her back. I'll do whatever it takes."

"Very good," said the Master Analyst once more. "Very good, indeed."

9

Ortego Outpost File Logs
Play Audio File 1560
Recorded: March 27, 2351

MITCHELL: *After the delivery of the sample, I have found myself utterly consumed. Upon my initial analysis, I could see nothing exceptional about the sequences in the native population's DNA, but after initial sequencing, it seems I was incorrect.*

The expressed traits of the sequence operate in much the same way as Doctor Curie and Sergeant Finn's, creating a kind of hybrid. Unlike theirs, however, which retain a mix of human and Variant DNA, the native sample appears to be a blend of Variant and the citizens of Everlasting. By this I mean, simply, that the natives living outside the city are as different as Doctor Curie is to myself. The natives are indeed hybrids, as we first surmised, but there is something else.

The DNA of the natives, while related to the Everlastians, is also similar to Earth's hybrids—the children created under Doctor Archer's experiments and research. This is more than I expected to find, but considering the similarities between our two planets' animal populations, it isn't entirely surprising.

I would need to examine a living specimen to see what effects this has had to be completely certain, but I would hypothesize that some, if not all, of the natives possess added physical abilities. While Sergeant Finn and Doctor Curie have enhanced senses and a higher white blood cell count, these individuals may retain other traits of which we are unaware. It would be most fascinating to examine or interview them to learn if any exist, but for now I must focus on the task before me.

The DNA appears to have multiple unique strands, each of which could very well hold the key to long term adaptability. Whether this proves to be a triumph or a fool's errand remains to be seen, but I shall continue down this path...to whatever end it brings.

End Audio File

The Waveguard
April 1, 2351

In the early dawn of the fifth day at sea, Sederin shouted from high atop the mast. "Land! Land! Land!"

The words broke through the deck and woke Terry from his restful sleep. He yawned and stretched, glancing to his left to find Lena's bunk empty. It wasn't surprising, as most of the people he'd encountered on this planet required so little sleep that it made him seem lazy by comparison.

The air on the deck smelled particularly fresh this morning, but with a hint of...what was it?

Something close to cinnamon, he realized, with a hint of fruit behind it. The crisp odor of baked treats riding the breeze, bringing hunger pangs. He clutched his belly in anticipation, leaning on the wooden rail toward the northern shore. There, a bustling dock with shops and traders, bakers, and sailing ships. What he found more remarkable, however, was the sheer size of such a place. Compared to Capeside or any of the other ports, this one seemed several times their size. How many people had gathered to live in this place, and why? Were there other cities in the world as large as this one? Until now, Terry thought Everlasting was the only place with such a population.

Perhaps there was more to the world than he first believed.

Beyond the little town, Terry could see a pass of cliffs ranging endlessly in the distance.

"Fair morning, Little Traveler!" came a jolly voice from behind.

A hand came down on his shoulder. Hux's many piercings glimmered in the morning light of the clear day, making Terry squint.

"It won't be long until you see my homeland. I hope you're prepared! Wait until you see the Wavemaster Arena. Oh, and the Maran Statue!"

"What are those?" asked Terry.

"Both are symbols of pride. The Arena is where wavemasters compete to prove themselves. I spent my younger years training alongside many other athletes. The statue stands at the entrance, representing the strength and willpower to endure such tests. Wait until you see it."

"You were an athlete?" asked Terry, surprised to be hearing this for the first time.

"One of the best!" declared the sailor with a hearty chortle. "I might not look it now, but in my time, I was quite the champion."

Terry had a hard time believing Hux could be even more intimidating than he already was. The wavemaster stood nearly seven feet tall, the same as Ludo, with hefty biceps and strong legs. How much tougher could one person get?

At the same time, Terry had seen some incredible things since arriving on Kant. Priests with unbreakable skin, monstrous animals the size of a small building, and a futuristic metropolis to name a few. Would he ever get used to seeing the impossible?

"There is no need for disguises, friends," declared Hux.

Terry, Lena, and Jinel each wore a shroud around their faces to cover themselves. They couldn't just go walking into Tharosa looking so out of place. The breathing masks were dead giveaways. Worse still, Terry's ears were round and small, not pointed like all the rest.

"Tharosa has many people arriving from all over Kant

every single day," said the wavemaster. "No one will notice any of you."

"What about our gear?" asked Jinel.

Hux smiled. "The people of Lexine wear extra eyes and machines as well, but none are given second looks. Not in Tharosa. We welcome all!"

"You don't think I'll stand out?" asked Terry.

"Not so, Little Traveler. Most will think nothing of you, except that you must be from far away."

Terry still hadn't told Hux about his true origins. Ludo and Ysa had accepted it, but only after several attempts at explanation. The concept of another world was more than a little complicated, especially since Terry barely understood it himself. Originally, he believed this to simply be another planet, rather than an entirely separate universe. Lena had explained this to him in some detail, though he still didn't entirely understand. In time, he'd try to tell his friends the truth, but right now there were other concerns.

"It's true," said Lena, speaking of Terry's appearance. "There's a tribe on the eastern continent of Liendis who have small ears like yours. Not exactly the same, but close."

"They're also quite small," added Jinel.

"Small?" asked Terry.

"A tall one might come up to your waist."

"That's beside the point," insisted Lena.

Terry handed the shawl to Ludo. "If Hux says we don't need to hide, then I believe him."

The wavemaster smiled. "As you should, Little Traveler! Now, come! Let us leave and get our footing."

The three of them—Ysa, Ludo, and Terry—followed Hux as he led them through the harbor and into the city.

As they passed by the various shops, Terry felt a flood of smells and odors—many pleasant, others ghastly. The streets were wider than those in Capeside, lined with carts and animals. Terry spotted several haddins and other animals pulling carts and vehicles, reminding him of Plead.

Terry wondered if the merchant had ever come here. If not, what would he say upon seeing such a place? Plead had often remarked on the complexity of this world, on the variety of people one could encounter.

"The world is so big," Terry had told the merchant.

"Bigger than any of us could hope to guess," Plead had answered.

I wish I could tell him he was right.

A Cold Room
April 1, 2351

Mei opened her eyes in her cell, groggy and tired. She sat up in her bed and rubbed her eyes, trying to focus and regain her composure. The last thing she remembered, she'd been injected with something. Another drug to—

Well, she had no idea, truthfully. The doctors never told

her much, nor did they speak enough to one another to give her any idea of what was going on. All she could do was scrape together bits and pieces from what she'd overheard.

The door opened and in walked Fentin. "Awake, are you?" he asked in his native tongue, seeing her standing with her hands against the transparent cell wall.

She said nothing.

He proceeded with his typical routine, cleaning his tools and preparing a dose of something. "You seem to sleep longer than the other one we had," said the doctor, thinking she didn't understand him.

What other one? Mei wondered.

Fentin placed the translator device on the table. "Do you understand my words?" he asked, this time in English.

"Yes," she said.

"Good. You should remain seated on the bed while I open the door, unless you want me to call someone."

She didn't argue. Not yet. Better to play this one smart and wait for the right opportunity. This was the first time she'd awoken before Fentin's arrival. She had to handle this the right way.

Mei remained still, placing her palms up as Fentin requested. He opened the cell door and motioned for her to come out. She did, standing and walking slowly to where he was, minding the cell walls. "Sit in your chair," he ordered, grinning that annoying grin of his.

She glanced at the metal monstrosity Fentin called a chair,

trying to hide her disdain. The seat was cold and hard, digging its edge into her thighs.

Fentin went to her side and began strapping in her wrist. He didn't seem too concerned with her, and it was no surprise. Mei was half his size, after all, and hardly imposing. He likely assumed he could overpower her if he needed to. Probably hold her down with just his body weight.

Maybe that was true, too. Mei didn't know. She'd never tested her strength against anyone in Everlasting, and she wasn't the strongest of the Variant children. Not like John or Terry.

Still, she couldn't just sit here and let this happen. Oh, no. Not by a long shot.

Right as Fentin tightened the first wrist strap, but before he could lock it into place, Mei jerked forward with her other hand, jabbing him in the throat.

Fentin fell back, gagging for air. He gasped desperately as his face turned red.

Mei untied herself with her free hand. Fentin struggled to stand before making a dash for the door. As it opened, Mei shoved him. He tumbled to the left, knocking his head into the nearby table as vials of blood were thrown into the air and shattered against the low ceiling. Dark crimson rained on them both, peppered with shards of glass twinkling in the dim light.

Fentin grabbed her, pulling her to the floor. She kicked him in the side of his throat, screaming as she tried to get away.

The doctor's eyes dilated as Mei scurried away from him. "H-Help! Someone help!" he yelled.

Mei fled into the hall, having no idea where she was going.

As she neared the end of the initial corridor, which merged with another perpendicular hall, she collided directly with a group of armed soldiers. Two of them grabbed her, but she shoved them away. They were dressed in Everlastian gear: dark blue armor with weapons meant to pacify, rather than kill. "Hey!" shouted one of them, clearly surprised.

She hesitated, uncertain of what to do. She couldn't get through that many people on her own. She wasn't John. She wasn't strong enough for this.

She took a step back. Maybe there was another way out, another path to take to escape. She just—

She felt a sting in her neck, a sharp, awful pain. She felt herself, expecting blood, but found nothing.

One of the soldiers had his weapon raised at her. "Target is down!"

In seconds, all the feeling in her body faded, each appendage useless as she collapsed onto the floor.

Back in the cell, lying in the bed, Mei was fully conscious, totally immobilized.

She had tried to make her escape, but couldn't even manage to get more than a few rooms down the hallway. Had she been a fool for believing such a thing was possible?

No, she thought, pushing the idea out of her head. *I can't just submit. I can't.*

Out of the corner of her eye, beneath the transparent cell

wall, she spied a vial of blood resting snug against the metal frame. She couldn't get to it from here, even if she could move.

She waited there for hours, unable to move. Unable to speak.

But after a time, some feeling returned, and eventually she managed to open her mouth and wiggle her fingers. The effect of the drug was wearing off.

As she sat up, finally, feeling the aches in her stomach and thighs, she noticed something in the corner of the cell, glimmering.

As she drew closer, she saw it was an empty vial. Fentin must have dropped it when she attacked him earlier, then left it here during the confusion.

A small crack ran along its edge. If she could break it, maybe file it down…

She heard someone down the hall—footsteps growing louder. Mei went back to her bed, stuffing the vial beneath her pillow. Her heart raced, and she took a deep breath. Easy, now.

She waited for the door to open, expecting to see Fentin and maybe an added guard. Instead, someone else had come. A man she'd met several times before.

Gel, the Master Analyst of Everlasting, the head of the Citadel itself, stared back at the girl in the cell.

And he smiled.

10

Ortego Outpost File Logs
Play Audio File 1592
Recorded: April 1, 2351

MITCHELL: *After running sixty-two tests of varying complexity, I have discovered what I believe to be the sequence responsible for Variant adaptability within the alien DNA. The next step is, of course, to find a way to use this to enhance the Lanrix drug without destroying or completely overwriting the present hybrid molecule we are already using.*

I believe the tests should take no less than a day, which means I will know one way or the other whether I have been wasting my time or not.

Either way, the project is nearing its end. For this, I am both thankful and uneasy. Thankful because I have pushed myself beyond what I believed to be my limits. Uneasy, because it means the work will end and I will need to look elsewhere to be productive.

I have always prided myself in my ability to self-analyze, so I am not naïve in what I have done. I understand that the reason behind my obsessive work ethic, at least in the last several days, is because of what has happened with Doctor Curie. I know that.

I also understand that when the project ends, this fear that I have, this anger, will not subside, nor will I find relief. There will need to be another distraction—another project—with which I can immerse myself. Otherwise, my overactive mind will be unable to rest. I'll be driven mad by my obsessive thoughts, and it will be for nothing. It would serve no useful purpose.

For that is the only value we can hope for in this life: to be useful.

Doctor Curie taught me that.

End Audio File

An Unknown Room
April 1, 2351

Mei sat in her cell, staring at the man before her—Master Gel, himself. "What are you…what is this?" She could hardly get the words out.

At the same time, she knew the answer was clear. Gel was responsible for her abduction. He'd imprisoned her against her will and enacted the medical experiments she'd been subjected to. It seemed so obvious now, after hearing his name in the hall the other day.

"It is good to see you again, Doctor Curie," said the Master Analyst. "It pains me to look at you in such a state, but I'm afraid I have no other choice. Your ineptitude in delivering a viable solution to the corrupted atmosphere has led me to seek my own alternatives."

"Alternatives? I was in the middle of finding a cure, you idiot!"

He smiled. "Indeed, you were, and I assure you that your research is continuing under the diligent eye of your assistant, Sophia Mitchell. However, that remains of secondary interest to us."

"What are you talking about?"

He approached the chair near her cell, sweeping his hand along one of the wrist straps, observing them, almost analytically. "You surprised everyone when you escaped, you know. No one expected such an outburst from one so small. Granted, your rebellion was short lived, but it was impressive."

"Get to the point, Gel," said Mei, trying to suppress the rising anger she felt in her chest.

"Your biology is a cross between two genetic sequences, as you know, which has given you a set of highly unusual, but natural abilities. It is because of this that we have seen to your imprisonment. You display a possibility in not only human potentiality, but also Everlastian, which is something that demands exploration." He raised the vial of her blood to the light, examining it. "Unfortunately, we have had some trouble mapping and replicating these genes on our own, despite our best efforts. For all our advances, we never reached the same threshold in genetics that your kind did. Perhaps we simply gave up too quickly, focusing on other areas which we felt were more vital to advancement. Regardless of these missteps, however, we shall strive for progress. You see, Doctor Curie, despite your alien origins, you represent the future of this great country. It is with you that we will finally achieve our true potential—the birthright we have been repeatedly denied."

"I told you already, I was working on a cure! You could have left the walls of this city without needing a gas mask. You could have—"

"We have no interest in your half-measures. What I want for my people is hidden somewhere in your veins, Doctor. What I desire is strength—the ability to protect ourselves from threats, not only from this world, but of the next. When you and your friends opened that portal and revealed yourselves to us, you brought the only true danger my people have known since the day the world fell. You came to us with weapons and abilities, displaying your arrogance. You are dangerous, even more than the savages who inhabit the wildlands, and I cannot abide it."

"I'm not the one who kidnapped someone trying to help them. Let's also not forget the civil war going on or the fact that you lost most of your Leadership. This city doesn't need an outside threat to bring it down. You're doing it to yourself."

Gel laughed. "Garden is a passing obstacle. They don't even realize the futility of their actions. You say they killed the Leadership, and you'd be right, but they didn't do that on their own."

"What does that mean?"

"My department secures and monitors all activity on the city's network. After being informed of a particular breach of information regarding the time and location of the Leadership's assembly, it stood to reason that Garden would attempt another attack. This breach was obvious right as it happened, but rather than attempt to stop their actions, I chose to step aside. I erased all records of it, then remained inside the Tower of the Cartographers to observe the aftermath. Most of the Leadership was taken out in a single assault, and I used the opportunity to bring you into custody."

"So, that's what this was all about. You saw a chance to seize power for yourself, so you took it." She scoffed. "You call us arrogant. Look at yourself, Gel."

"Call it what you will, but I did what had to be done. The Leadership had grown complacent, stalling on action for decades, unable to do what is necessary. When we first discovered your people, I advocated for your imprisonment and seizure of the gate. My colleagues ignored me, even after witnessing Johnathan Finn kill an animal seven times his own size. Even then, they did not see what I did. They did not recognize the threat standing before us. A threat which I alone have quelled."

"You're deluding yourself, you—"

"Enough!" he snapped, and it made her stiffen. She'd never heard this man raise his voice. "I will have no more argument. As we stand here, Johnathan Finn is on his way to die. The rest of your people will follow."

"What are you doing to John? Hey! What are you talking about?!"

He smiled at the display. "Nothing more than he deserves."

Gel placed the vial of Mei's blood on the end of the table. He walked to the hall and motioned for Fentin to come inside. "Proceed with the next experiment. Inform me of the results."

"Yes, Master," said the man.

"It was good to talk with you today, Doctor Curie," said Gel, looking back at her. "Now, be a good girl and stay in your box."

Ashby Harbor, Tharosa
April 1, 2351

Terry followed Hux to the outskirts of the seaside town of Ashby before stopping. He approached a large two-storey building, about to go inside. "What are we doing?" asked Terry, trying to understand the plan.

"Ashby only has one lodge. I need to make sure there's room for everyone," said Hux.

"Shouldn't we first contact the local authorities and get on with it?" asked Jinel, rather impatiently.

"It will take at least a day to acquire the supplies. Before that, we will need to speak with the queen."

"What queen?" asked the soldier. "Why can't we simply get our cargo and leave?"

"Any purchases from the mines must be authorized by Her Majesty, personally," explained Hux. "Be easy and wait a while. I'll procure what we need."

Hux went inside and began talking with the woman at the counter. A moment later, he returned with three coins. He gave one each to Ludo, Jinel, and Terry. "Present these when you return and she'll show you to your room."

Terry accepted the coin, examining it to see a portrait of a ship on one side and a mountain on the other. He was surprised at the craftsmanship. The ship looked exquisite, with every point rendered in fine detail.

Lena reached out with her arm, catching Ludo's wrist. "Easy," said the farmer.

"I think I need to rest," said Lena.

"It's your mask. You're exerting yourself too much," said Jinel.

"I don't think that's the problem. I suspect there is a crack in the seal of your filter."

Jinel went to her and tried to examine the gear. "That's possible, but I'm not a mechanic."

"Can you wait here with her while the rest of us go get what we came for?" asked Terry.

"I didn't come all this way to stay in a room," said Jinel.

"I'll wait with her," said Ysa.

"We both will," echoed Ludo, lifting her back up.

"Thank you," said Lena, still breathing shallow breaths.

Ludo and Ysa took her inside while the others looked to Hux. "Ready to see the city?" he asked.

"Let's get what we came for and go," said Jinel. "There's a war to win."

He nodded, then motioned for everyone to follow. They

made their way through the streets, passing dozens of people. Many carried different looks about them, a variety of clothing styles and physical features. One or two even wore metallic masks and goggles. It seemed Hux's claim was true. This town, more than any others Terry had come across, was filled with travelers from all over the world.

Along the wall they found a gate with three men standing watch. "Barniby!" yelled Hux in a jolly tone.

A stout man, similar in size to the wavemaster himself, snapped around to see who called him. At this, he grinned and raised his hands. "Hux, you old pirate! I knew I recognized that voice!"

They embraced, smacking each other on the back. "It is good to see you again," said Hux.

"I was sure you wouldn't return for another three weeks. Did something happen on the sea?"

"Indeed! There's an emergency that needs taking care of. Do you know if the queen is accepting visitors today?"

"She isn't," said Barniby. "But my mother would make an exception for you, Hux."

Hux smacked his chest. "Thank you! Might we go there now?"

Barniby nodded, turning to the other watchmen. "Wait here while I take Hux to the court."

"Yes, sir," said the guards.

"Who is the queen, exactly?" whispered Terry as they started walking out of the city.

"Barniby's mother," answered Hux. "She is a noble and generous woman."

"Wait, so you know the royal family personally?" asked Terry.

Hux chuckled. "Barniby is my cousin. My father is his mother's brother."

Terry's mouth fell open. "The queen is your aunt?"

"Indeed!" said Hux with a grin.

Terry looked at Jinel. "Did you hear that?"

"Our friend Hux is royalty, it seems," she answered.

"Not quite," said the wavemaster. "Only the crown itself is considered royal. It does not extend beyond the person who wears it. Barniby and I are the same as anyone else."

"But isn't Barniby in line to be king?" asked Terry. "Isn't that how it works?"

Hux raised his brow curiously. "What sort of method is that for electing a ruler?"

"A long time ago, back where I come from, those things went from parent to child," said Terry.

Hux laughed. "Such a silly thing! Your country is strange, Little Traveler."

"How do you do it, then?"

"There are six houses, each with their own families. A member of a house is chosen as a representative on the Council of Six. It is from those individuals that the crown is chosen. The crown cycles from one head to the next."

"How long does it last?"

"Five years, and then it rotates to the next house. It's fair this way to everyone, and it forces them to work hard to get things done. My aunt has been queen during this time, but soon the crown will change heads again, and the cycle will continue."

Terry tried to imagine the process in his head, but found it somewhat odd. Houses? Rotations? It seemed so foreign. Nothing like the history books he'd grown up reading at the Academy.

The group made their way along a wide road, surrounded by a valley that stretched on into the distant cliffs. The mountains surrounded the valley and looked to continue in both directions to some unknowable end.

To think, this was only the start of this new land. The beginning of the rest of the world.

PART II

Man is free at the instant he wants to be.

– Voltaire

To different minds, the same world is a hell, and a heaven.

– Ralph Waldo Emerson

Every parting gives a foretaste of death, every reunion a hint of the resurrection.

– Arthur Schopenhauer

11

Leadership Report 228302.452
Recorded 04.1.884
Subtitled: Update 109

GEL: *Do not argue with me, Vivia June.*

JUNE: *Sir, if we allow Garden to access this information, Master Kai's life would be—*

GEL: *You needn't concern yourself with such details. Simply perform the task I have placed before you.*

JUNE: *It only seems—*

GEL: *Do you trust me, Vivia June?*

JUNE: *Sir?*

GEL: *Everything I have done, has it not been for the good of Everlasting? Have you not witnessed it firsthand?*

JUNE: *Of course, Master Gel. I would never question your dedication.*

GEL: *Then I ask you again: do you trust me to do what is best for this city?*

JUNE: *I… Yes, sir. I do.*

GEL: *Good. Now, go and see it done. Contact me once the attack is over.*

JUNE: *Y-Yes, sir. All is for the good of Everlasting. I will see your will done.*

End Audio File

Galathane City, Tharosa
April 1, 2351

A SET of stairs greeted them at the base of the mountain, rising high into the cliff. They climbed until they reached the entrance—a tall gate four times Terry's size.

Barniby motioned at the guards as he approached them. As he did, the two returned the gesture and promptly opened the gate. Each of the men, who were both thick with muscle, holstered their swords. They each took hold of a crank and turned it, throwing their backs into it. The gate rose, echoing through the cavern walls and rattling Terry's chest like thunder.

The group stepped inside, finding themselves surrounded by eccentric stone walls, with chandeliers and sparkling jewels high above their heads, rising high into the mountain. Terry nearly fell back as he bent his neck to see the ceiling and all the enchanting objects. It was all so elegant, though perhaps a bit unnecessary.

"Everything in this hall represents a hero lost at sea," whispered Hux, almost reverently. He pointed at the nearest one, a gem the size of Terry's fist—green and reflective, with a border of metal surrounding it with unknown writing. "Wavemaster Tarda. Killed in the Lexine War. He destroyed twenty-seven enemy ships and saved Ashby."

Terry nodded, bowing his head a little. The heroes in this hall were not his own, but he would show them respect. Not for them, for they were long dead, but for the man beside him now. The wavemaster who had risked his own life to find and save Terry's. That was worth whatever he could give.

The end of the hall opened into a massive cavern, larger than any he'd ever seen. Along the massive walls, long and winding walkways had been carved, with dozens of people going here and there. The sight reminded him of Central, the city of his birth. The difference being that these people didn't live in fear of what lay outside their doors.

There were also homes within the stone, carved doors and windows making for some elaborate designs. High above it all, Terry saw the sky between the rocks, filling the domain with its light. "You can see the clouds," he remarked, spotting a bird as it entered and perched on a crack.

Hux nodded. "A fine display, isn't it?"

"Are we going to the throne room?" asked Terry.

"Not today," said Barniby, motioning to one of the larger

homes near the rear of the cavern. "The queen is in our home this afternoon. My father is preparing dinner as we speak."

"How exciting!" declared Hux. He bent to Terry's side. "Uncle Senna makes the best Haddin stew you've ever had."

"I've never had that," said Terry, and he wasn't so sure he wanted to try.

Terry sat at the end of a long table—the largest he'd ever seen outside of the Academy. It reminded him of the cafeteria where all the kids would gather to eat, getting their trays from the line, sitting together and talking, making fun of one another, laughing.

For a moment it was like he was there again, surrounded by friends and classmates, the smell of soy burgers and corn bread in the air. His mouth watered at the thought of it.

At the far end, a woman sat in humble clothes. Her name was Porcia Castchian, queen of this country and Hux's aunt. Despite all of this, she had no air of royalty about her. Rather, she reminded Terry of Ludo's grandmother, smiling and warm, a pleasant look of quiet kindness in her eyes. "It is good to have so many visitors," she said to the crowded table.

Jinel sat beside Terry, saying nothing. He could almost feel the urgency radiating from her, but she would have to endure the customs if she wanted her weapons. According to Hux, it was customary to feast together when a relative came home, even in an event such as this. As soon as the meal concluded,

Hux would present his aunt, the queen, with a request for the metal.

With any luck, the transaction wouldn't take long.

"I'm sorry to tell you that your request is impossible. The mines are currently inaccessible," said the queen, sitting in her cushioned chair. She frowned upon speaking the words, clearly displeased with the situation.

Dinner had concluded a short while ago, leading straight into the request. "Don't you keep reserves in a vault or a storeroom?" asked Jinel.

"Certainly," remarked Portia Castchain. "But those supplies are for our own needs. Without access to the veins in the mines, we must use our stock cautiously."

"But we need it to save people's lives," pleaded Jinel.

"I trust your words, but just as you place value in your own kind, so, too, must I. As the queen of this country, it is my sworn oath to put my people first."

Terry could hear Jinel's pulse pounding, even beneath her armor. She was understandably livid, having sailed five days to get here, stuck behind a breathing mask. "We'll figure it out," Terry assured her. "What's the issue in the mines?"

The queen looked at him, eying his ears but saying nothing. "Our workers are missing. Many are blaming the Sneaks."

She said the final word like it disgusted her. "What does *that* mean?" asked Jinel Din.

"Creatures," said Portia. "We've encountered them before, but they've never attacked anyone. It's the first time."

"They're in the mines?" asked Terry.

The old woman nodded. "Before this season, we had free reign over the tunnels, but for some reason they recently attacked us, dragging our people into their nest. We have no idea what has changed their behavior."

"You didn't go after them?" asked Jinel.

"What few soldiers we have were sent to investigate, but not many returned. The animals are too fast to fight, especially in such closed spaces."

"Where are the rest of your men?" asked Jinel.

"Most of our forces have been deployed to the eastern front," said the old woman.

"What's going on out there?" asked Terry.

"A small conflict," she answered. "The fifth house has had their ships attacked by the neighboring island tribes. Many were killed, so something had to be done."

"It should be quick," said Barniby. "A few months at most."

"That's too long to wait," said Jinel.

"It is the only way. Until the mines are safe to work, we cannot lend you any of our supplies, including oryx metal," said the queen.

"Oryx metal?" asked Terry.

"Orinchalium. That's what they call it here," said Jinel. She looked at the queen. "What if I go in and find whatever's threatening your miners?"

"You alone?" asked Portia Castchain, then laughed as if it were a joke.

"I'm serious," insisted Jinel.

"But you are just a girl. How can you—"

"I'm a soldier of Garden. I'm no stranger to combat."

"Nonetheless, I cannot permit such a reckless act. We don't need another death on our hands."

"I'll go with her," said Terry.

"Still, that is only two. It is hardly—"

"As will I," decreed Hux, grinning widely.

Barniby laughed. "If the three of you are going, My men and I will join, too. We can't have a pirate and some foreigners handling our problems for us."

"Is that enough?" asked Jinel.

The queen looked at both her son and nephew. "You understand the dangers of what you're asking."

They both smacked their chests. "It is for the good of our house," said Barniby.

The queen hesitated, taking a moment to consider their proposition. She tapped her chest with her fist. "Very well. I welcome the help, but please be careful."

"Thirty armed conflicts and I'm still standing," said Jinel Din. "A little animal won't be the thing that takes me down."

12

Ortego Outpost File Logs

Play Audio File 1612

Recorded: April 2, 2351

MITCHELL: *It worked!*

Despite my many reservations on the likelihood of success, the alien gene responsible for Variant compatibility has been successfully fused with the Lanrix drug. I have no words for what I am feeling, except to say that…I only wish Doctor Curie was here to see it. If this new formula works…if we can use this to cure Variant exposure once and for all, then everything we have worked for will be worth it. Archer's dream, for all its flaws, will be realized.

I don't know what will happen next. I don't even know if the drug will work once it is used on a subject. Because of this uncertainty, I have taken to using my own cells in order to test the viability of the new blend. If it holds and proves viable, I will proceed with human trials. In other words, I will use the cocktail on myself.

I am sure the board would protest this decision, but it is the fastest method available to me, and I must follow it. Everlasting is in disarray. If Garden succeeds in destroying the domeguard, the city will succumb to the elements and fall, leaving an entire population to suffocate. Doctor Curie, if she is still alive, will be placed in further danger.

I cannot let that happen. One way or the other, I shall have my results.

End Audio File

Everlasting
April 2, 2351

John sat with a group of Everlastian soldiers in a hangar bay, waiting to receive his new weapon—a short rifle capable of firing the nerve toxin with exceptional precision. This would make it much easier to subdue and capture the soldier and rebel leader Jinel Din, thereby granting them the leverage to discover Mei's true location and, with any luck, extract her safely.

A woman approached with a case in her hand, stopping in front of him. She presented it like a gift and he took it, curiously. "Is this it?" asked John, staring at the gray box.

"I was asked to retrieve your personal rifle as well," she said, ignoring his question.

He cocked his head, thinking he must have misheard her. "What?"

"Your weapon cannot be allowed onboard the ship, per Master Gel's request," said the woman.

"Why the hell not?" asked John.

"Due to the fatal nature of the ammunition it contains, your firearm brings too great a risk to the mission at hand. It is far more efficient to—"

"I'm not giving you my gun," he said, flatly.

"But, sir—"

"No. Not doing it."

She started to say something, but stopped. Her eyes dilated, indicating she was receiving something through her implant. "Ah, very well. Master Gel says he will allow you to carry your rifle, but asks that you please refrain from using it."

"Don't worry. I'll use yours instead. I'm just not giving mine up."

"Of course. Thank you, Sergeant." She gave him a slight bow, and left.

He sat there staring at the box, which looked more like a briefcase than anything. Searching and failing to find any sort of mechanical lock, he instead discovered a small rectangular piece of black material. Touching it, he felt the casing tremble in his hands, then snap open. "Must be some kind of scanner," he muttered.

Inside the box was a small pistol, the same kind he'd seen some of the soldiers carrying all over the city. John still recalled the first time he encountered one of these, back when Lena Sol and her team had arrived at the portal site and, incidentally, paralyzed nearly every single member of his team. This was the first time he'd ever wielded the weapon himself, which was fine. He much preferred the comfort and familiarity of his own rifle over this tiny piece of alien tech.

He touched the pistol in his hand, wrapping his fingers around the grip. The basic design was the same as any other sidearm, but with a few alterations. For one, the barrel was about half the size of a standard pistol. The weapon was also much lighter than he expected, maybe about a third the weight of a normal gun. Regardless, as long as it worked when he aimed and pulled the trigger, he couldn't complain.

Gel's request for John to come alone, without his team, still bothered him. He wasn't used to working with another group of soldiers, especially considering these people weren't even human. They also had completely different training and backgrounds. Nothing like his own. How could he trust them to have his back out there? How could they trust him?

It might have been a mistake to do this alone, but oh well. Too late to go back now. Gel had made a fair case regarding the need for secrecy, stating that Garden had eyes almost everywhere, including in his own department. Besides, with Mickey and Hughes injured and recovering, John's team needed a break. He knew better than to ask Short or Track to join him, not when their minds would be heavy on their friends. The rest of the team—Brooks, Meridy, Hatch, and all the others—needed to stay back and guard the portal and their camp, should anything else happen. The Blacks currently served as the only line of defense between Kant and Earth, so it certainly wouldn't do to spread their numbers too thin.

But still, John couldn't help but feel like he was missing something. Another set of eyes to watch his back. Another voice to tell him when to be on guard. He didn't trust these Everlastians, not as much as he wanted to. Not when Mei was missing in their city and he couldn't find her.

As the soldiers formed up and boarded the Red Door, John lifted his pack and slung it over his shoulders, tightening the straps. He took another look at the bay, then climbed into the aircraft's side.

The journey would take a few days, according to what Gel had told him. First they would touch down in the Northern Ilse at the Love and Grace Laboratories, whatever that was, to pick up a few personnel more familiar with the terrain and local wildlife. From there, it was only a short flight to the continent. John had no idea what to expect from this trip, but he hoped it wouldn't take long. Every second he was away from Everlasting was time away from wherever Mei was being held.

The Red Door shuddered, lifting off the bay landing pad. It eased its way through the outer door and into the sky above the trees. In the distant horizon, two suns dipped, reflecting midafternoon. *I'll find you, Mei,* thought John, looking back at the city as it fell into the distance. *No matter what it takes, no matter what I have to do, I'll bring you home. I swear.*

Galathane City, Tharosa

April 2, 2351

Terry awoke the morning after his meeting with the queen, opening his eyes to the suns' light as it pierced the open window of the seaside lodge. The cool northern breeze blew through the opening and caressed his cheeks, reminding him of how far he'd recently traveled. It was a stark change from the warmth of Ludo's farm or the sickly cold of the underground Garden base. Here, the chilled air felt fresh and invigorating. The usual grogginess of waking up ceased entirely, replaced with a burst of energy.

"Time to seize the day," exclaimed Hux, who had taken the twin bed near his own. The sailor was already on his feet and ready to go. "We have much to do before it's done."

Terry could already hear people in the hall, shuffling around. Ludo's voice stood out as he proclaimed a good morning to anyone who would listen. At the same time, Terry observed, Jinel was lecturing Lena to stay put and out of trouble, back in their room.

He leapt up and got dressed, following Hux to meet the others. Lena stayed behind with Ysa and Ludo, who promised to have dinner ready by the time the rest of them returned. "I want to see the market here and try the food. I'll have a feast for you!" exclaimed Ludo, always eager to feed his friends.

Lena gave Terry a hug before he left. "Be careful," she said from behind her breathing mask.

He smiled. "No need to worry. I've got Hux and his cousin to help me, and don't forget about Jinel."

Jinel Din grunted. "The sooner we finish, the better."

Hux, Terry, and Jinel made their way through the city gate

and toward the mountain. Barniby met them at the stairs, sword in hand and with an eager expression on his face. He beat his chest with the hilt of his weapon. "Fair day, cousin Hux!"

"Fair day!" returned the wavemaster.

"Follow me, friends, and let's make quick work of this."

They traveled through the cave city and into a series of long corridors. The mine entrance was some distance from the Galathane City, deep in the heart of the mountain. They passed by many splintered paths along the way, which Hux explained had once led to other mines, but were now bled dry of resources. "Why did they stop?" asked Terry, upon hearing this.

"For many reasons," said Hux. "An underground river blocked progress, while an unstable wall collapsed another. The miners dig and dig, sometimes in several places at once."

The tunnel descended as they went, which took them over an hour to traverse. When they reached the actual entrance to their destination, they found a massive metallic door. Terry stared at it with some curiosity, gripping the hilt of his sword. "Is this the same metal as—"

"Indeed, it is," said Barniby. "Oryx metal, like the weapon at your side."

Hux touched the door. "Not pure, though. The crafters use it along with other ores to create a sturdy blend. Only a fraction of it is needed to strengthen other metals beyond their own capacity."

Barniby nodded. "Exactly right." He gripped the handle.

"Ready to go inside?"

Jinel checked her rifle's safety, then nodded. "Let's make quick work of this."

"You heard the fine woman," said Hux.

Barniby gripped the handle and pulled, opening the door and flooding them with a foul and ancient taste. "In we go," he told them, and together they entered the mines.

The Red Door
April 2, 2351

THE NORTHERN ISLES was home to the Love and Grace Laboratories, a small outpost of about fifty scientists and analysts from Everlasting. There were many similar locations scattered all across Kant, but each had a separate purpose. Love and Grace was created specifically to observe and catalogue all life in the nearby region, which included the country of Tharosa and its many islands. At least, that was what John had been told during his short briefing ahead of the mission.

The Red Door flew across the snow-covered peaks of the Atlian Mountains beyond Everlasting and headed straight to the Northern Isles. It took only a few hours to reach, which was fine with John. The sooner he landed, the sooner he could proceed with the next portion of the mission and eventually return to the city. He had no desire to be out here, except for the eventual goal of finding Mei, and afterwards Terry. He'd come to this planet seeking his friend, but along the way he'd lost another. What good was he if he couldn't even keep the ones closest to him safe? What kind of value did he have?

He pressed his head against the aircraft window. *No,* he thought. *I'll find them both and bring them home. Whatever it takes, I'll do what I have to do. I'll—*

The Red Door shuddered, beginning its descent. John could see the labs below, white and gray domes, dotting the island like mushrooms on a log. It looked like a nice place, and any other time he might enjoy a tour, but his time was precious and the job couldn't wait. With any luck, the ship would soon be in the air again.

On the landing platform, a team waited to greet him. He recognized one of them immediately, a woman with familiar eyes.

"Welcome to Love and Grace," said Emile Res. "It's good to see you again, Sergeant Finn."

"Emile, is that you? I didn't know you'd be here," he said, surprised to see her. Emile had been one of the first few people John had met after arriving on this planet, along with Titus Ven and Lena Sol.

Emile waved. "This is my permanent duty station. I was only with the investigation team because of my archeological expertise. The technology used in constructing the portal is ancient and outdated, but I have some experience with it."

"I'm sure the team misses you now that you're gone," said John.

"The feeling is mutual. Be sure to give Bartholomew and

Zoe my best whenever you see them."

He nodded. "Did anyone tell you why I'm here?"

"Of course," she answered, as though it were obvious. "You are after a wanted fugitive. I'm set to join you as well, per Master Gel's orders."

Her words surprised him. The mission stated something about a few extra crewmen, but nothing regarding Emile. Maybe he simply missed the name at some point. "What are you coming with me to do?"

"Our research team is in charge of cataloguing and charting this region, so I have more than enough experience to assist."

"I'm just surprised it's you," said John.

"Master Gel selected me for that reason, actually. He believes you will be more comfortable working with me as opposed to a stranger." She smiled. "Familiarity breeds productivity."

"I guess it does," he said.

"Don't worry, nearly everyone on our team has an intimate understanding of the cultures and customs in this region, as well as the geography. I can tell you where the predators are and what to avoid, too."

"Sounds like you know your stuff," said John.

"Says the veteran soldier," remarked Emile.

She led him through the hangar and into the facility. Unlike Everlasting, which had been pristine and clean, not a speck of dirt to be found, this facility felt lived-in and real. Walking through the halls, he saw supplies strewn about, with dust on the windows, and places where the dirt had been dragged in. When asked about it, Emile shrugged. "We're not prudes like the people back home. Can't really be that way when you live in the real world."

"I thought everyone was afraid of contamination," he said.

"We are, but the fear is overblown. You can't get hurt from the gas unless you breathe it in. Even then, it doesn't do anything more than suffocate you. We go outside all the time with nothing but our regular clothes and a filtration mask. We only wear the full body suits if we're exploring a new area."

"Why's that?"

"Sometimes you find radiation swamps, maybe some chemical waste from before Extinction Day. It's hard to predict unless you know the area. When I visited the portal site, we had concerns about the energy supply powering the facility." She paused. "Oh, and sometimes it simply helps to have the armor in those suits. You've seen the wildlife. I'm sure you understand."

John recalled the attacks on his camp and the many animals he had to put down before finally securing the site. "I have an idea, yeah."

"While the ship refuels, is there anything you need to do?" asked Emile.

John felt his stomach growl. "I haven't eaten since yesterday."

She laughed. "Not a problem, Sergeant. We might be out in the wild, but that doesn't mean we don't have the essentials. Let me show you the dining room."

13

Leadership Report 228876.909
Recorded 04.2.884
Subtitled: Update 111

JUNE: *Sir, the attack is underway. Garden has infiltrated the building. It should be over soon.*

GEL: *Very good, Vivia June. How long before they reach Master Kai's location?*

JUNE: *Approximately six cycles, by my estimates. Not long at all. Shall I keep you informed of their progress?*

GEL: *No need. I will send in our defense force to counter their assault once they take the Master's floor.*

JUNE: *Understood, sir. What else would you have me do?*

GEL: *Do you still have the device in your possession?*

JUNE: *Of course, sir. I brought it with me to the new facility. The* *original box was damaged in the previous attack, but the core device is still safe.*

GEL: *Very good. I want you to activate it as soon as this transmission ends.*

JUNE: *To clarify, you wish for me to destroy this outpost?*

GEL: *Yes, that is exactly right…and I would like you to remain behind with it to ensure its success.*

JUNE: *S-Sir? Can you repeat? Did you say—*

GEL: *You must activate the bomb and remain behind. It is essential, Vivia June.*

JUNE: *But, sir, I…I don't entirely understand.*

GEL: *You are the only one with intimate knowledge of what has taken place in this city. The only one besides myself with an acute understanding of the steps we took to ensure our country's survival. If anyone connects you to Master Kai's death—to the fall of the Leadership—it would undermine everything we have worked to create. It would destroy Everlasting. Do you understand?*

JUNE: *I…I do understand, but—*

GEL: *What you do now—the sacrifice you are making—it shall ensure our people's survival. There can be no other way. Do you have the device with you? Is it in your current possession?*

JUNE: *Y-Yes…Yes, sir, I have it here. I—*

GEL: *Then speak, Vivia June. Repeat the words of our country.*

JUNE: *All…All is for the good of Everlasting, sir.*

GEL: *Again, Vivia June. Say them once more.*

JUNE: *All is for the good of Everlasting. All is for the good of Everlasting.*

GEL: *Let go now…and see it done. Say the words.*

JUNE: *All...is for the good of Everlasting...All is for the good of Everlasting...All is for the good of Everlasting...All is for the good of—*

End Audio File

Galathane City, Tharosa
April 2, 2351

The tunnel was dark and thick with dust.

Jinel activated the light on her rifle, filling the mine, and startling Barniby. "What is that?" he asked, shielding his eyes.

"It's like a torch," explained Hux, who had already witnessed the light while aboard his ship.

"A torch?" asked Barniby.

"Technology," explained Jinel. "It's artificial."

"It reminds me of the sailors from Lexine. They bring all kinds of strange things. Is that where you are from?"

"Jinel is from far away," said Hux, glancing at her. "Not Lexine, but some other country."

"Let's keep going," muttered Terry. It was best to ignore questions about Everlasting, at least for now. No need to send Barniby into a state of shock when he needed his wits.

"Follow after me," he explained, removing a small torch from the wall, then lighting it. The flame came alive in seconds.

They moved through the mine with some haste, passing a few corridors in the process. Terry wondered why they weren't checking everything, but Barniby seemed to know where he was going.

After some time, they arrived in a larger room with multiple passages branching off in various directions. Several tools littered the ground, no order to them. "This is where it attacked last time. One soldier was dragged—" He looked around, then pointed to the farthest tunnel. "—that way."

"Did no one else try to save him?" asked Terry.

"The Sneak's leg stabbed the miner's chest, cutting straight through his heart. He was dead before anyone could stop it." Barniby frowned. "It dragged the poor fellow by his ribcage."

"That's a nice image in my head," said Jinel, aiming her light in the implied direction.

Hux unsheathed his sword. "Chin up! Let's end this monster so it can't hurt more of our countrymen."

They followed the path before them, towards the deeper recesses of the mine. "Look there," said Jinel, aiming her light at the ground. There were streaks of red scratched into the dirt. Obvious tracks led further into the dark. "The trail is still fresh."

Barniby gave a knowing nod. "It hasn't been more than six days since the mine was closed. Without any workers to disturb the ground, it should still—"

Terry paused as he heard a shuffling noise coming from somewhere far away. "Wait," he said, touching Barniby's shoulder.

"What is it?" he asked.

"Quiet a moment, " said Hux. "Our friend here has a talent. Let him use it."

Barniby watched Terry with some curiosity, no doubt full of questions, but said nothing, abiding his cousin's advice.

Terry closed his eyes, picking up the sounds of the distant places buried in the mine. The unknown, untouched caverns beneath the manmade halls…

…and he heard a sound.

Tick…Tick…Ticka…

It was difficult to make it out, so Terry focused harder. He pushed everything away, filtering what he could: Hux licking his lips…Barniby's racing heart…Jinel's heavy breathing through the filter of her mask…rodents in the darkened corners.

Beyond them and between, Terry heard the sounds again, and this time with more clarity.

Ticka. Ticka. Ticka.

Ticka. Ticka. Tee.

Ticka. Ticka. Ticka.

Ticka. Ticka. Tee.

He heard and felt the rattling noise, and a shape formed in his mind. A massive piece of machinery, hidden somewhere far below.

And with it…something else…clamoring and clawing, scratching the dirt as it walked.

Sk sk sk sk sk sk sk, along the dirt it crawled.

Sk sk sk sk sk sk sk, came the creature hence, and louder still it grew.

"It knows we're here," said Terry. "It's coming this way."

"Finally," Jinel said as she squeezed the rifle's grip. "Let its suicide march begin."

THEY FOLLOWED the bloody trail along the mine, curving and winding through the tunnels until they found its end. "Looks like the trail stops here, but where did it go? I see no body," observed Barniby.

"It stopped bleeding, I suspect," said Hux, pointing to the ground. "The tracks continue on, if you look close."

Sure enough, the dirt was covered in marks, leading further in, but even without the trail, Terry could still hear movement in the walls as they drew closer. They wouldn't have to wait for long. "We should find an open room," he said, eyeing Hux.

"Right," said the wavemaster. "Barniby?"

"Not far. Follow, friends," he said, leading them through the tight space. As it opened, they found another work area, littered with stone and rubble. Holes in each of the walls marked unfinished progress.

"Look there," said Jinel, shining her light on one of the holes. The black rock glistened.

"Oryx metal," said Barniby.

"I don't see any other tunnels. This must be the deepest part of the mine," said Jinel.

"Your guess is right, but I see nothing different here than—"

The sound of movement filled the walls. They all heard it, stirring at the noise.

Sk sk sk sk sk sk.

Jinel turned her light to the left and right, searching for any sign of the enemy, any hint of an attack.

Sk sk sk sk sk sk.

It seemed to come from all angles, echoing in the cavern. They bunched together, facing all sides.

Sk sk sk sk sk sk.

Sk sk sk...

Sk...

All four grew still and quiet, not a breath rising from their chests.

Jinel aimed her light again at the opening where the black stone stood.

Terry drew his sword, waiting for what came.

Waiting...

Waiting...

Sk...

The reflective ore moved inside the stone, a metallic limb reaching out of the wall. As it did so, several bursts of red light pulsed from one end of its body to the other, deep beneath its glossy, black design. "There!" shouted Jinel Din, bracing her weapon. "It's here!"

The creature leapt to the ground, its onyx body glistening under the light of Jinel's gun. It moved across the ground with its many limbs—six, no eight, no, ten—digging up the earth.

Jinel let lose her weapon, firing wildly into the beast. Bullets slammed against its arms, but it continued moving without pause. Its limbs grew and receded with each step, their number constantly shifting. What sort of beast was this?

Hux raised his spear, preparing to attack, motioning with his other arm for Jinel to stop firing.

The moment she did, Hux and Barniby engaged, dashing towards the monster. It backed away in response, dodging their attacks, climbing onto and along the wall so fast the two men couldn't keep up, especially in the dark.

Jinel tried to find the creature with her light, but it continued to evade her. Its limbs pulsed with a red glow, allowing Terry to spot it as it lunged toward the opening in the wall. He ran at it, his weapon drawn, hoping to stop its escape.

At the last second, right as his sword was about to strike, the Sneak reacted by spreading its body into a different shape, consuming Terry's blade and, subsequently, his hand.

It clung to the wall with part of him inside of it, dragging him toward the hole. "It's got me!" he screamed to the others.

"Pull it back!" shouted Jinel.

Terry did, but felt a sudden heat inside his hand, burning like fire. He screamed in pain as the creature dragged him into the opening of the wall. "Help!" he cried. "I can't get away!"

But before his friends could get to him, Terry was inside the wall itself. The gap opened into a massive hole, and he fell into it, the force of the Sneak pulling him deeper into the earth below, crashing into stone and darkness, falling to some unknown end.

Terry opened his eyes in the dark, unable to see anything. The air was thick with dust, and he coughed as he breathed.

His head was pounding. He could barely think. How far had the creature taken him? How deep into the earth had they gone?

Ticka Ticka Ticka, came the awful sound.

Ticka Ticka Tee...

There it was, close enough to touch. The noise from before, the unknown thing from somewhere in the stone...he was close to it now.

Terry focused his mind, shutting out the pain in his skull and hand, and igniting his eyes to see.

As he opened them, the room filled with a blue tint, and all at once he saw it there. A mammoth *thing* without a name.

A massive machine stood tall and wide, metal arms piercing into stone, digging into the stone walls all around. The machine continued in its ramblings, muttering noise and filling the cave, performing some unknown task.

But for how long?

Its center flashed with a sudden emerald glow, followed by the noise again.

Ticka, came the bulking mass. *Ticka Ticka Tee.*

Terry rose to his feet, spotting his sword a few meters from his side. As he reached for it, he felt the pain and recoiled. His fingers were covered in cuts, reaching down along his palm and wrist. The pain of the wounds was overwhelming.

He tried to block out it, push the pain away, but it wouldn't leave him. For whatever reason, he couldn't adjust.

Can't focus on it, he thought, grabbing the sword with his other hand. *Have to find a way out of here.*

A shadow moved in the corner of his eye. He flinched at it, turning quick to see something scurrying away along the wall. He stared at the space along the stone, waiting and watching for—

The glowing red light from within the mobile machine danced from one end to the next, revealing the monster. "I see you," muttered Terry, and he walked forward.

The creature continued its crawl, passing broken stone and shards of metal, finally touching the level ground once more. It moved fluidly along the earth toward the central machine. As it neared the massive object, a large hatch opened, sliding up to reveal a burst of green light. The Sneak raised itself to the edge of the opening and shuddered, letting out bits of itself into the device. Bits of—

No, it was vomiting chunks of something else…a kind of ore. Could it be feeding the larger machine?

Terry ignored the thought. He had no context for what was happening. All he knew was that he needed to escape this place, but the only way to ensure success was to kill the one responsible.

He stepped forward, his weapon ready. He hadn't spent much time using his other hand to fight, but with some luck it wouldn't matter. He'd have to be fast.

Terry launched himself at the belly of the large device, at

the little thing at its core, and struck.

His sword cut through the creature's side, slicing a piece of its body away.

The chunk of the beast fell to the ground, and it turned to look at Terry.

Except it didn't, he realized. It couldn't, for there were no eyes to see him. No face or mouth or features. Only the mass itself, bobbing and moving, and…reforming.

The monster's metal flesh, which the sword had cut, came together and expanded, rebuilding on itself. A ball of midnight, reshaping.

Terry watched with disbelief. "What the—"

The Sneak leapt at him with ferocious speed. He dropped to a knee and rolled to his side. The beast cut into his arm as it passed.

Blood poured out of his flesh, bringing a shock of unexpected pain. He yelped as it burned, igniting his whole body.

The creature landed a few meters behind him, and he quickly turned to follow it, minding his guard.

Terry braced himself, slowing the moment long enough to raise his guard and block the attack. The Sneak hit his sword, deflecting to the ground, readying itself once more.

How was it able to hurt him so badly? Why couldn't he stop—

It came at his feet this time, and he met it with a thrust of his blade, piercing its body and severing a chunk from the larger mass. The monster gave no pause, reforming itself immediately.

The Sneak lunged at him, but he deflected it, sending the

blob of morphing metal into the nearby wall. In mid-air, the monster changed, extending its tentacle arms behind, catching the wall. It bounced, projecting itself back at him.

The sudden action took him by surprise, but he managed to avoid the oncoming threat, if just barely. The metallic beast slid beside him, sweeping the hilt of his sword, slashing his hand in the process. Terry let out a cry of pain. Despite his concentration, the Sneak was still penetrating his defenses, still hurting him.

The beast's razor sharp body shuddered, forming different arms and blades, and it moved across the ground like a demonic spider.

It went toward him, scurrying between his legs. He leapt into the air, high above the monstrosity, and struck its flesh in one solid motion.

A chunk of the monster fell away, landing like gel several meters away. The animal tried to reform, but something was obviously wrong with it. Its flesh trembled as it attempted to redistribute its weight to the missing section, but it couldn't get there. *It must not have enough left,* thought Terry. *Time to finish this.*

He ran at the creature and unleashed a flurry of attacks, swiping its body with his cold orinchalium blade. The monster fell in halves, and with another quick stroke, into quarters.

The pieces let out drops of liquid, attempting to reform and come together, but Terry refused to give it the chance. He sliced each section into smaller and smaller pieces. Before it was done, the Sneak had been disassembled into tiny fractions of itself.

He watched them for a long time, waiting, but the creature

never rematerialized. He'd killed the beast at last…if it was ever truly alive to begin with.

Several minutes later, he heard a voice calling to him.

"Terry!" shouted someone from beyond the walls.

It sounded like Barniby.

He ran to the back of the cave, to the place where he'd fallen. "I'm here!" he yelled back.

"Did you hear that?" asked Hux.

"He's alive," said another, whose distorted voice could only be Jinel.

"Terry, do you hear me?" asked Hux, shouting down the hole. "The opening is too narrow for me. Can you climb?"

"I don't think so!" he returned.

"We'll find a rope," shouted Jinel. "Don't go anywhere!"

"There's something here," said Terry. "A machine."

"What sort of machine?" asked Hux.

"I have no idea," he said.

"I'll come down and have a look. Stay where you are!" yelled Jinel.

"I don't think that's going to be a problem," muttered Terry. He turned back towards the hulking object at the center of the cavern. "There's nowhere left to go."

Terry sat beneath the hole in the cavern, staring at the machine and the debris surrounding it. What purpose did a thing like this serve, and what was it even doing here? From what he could tell, it was more advanced than the machinery on the surface, but given how little he knew of Galathane City or Tharosa, it was impossible to say.

The others returned after a short while, a length of rope dropped from the opening. A few moments later, Jinel began her descent into the cave.

As she moved between the stone, Jinel scraped the sides with her boots, kicking dust. Her light shined down on his location as the weapon dangled from her side.

"Easy coming in," said Terry, watching as several pebbles hit the bottom of the crevice. The last thing they needed was a cave in.

"Not to worry," she said, reaching the ground and raising her light. "Now, let's see what you're—"

The sight of the machine left her stunned, its hulking mass filling half the cavern. "That's what I was talking about," said Terry.

"Unbelievable…is this still operational?" She walked toward it, waving the light from one side of it to the next, searching.

"What is it? Do you know?"

"The technology looks to be pre-Extinction Day," she said.

"You mean before Variant?"

"This is a metal purifier."

"A what?"

"The miners insert ores into the machine and it extracts whatever impurities the metal has. I've never seen one in person, but I remember the database entry."

"The Sneak that attacked us was feeding it," said Terry.

"Feeding?" she asked.

"It was giving it something, like chunks of metal or maybe rocks. I don't know."

"Wait," she said, stiffening. "Where is that thing? Did you kill it? Did it run off?"

"It's dead, I think," he said, pointing to the various pieces.

She squatted down and examined them, nudging one of the blobs with her gun. "Interesting," she whispered.

"What do you think it is?"

"You don't know?"

He shook his head. "Should I?"

"This is a machine."

"Like a robot?" he asked.

"A construct, made up of what appear to be micromachines."

"Micro?" he asked.

She reached out with her fingers and touched the metal. It trembled, reforming slightly, and then relaxed. "Tiny machines built to perform a certain task. They often come together to form a larger assembly like the one you fought against. The technology is very old."

"How do you know about this?"

"Everlasting uses them in repairs, but we moved away from the technology a century ago. We only use them for a few things now."

"Why?"

"Orinchalium is the primary metal used to create them, but as you already know, the metal is exceedingly rare."

Terry looked at the cut on his palm. No wonder this machine was able to hurt him. It was made of the same metal as his sword. "I see. So, what are they for?"

"You remember the sentry units you fought?" she asked.

"The Guardians? Sure, but I don't think they—"

"Those didn't use them, no, but some do. The micromachine sentries are remotely controlled via satellite uplink, while the ones you fought relied on a pilot."

"Are they just different models or something?"

"No, all the sentries started with a similar design, but over time most of them had to be refurbished. It's been two centuries since the last one was constructed, and they've all taken a beating. Over time, our engineers had to replace their parts and alter how they functioned."

"So, that means there's still a few micromachine Guardians somewhere in the wild." If they were anything like the little one he'd just fought, they wouldn't be easy to kill. "That doesn't sound good."

"Why do you think I came all the way to this continent?" she asked, approaching the giant machine. "All the other sentries have to rely on a pilot, which we can kill, but the other kind—the ones made up entirely of micromachine orinchalium…well, the only thing strong enough to stop them is more of the same." She shined her light on the sword in Terry's hand. "That's why this mission matters. Without that metal, none of us stands a chance."

14

Ortego Outpost File Logs
Play Audio File 1627
Recorded: April 3, 2351

MICHTELL: *So far, the fusion is holding strong. I've tested it on my own cells and the mix appears to be stable, although I will need to modify a few things. The next step, barring any complications, would require me to perform an injection on a living creature. Preferably, if I had one available, a rodent, but I don't have time to order one from Central.*

Instead, as I have stated previously, I will be using the mixture on myself. In fact, I have the needle in my hand as I speak. I am certain others would criticize me for what I am about to do, but I don't care.

Given the recent upheaval in Everlasting, the time for experimentation and waiting is over. If the walls fall—if the city loses all of its protection from the gas—thousands of innocent people will die.

The reaction will be fast, and I'll know quite soon whether I've wasted my efforts or not.

Now, then…

Time to change the world.

End Audio File

The Red Door
April 3, 2351

Johnathan Finn was already waiting inside the ship when Emile finally arrived.

"I thought I'd beat you here," she said when she spotted him.

"I like to be early," he answered, thumbing the safety belt around his waist.

She took a seat across from him. "That so?"

"Not really," he admitted. "I'm just in a hurry to get back."

"Your concern is understandable, given the situation."

He only grunted. As much as he appreciated her sympathy, talking about Mei wouldn't do him any good right now. He had to focus on the job. Go find this Jinel Din and bring her back to Everlasting.

Get her to talk. Find Mei. Focus on the task.

The aircraft roared to life, shaking their seats as it began to lift. "It seems we're on our way," remarked Emile.

"How far away is our target?" asked John.

"Satellite feed shows her ship docked in a harbor, south of a mining city. She was tracked into the mountain and hasn't been seen since."

"The mountain? How are we supposed to find her?"

"Wait, of course," said Emile. "She has to come out at some point."

The Red Door left the hangar and took off toward the north, headed for its goal. Another continent to the north. Before this day was through, John would find his target. He'd finish the job and get his answers.

One way or the other.

Galathane City, Tharosa
April 3, 2351

"You heal pretty fast," said Jinel, checking the bandage around Terry's hand, followed by his shoulder. "Remarkably fast, actually."

Terry and his friends sat inside the queen's house, waiting for lunch. Having fulfilled their promise to retake the mines, the group was invited to relax and discuss the terms of their agreement. That is, authorization to receive their payment of orinchalium. A well-deserved prize.

"His wings stretch far," explained Ludo with a large grin. "I taught him everything he knows."

Terry laughed. "It's true, he did."

"You taught him how to heal faster?" asked Jinel, clearly confused by the notion.

Lena stood right beside him, observing the place where the wound had been. "Accelerated healing factor is inherent to the priest class, usually induced through various forms of meditation. However, if I understand correctly, Terry, you were able to do much of this before you learned how to focus your mind."

"Sure, but it wasn't even close," he said.

"Still, your biology is very distinct, even more than the naturally evolved population on Kant, such as Ludo and Ysa here," explained Lena.

"If it weren't for them, I would probably be dead," said Terry, smiling at the couple. "They taught me how to survive."

"Terry has come far," said Ysa, her voice as elegant and soft as ever.

Ludo placed a hand on his shoulder. "It is so."

Hux bellowed out a roar of laughter. "What a crew we're shaping up to be."

"What is all the noise down here?" asked the queen, entering the hall from the kitchen, a wide smile on her face. She was holding a tray of baked treats, the scent of which had filled the room long before she arrived.

"Only friends speaking loudly, Majesty," answered Hux.

"Sounds to me like family, nephew, but still think nothing of it. Everyone, come with me and let us eat. There is much to discuss regarding your contributions yesterday."

"A fine day it was," called Barniby from the kitchen.

"With many more to come," said the queen.

Terry explained to the queen what he found in the mine, leaving out a few select details. For example, the queen didn't need to know that the only reason Terry knew what the machine did was because of Jinel. If anyone learned where she was from, it could pose a danger to her, since Everlasting was so revered. People might think she was a god, while others might try to kill her, as Hux had suggested.

No, it was better to stay as far away from that as possible, so instead he told a lie, claiming he'd seen the purifier in other areas of the world.

"I see, so the Sneak was a machine, guarding its nest," mused the queen.

"In all likelihood, it was only trying to do its job, but at some point, malfunctioned," said Jinel.

"Whatever the case, it's gone now," said Lena.

"Indeed, it is," said the queen.

"Which means you can send your miners back in," finished Jinel.

The old woman nodded, smiling. "I suppose you'll want your oryx metal, as we agreed."

"If you don't mind," said Jinel.

"Rest easy. Barniby has already left to secure it for you. It will be brought to Hux's ship right away."

"Thank you, majesty," said Hux.

"You are most welcome, nephew," she said, cheerily. "Shall

we eat now? I've spent all morning meeting with my staff about this matter and I must admit I'm quite famished."

After lunch, the crew departed, waiting as Hux embraced his aunt and said his goodbyes. The jolly sailor smiled brightly at her, kissing her forehead. "Safety to you, majesty."

She tapped her chest with her shaking fist. "To you, nephew Hux, and please come home to us soon."

He returned the gesture, bidding her farewell.

It was snowing when they arrived at the city gates, and had been since the night before. By now, the field was covered in a sheet of white flakes, transforming it.

"Something wrong?" Jinel asked, glancing at Terry as they reached the steps.

"It's been a while since I saw snow," he said.

"When was the last time?" she asked.

He thought back to when he arrived on this planet. As the portal spit him out onto the mountainside, along with pieces of the Ortego facility. He remembered the fear and confusion he felt, the sudden touch of ice, the shock of the world before him. The sight of two dancing suns. He had been afraid that day, a frightened child in the wilderness.

But that was a long time ago…and he was older now.

An easy smile formed, and he looked at his friends, who each stood beside him. "I can't remember, but it feels like a lifetime ago."

"I believe I know what you mean," she answered, and he knew it was the truth.

The Red Door
April 3, 2351

THE AIRCRAFT FLEW across the sea of clouds, parting them like saltwater. The continent of Tharosa was just ahead, growing larger in the distance, though it was hardly visible behind the building snow storm. John stared out the window. "This could be a problem."

"If the storm gets any worse, we'll have to wait it out," said Emile.

"What's the forecast? Do we know?"

"Looks like a few more cycles before we arrive, according to Analytics."

John reached into his pack and removed his headgear, a thick beanie to cover his head and ears. "Good thing I brought this."

"We have masks if you'd like one. They'll shield you from the cold," said Emile.

"Thanks, but I'm fine with my own gear," he said. The ship passed through the storm with only a minor bit of turbulence. As it neared the continent, the Red Door began its descent. John spotted mountains first, followed by the harborside village. They'd come from the east in order to land in a nearby field so as not to alarm anyone. "Do we have a read on the boat?"

"Still docked," she answered.

"We need to get to them before they leave," said John.

"Agreed."

"That means leaving the ship before the storm ends."

"Maybe for you and your team," she said. "I'm staying here."

"What's the point of bringing you if you're not going?"

"The orinchalium in Jinel Din's possession, if she's been successful, needs to be analyzed. I'm not leaving the ship until you've captured her." Emile shuddered. "That woman is dangerous."

John lifted his Everlastian pistol, looking it over. "I guess that means we'll have to take her down fast."

"Her accomplices, too," added Emile.

"Right," said John, holstering the weapon.

The ship landed after a short moment, and the outer door unlocked automatically. John got to his feet, looking over the cabin and the dozen soldiers he'd brought with him. "Are we ready?"

The men raised their fists, giving their salute.

"Alright." He pressed the unlock button, opening the door. A strong wind hit him, stinging his cheeks. "Move out!"

The harbor was nearly covered in snow by the time they reached the ship. Hux went in to check on the cargo while the others waited on the dock, which had already emptied for the day. "Shame. I wanted some snacks before we left," said Ludo.

"Don't worry," said Ysa. "Lena asked the innkeeper to buy some. They are on the boat."

Ludo's face lit up. "Truly?"

Lena handed him a piece of wrapped meat. "We noticed you had an affinity for dried sempter fish and raginello cheese, so we made some requests."

"So kind!" He took the food, grinning.

"Ludo is easy to please," remarked Ysa.

"It would seem so," said Lena, trying not to laugh.

Jinel and Terry stood a few meters away, watching Hux's crew walk along the deck of the ship. The young soldier cleared her throat. "Mind if I ask you a question?"

He nodded. "What's up?"

"Are you doing this because you believe in Garden?" she asked with her muffled voice.

"Garden?"

"Yes. I realize now I haven't asked how you feel about all this. Did you agree to assist us because you understood the cause? Because you wanted to change things?"

He thought about the question, then shook his head. "Not really. I'm not much of a revolutionary, and I don't know enough about your politics."

She blinked. "Then, why?"

"I was being held hostage in that lab, but you saved me. You got me out. Maybe it's stupid, but I'm doing this because it feels like I should. Because I have a debt that needs paying."

"So, you owe Garden your life? That's why?"

"No," he said, looking at her. "Just you. You're the one who saved my life. You walked me out of that place when bombs were going off. The least I could do is help you. Besides," he added, "you're my friend."

She stared at him. "Your friend?"

"You and them," he said, motioning to Ludo, Ysa, and Lena. "And Hux, of course."

She looked at the others, who were laughing amongst themselves. "I see. Well, thank you, both for agreeing to help me and…for the rest."

"The cargo is set!" called Hux as he came out from the cabin. He walked to the bow of the ship and smacked his chest. "We can leave right away."

"Shouldn't we wait for the snow to stop?" asked Terry.

Hux scoffed. "A little ice never stopped this old ship!"

"Rightly said, dear Hux!" shouted Ludo. "Let us—"

"Hold," said Ysa, touching her husband's wrist, quieting him. "Listen."

Ludo said nothing, but closed his eyes instead.

"What is it?" asked Jinel.

"Wait," said Terry, and he followed his friend's lead, shutting his eyes and focusing his mind. With the strength of his senses, he listened, shutting out the distractions. The gushing water beneath the docks. The soft wind, carrying the snow. The people in their homes, laughing, talking, arguing.

Far beyond the walls of the village, an engine rumbled steadily in a field. Two dozen feet shuffled in the snow-tipped grass, running in this direction.

"Do you hear it?" Ysa asked him.

He opened his eyes. "Are those soldiers?"

"Soldiers? From where?" asked Jinel.

"I don't know, but it sounds like an aircraft just unloaded some people."

"Everlasting," muttered Jinel. "Could it be they've found us?"

15

Ortego Outpost File Logs
Play Audio File 1634
Recorded: April 3, 2351

HARPER: *Wait a second. Are you saying you injected an untested immunization without clearing it with the board? Please tell me I misheard that.*

MITCHELL: *That's correct.*

HARPER: *Good God, Mitchell! What the hell were you thinking? You could have died.*

MITCHELL: *True, but I didn't. I'm still alive.*

HARPER: *That's not the point and you know it. You defied procedure and put yourself in serious danger.*

MITCHELL: *Nonetheless, it seems the vaccine works. I've performed multiple tests since injecting myself and—*

***HARPER**: You haven't experienced any negative side effects?*

***MITCHELL**: Not a single one. Based on the data before me, it would seem we now have a viable solution.*

***HARPER**: Well, be that as it may, it doesn't excuse your behavior. You understand that, don't you?*

***MITCHELL**: Certainly.*

***HARPER**: You'll have to appear before the board for a special hearing to discuss the ramifications of your actions. However, given the results, I'm sure they'll opt for a lighter touch.*

***MITCHELL**: Ma'am?*

***HARPER**: You've just cured Variant, Sophie. The board isn't going to throw you away for taking a few risks, even if they were stupid ones. The rest of Central would lose its mind.*

***MITCHELL**: I only did this because time was a factor. Everlasting is in the middle of a war and they need this medicine.*

***HARPER**: Then give it to them. Test the formula on one of their own first, but go ahead and begin full production.*

***MITCHELL**: Titus Vin and his crew are on their way as we speak. Master Gel has agreed to let us test the cure on a volunteer. I'll take proper safety procedures this time, but I believe the vaccine will hold.*

***HARPER**: We'll need thousands of doses, and soon, should this actually work. Inform me as soon as you know the results of the test. I'll have our labs stop everything to focus on replicating more inoculations.*

***MITCHELL**: Thank you, Dr. Harper.*

***HARPER**: If all of this works out, Sophie, believe me, I'll be the one thanking you.*

End Audio File

Ashby Harbor, Tharosa
April 3, 2351

Terry and his friends ran through Ashby like their lives depended on it, knowing that was likely the case. The Everlastian troops were coming, bringing conflict with them. There would be no respite today. No chance to flee or hide.

Terry and Ysa ran together at the head of the group, with Ludo and Jinel following behind. Hux remained at the docks with Lena, preparing the ship for departure.

They came to the edge of the town just before the gate, kicking snow as they arrived. Already, Terry could see the ship in the distant field, a squad of soldiers gathering around. Each of them wore a mask or a helmet, blocking their faces.

"Not as many as I thought," observed Ysa, rather calmly.

"They're tougher than they look," said Terry.

"Do they fly?" she asked.

Jinel and Ludo slid to a stop beside them. "Everlastians don't fly," said Jinel, hoisting her rifle from her side, readying it. "But they have guns and armor, and that makes them tough to kill."

Terry raised his brow at the soldier beside him. "Don't count us out yet. We've got a priestess, an Everlastian field commander, a farmer, and a mutant kid from Central. What's an army to that?"

"Don't forget the wavemaster and the analyst," said a

female voice from behind. Terry turned to see Lena standing there with Hux at her side. "You didn't think we'd leave you to it, did you?"

"What about the ship?" asked Terry.

Hux beat his chest. "My crew is here and needs its captain."

"I can't do much without a weapon, but I'm here if you need me," said Lena.

"Any ideas?" asked Jinel.

"We can't let them near the city," said Ludo.

"We could engage them in the field," said Jinel. "Flank them if we can."

Terry nodded. "Okay. Let's split into two groups, then meet in the middle."

"Wait," said Ludo. "Are you certain we should fight them?"

"If we take the ship, the satellite will track our movement," explained Lena. "They'll follow and sink the *Waveguard* before we're halfway there."

"Sink the *Waveguard*?" asked Hux, appalled.

"It won't come to that," said Terry.

"Here," said Jinel, looking at Lena. She handed her the rifle. "Stay here and fire from a distance. Use the guided scope like I showed you the other day."

"I-I remember," said Lena, taking the weapon.

Jinel took a pistol from her waist and switched off the safety. "We'll hit them hard and quick, before any of them have a chance to react. Are you ready?"

John watched as the Everlastian soldiers unloaded from the Red Door, their boots hitting the snow, flattening the mound until it was nothing but hard ice.

They gathered together in a circle around him, waiting for orders, prepared to move ahead.

Once the ship had unloaded, the door raised and locked back into place.

John lowered his goggles to cover his face. "We're going to the docks first. I want everyone behind me!"

The soldiers raised their fists, acknowledging the command.

John jogged through the field, each of the twelve behind him. The wind was picking up, pushing snow along the ground. With any luck, the villagers would be indoors and out of sight. He wouldn't be able to live with himself if a civilian was injured…or worse. If only he had his team with him. People he could trust. People he knew. Not these aliens with their unknown procedures.

Gel had assured him that the troops were more than capable. He claimed they were fully trained to avoid such situations, but John couldn't know for certain…not until he was in the middle of a firefight with them. That was the true test of a man's character, the only way to know his soul.

Terry and Ysa crept between the trees on the side of the field, watching the soldiers as they trotted toward the village. On the other side, Ludo, Jinel, and Hux were doing the same, preparing to attack.

Jinel reached the opposite end, crouched behind one of the thicker trees. She couldn't see Terry, but he had assured her that he would be watching, and it was true. With a slight raise of her hand, she formed a fist, then brought it down, signaling the attack.

Terry tapped Ysa's wrist, and together they burst through the tree line and straight into the field.

On the other side, Jinel's team did the same, setting their sights on the enemy troops. The commander of Garden fired with perfect precision, blasting two of the soldiers in the head, ending them.

The other soldiers reacted instantly, opening fire on the rest. One of the shots hit Ludo, knocking him into the snow.

"They're using the toxin!" shouted Jinel. "Don't let them hit you!"

Ysa slid beneath the line of fire, knocking one of the men to the ground, throwing snow into the air around the crowd. With a series of quick hits, she shattered bones, tearing a scream from the man's throat.

She grabbed his weapon and tossed it into the clearing, then turned on another one.

"Stop her!" shouted one of the soldiers, but his voice was strange, not muffled from a breathing mask, but clear and distinct.

Familiar, too.

He wore a separate uniform from the rest, a strange mask

on his head with goggles. The design wasn't Everlastian, but still familiar.

Hux charged like a bull into the field, stampeding into two soldiers and grabbing both their heads, one in each hand, and burying them in the ground.

Another set of troops took aim at the wavemaster, preparing to stop him. Seeing this, Jinel tried to draw their attention, shooting one in the leg. The other soldier unloaded his weapon onto her, but she was already back behind the tree.

A shot hit one of the men in the side of his shoulder. It came from the city walls. There, Lena Sol was crouched with Jinel's rifle, aiming at the crowd. She pulled the trigger, taking a slow and steady breath, and fired, tagging another in the arm.

Terry kept his eye on the man who appeared to be their leader, the one without the mask. "Hit them quick!" the stranger cried, then fired his own pistol, tagging Hux in the foot.

The wavemaster stumbled, pausing momentarily, and then collapsed.

"They're using the toxin!" shouted Jinel.

Can't give them time to get the rest, thought Terry.

He dashed at the soldiers, his weapon extended. One of the men fired at him, but he deflected the shot with his blade, and continued forward.

Terry drew in close, disarming the nearest soldier. He raised his sword to him, aiming to stab him in the leg. He didn't want to take anyone's life today, only injure them.

But before the blade could make its mark, the leader of the

squad came upon him, knocking Terry back. The leader stood between them now, his pistol drawn and aimed. "Back off!"

But Terry wouldn't have it. He readied himself to begin again, steadying his stance.

"I'm warning you," said the man with the mask. His words didn't match his lips. He had to be using a translator, the same one Lena had told him about…but what was a foreigner doing with Everlastian soldiers? Unless…

"Who are you?" Terry asked in English.

The man hesitated at the change in language. He pressed his hand to his collar, and there was a click. "You speak English?"

"My name is Terry and I'm from Earth," he said. "Now, who the hell are you?"

John stared at the wild man before him, the one speaking the language of his home world. The savage with the mad, unkempt hair and unusual clothes. The man who had just called himself Terry. "What did you just say?"

"I said my name is Terry. Who the hell are you?"

John lowered his weapon. "Terry?"

"Yeah…do I know you?"

John removed his mask, revealing his tired face. Terry's eyes widened, a shocked expression overcoming him. They both stood motionless for what felt like a long moment, saying nothing.

"Oh, my God," Terry finally muttered, his mouth hanging open. "John?"

John nodded, uncertain of what to do or say. He'd spent so much time looking for the person in front of him, never knowing if his hopes were wasted, never knowing if the friend he knew was even still alive. "I can't believe it's you," he answered, almost choking on the words. "How…what are you doing here?"

"I'm—"

A sudden burst of weapon fire sounded from behind him, bringing John out of his daze. "Everyone, stop firing. Stop!"

The Everlastian squad came to a halt, but didn't lower their weapons. Instead, they kept their sights fixed on the enemy. One in the tree line, one behind the city wall, and three others immobilized in the snow. Two large men and a bald woman with tattoos.

"Why are you helping Everlasting, John?" asked Terry.

"Mei's been taken hostage. I need to find the one responsible. A terrorist who knows where she's being kept."

"Terrorist?"

"Garden. They abducted her," explained John.

"But I've been with them. I didn't hear anything about that."

"Then you've been lied to," said John. His eyes fell to the snow. "I know it's true. I've seen the intel."

Terry looked at the person in the woods. A female wearing a breathing mask and armor. "Is this true?" he asked, yelling across the field. "Did Garden kidnap Mei?"

"Leadership lies!" she returned. "Garden would never do anything to you or your people! We have one goal: to overthrow the dictatorship in our city and bring peace to our people!"

"Who is that?" asked John. "Is that Jinel Din?"

"How did you know her name? Is she the person you're after?" asked Terry.

Finally, thought John. Now he could finish this and return to the city. He'd save Mei and then they could all go home. "Terry, listen to me. That woman knows where Mei is. We have to bring her in!"

Terry looked at Jinel, blinking curiously. He shook his head. "Jinel saved my life. She wouldn't—"

"Whatever she's telling you, it's not true. She's just using you. These people are terrorists. They need to be stopped."

"But—"

John started toward the trees. "Don't worry, Terry. I'll handle this right now. You'll see." He raised his pistol, aiming at his new target. "Come out, Jinel Din! You're coming with me!"

"John, stop!" begged Terry. "You're making a mistake!"

"Sorry, but we don't have a choice," he answered. He didn't like going against his friend's wishes, but given the current stakes, he couldn't take the risk. He had to ensure Mei's safety, no matter what.

John stared at the woman in armor, this terrorist commander who had plagued Everlasting for so long. He would have to be quick to outgun her, but given his reflexes and speed, he knew it wouldn't be a problem. Just slide to the left and tag her with the toxin. It would only take one shot. Maybe two.

He stopped a few meters from her, staring her in the eyes.

John took a deep breath, clearing his mind. He could do this. He could save Mei. Save Terry. All he had to do was breathe.

One.

Two.

Three.

And go.

Terry didn't know what to do. He was finally reuniting with his oldest friend, but it came at the cost of another's freedom. No doubt, John believed what he was saying, but there was no way Jinel could be responsible for Mei's kidnapping. Yes, the woman had committed acts of violence against the Leadership, but she'd never done anything to suggest she was capable of such a betrayal.

Or would she? He had to admit he'd only known her for just over a month, which wasn't long enough to truly understand a person, but…

Still, he'd spent time with Jinel, fought alongside her. He understood her motives and what she was after, and he knew that all she really wanted was to save her people. Whether or not she was right in this, he couldn't say, but he had no doubts that she believed it. She'd also saved his life, brought him out of that lab and taken him to freedom. He'd trusted her enough to cross an ocean, to come all the way to Tharosa to find a way to stop the war. She had always looked out for him. She'd always told him the truth.

The Everlastian soldiers stood between Terry and John, their attention divided. If he could get around them, somehow, he might be able to stop his friends from fighting. It could be possible to talk this whole thing out. If he could just—

John broke into a mad dash in an instant, opening fire on Jinel Din. He slid in the snow, letting loose a barrage of shots, nearly hitting her. She managed to move behind the massive trunk, keeping it between them, unable to return fire.

The move opened her to an attack from the other soldiers, who now observed her clearly. They raised their weapons, preparing to strike her down with the nerve suppressor. "Stop!" demanded Terry, but a few of them raised their guns to him, warning him to stay put.

Terry focused his mind and cleared himself of all thought, all distractions, and in that single moment of tranquility, released his inner calm.

He raised his blade and attacked the squad, dodging their shots as he moved across the glade. He cut the first rifle down, splitting it in half, taking the man's trigger finger with it. The soldier screamed in shock as Terry continued to the next.

With a quick parry, Terry knocked the second rifle to the side, nearly throwing it from the man's hand. He moved in and stabbed him in the arm, forcing him to drop the weapon.

He pushed his way through each of the soldiers, disarming them as he cut through the crowd. A pool of warm blood pooled in the middle of the white field. The men ran in terror, back towards their ship, while others passed out where they had collapsed.

"Terry, stop!" ordered John.

"They've brainwashed him. Don't listen!" yelled Jinel.

"Both of you need to stop!" demanded Terry.

John aimed his pistol at the Garden soldier. "Not until I have her. Not until I get Mei back!"

Terry lunged at his old friend, going for the weapon in his hand. Terry pressed him back against the nearest tree, pinning him to the bark as John refused to let go of the pistol, continuing to fire into the leaves. "Stop it!" yelled Terry.

"Let me go!" barked John, and he kneed Terry suddenly in the belly, pushing him back.

Terry staggered, surprised at John's strength.

John raised his weapon. "I don't want to hurt you, but—"

"Neither do I!" snapped Terry, taking one of Ludo's daggers from his waist and throwing it towards the pistol. It struck the weapon, forcing it free of John's grasp.

Terry took the chance to attack. He ran straight at him, but John reacted quickly, raising his leg into Terry's stomach, grabbing him by the arms. John rolled on his back, bringing Terry above and behind him, throwing him into the snow.

The two rose to their feet and attacked. As John threw a fist, Terry took his wrist and turned, pressing his back to John's chest, elbowing him in the stomach with so much force it sent him sliding backwards, kicking snow into the air.

John returned immediately and slid towards him, sending snow into Terry's face. From behind the white cloud, John sprang forth at him, knocking him in the chest with his head like a battering ram while grabbing both his sides. John lifted Terry and pushed him back into the nearest tree, cracking the wood.

Terry brought both his hands down on John's neck, striking him repeatedly. John let him go, and Terry caught himself on a branch. He reengaged, sprinting forward. A few meters from his target, he leapt high into the air, releasing a series of swift kicks, aimed at John's chest.

John braced for the assault, blocking with his arms crossed and his head down, his feet planted where he stood.

As Terry began to land, John grabbed hold of his ankle and swung him to the ground.

Terry hit the earth with a deep thud, snow billowing into the air.

He staggered to his feet, unsteady and nearly falling.

John reached for the rifle on his back, the one he'd ignored until now, and aimed it squarely at Terry's face. "Don't move!"

But Terry wasn't listening, and attacked. John's finger brushed the trigger, nearly firing, but he checked himself. Instead, he slammed the butt of his rifle into Terry's shoulder, redirecting him.

Terry spun around, recovering quickly. When the rifle came again, he dodged, using John's own momentum to catch the gun and disarm him.

In that same instance, Terry raised his foot, and with a single, perfect strike, slammed it into the soldier's chest.

The impact sent John flying, snapping low-hanging

branches and scattering dead leaves. A splash of blood exploded from his mouth as he landed and slid into a tree trunk.

"John!" called Terry, frantically, once he saw the blood.

The seasoned soldier wasn't moving.

John sat with his hands crossed, smiling a big, bright smile, and laughing. Today was the day he went to school. Today was the day he got to grow up.

"Do you have everything you need, Johnny?" asked his mother. They stood together at the train station, along with his brother, Trevor, who had only just graduated from the Academy himself.

John nodded. "Yup!"

"Good," she said, giving him a hug. She nuzzled his cheek with her nose, and he giggled. "You know we won't get to see each other for a while, but you're going to be tough, right?"

He grinned. "Yeah, I'm tough!"

"Remember what I told you, Johnny," said Trevor.

"Stay out of trouble," said John, repeating the advice he'd been given.

"Right," said his brother. "And you're bigger than the other kids will be, so don't be a bully."

"No way," said John, shaking his head. Trevor had told him about how sometimes kids could pick on other kids. John would never be like that. Not in a million, billion years. Not ever. "Only cowards…um…" He tried to remember.

"Only cowards hurt those weaker than themselves," Trevor reminded him. "Got it?"

"Yeah, I remember," insisted John, smiling.

Trevor beamed, then tussled his hair. "Good man."

"You won't see us for a while, but don't ever forget how much we love you, Johnny, and when you're done at school, you can come home to us," said his mother. Her eyes were beginning to tear up. "You're a good boy and you have a good family. You know that, right?"

Trevor placed his hand on their mother's shoulder. "It's okay, Mother. He understands, just like I did when I left."

"Yeah, Mom, I know," John assured her. He leaned in and hugged her again. "I won't forget. I promise."

"You better not," she answered, squeezing him with everything she had. "Never, ever. You hear me, baby?"

He kissed her warm, wet cheeks. "Never, ever."

JOHN OPENED his eyes in the snow as blood poured from his nose and mouth. He felt the sting of the cold suddenly, as though for the first time today.

He raised his head, wheezing as he gasped for air. "Ungh…" He turned on his side, holding his stomach, suddenly remembering where he was.

A thin line of blood dripped along his cheek.

Someone was running toward him. It was Terry, he realized. Oh yes, that's right. His old friend. "I'm so sorry!" Terry yelled as he arrived. "Oh, my God. Are you okay?"

John felt his stomach. A sharp pain in his abdomen and chest, but nothing broken. "I'm…good," he muttered.

"I didn't mean to hit you so hard," said Terry.

John raised his hand. "It's fine."

"Oh, man," said Terry, examining John's face. "Your nose is—"

John wiped the blood with his sleeve. "You got tough while I was gone," he said.

"That's your response to me breaking your nose?"

"Not broken. Relax."

"What about your ribs?"

John forced himself to sit up. He leaned back against the nearby tree trunk and let out a sigh. "I'm okay."

"Dammit, John. Why didn't you listen to me? I tried to tell you—"

"I know," he muttered, raising his eyes to look at the falling leaves.

"What happened? Why were you after Jinel? Can you explain it to me?"

"I just wanted to help," he said, clearing his throat. "I…"

"Help?"

"Mei, she…they got her and I…" A sudden lump formed in his throat. "I just wanted to help…I…"

Terry took a few steps closer. "John?"

"I just wanted to get her back, Terry," he said, his voice cracking.

"What are you talking about?" asked Terry, sitting next to him.

The wind blew, and flakes of snow lifted from the ground, scattering in the air in front of them.

"I don't know what to do. Terry, tell me, what am I supposed to do?" The words came quickly, uncontrollably, and he didn't know what to say. He didn't know what to do or what to think or what to feel and…

…and for the first time since all of this began, John let it all come riding out of him. The loss he didn't want to have. The hole in his heart that Mei had left. That had grown bigger with every person he had lost.

Tears bled out of him, gushed like a river of grief until he could scarcely breathe. He didn't even try to fight them. He didn't have the strength for it anymore.

"I couldn't save her. They took my Mei and I couldn't stop them, Terry. I couldn't stop them and I couldn't make it right. You…I couldn't save you, either, back when you left. No… when you were *taken*. I couldn't…" He gasped the cold air and it burned his throat. "I couldn't…I couldn't save my mom. My brother. Everyone. They're all—"

But before the rest could come, Terry's arms wrapped around him, squeezing him tight. John felt everything dissipate —all the walls blocking his grief and fear—and he let it all go. "I'm sorry," he cried, pressing his eyes into his friend's shoulder.

"I'm sorry I couldn't find you sooner. I'm sorry I couldn't do what you needed me to do."

"You did find me, John. You came all this way and you did it. See? I'm here. You did it," he said, this man who had been his friend…who was still his friend.

John had come so far to find him, traveled to another world —another universe—to see this boy again, his oldest and greatest friend. His brother. And he was alive. Oh, God, he was real, sitting next to him, here in this distant place.

Here, beneath an ancient forest, surrounded by the falling snow.

16

Ortego Outpost File Logs
Play Audio File 1641
Recorded: April 3, 2351

MITCHELL: *Thank you for taking my call.*

GEL: *Of course, Sophia Mitchell. I understand you've obtained what you believe to be a cure to the gas that plagues us so?*

MITCHELL: *That's correct. I've tested the compound on both myself as well as Titus Vin and it would seem the results are the same. Both he and I are now entirely immune.*

GEL: *Absolutely remarkable. Are there no side-effects? Have you observed anything abnormal?*

MITCHELL: *None whatsoever. In fact, Titus says the air feels the same as it does in Everlasting, and I'd have to agree.*

GEL: *Excellent. When can you have the first shipment delivered to us? I would like to begin inoculations as quickly as possible.*

MITCHELL: *We're synthesizing them now. I should have the first hundred by the end of the day.*

GEL: *Very good. I understand. Please, Sophia Mitchell, the sooner you get them to us, the better. Our people are in dire need.*

MITCHELL: *I won't rest until I do, I assure you. If I might inquire on something else, before we disconnect.*

GEL: *Of course. Please, go ahead.*

MITCHELL: *Have you any news on Dr. Curie?*

GEL: *Ah, yes. Has Sergeant Finn told you of his current mission?*

MITCHELL: *He only mentioned he needed to leave the continent to help you with something. He didn't say much more.*

GEL: *That is because I told him not to. There are spies everywhere, you see, but I'm sure it won't hurt to tell you now. He is currently tracking a terrorist in the hopes of finding Dr. Curie's location. We believe she is being held prisoner in a Garden facility. If this investigation proves accurate, we should find her soon.*

MITCHELL: *Are…Are you certain?*

GEL: *I cannot say definitively, but I am confident we will yield results, should Sergeant Finn succeed.*

MITCHELL: *That's wonderful news! Thank you!*

GEL: *You are most welcome. It is the least we can do, given the situation.*

MITCHELL: *I'll do everything I can to get the medicine to you, Master Gel. Please, just find Dr. Curie.*

GEL: *We will do our best to bring her back to you. I give you my word.*

End Audio File

Somewhere in Everlasting
April 3, 2351

Fentin stood beside the countertop fumbling with a vial of Mei's blood. He marked it and put it aside, moving on to the next genetic sample. He did this multiple times a day, usually after extracting the material directly from Mei's body.

Strapped to her chair, here in this place, all she could do was watch as little pieces of her were organized for later exploitation.

She twisted her hand in the strap, trying to loosen them, but failing. *Wait until I get out of here,* she thought, burning a hole in the back of Fentin's head with her stare.

As though he could sense her, Fentin turned around. "It's almost time for sleep," he said, using the translator beside him.

"Screw off," she muttered.

He smiled, almost innocently, and turned around to continue his work.

The door opened a second later, and in walked Master Gel. He'd taken to visiting Mei on occasion, usually to see how Fentin's progress was going, but also to mock her. She wagered he enjoyed the situation more than he let on. Somewhere, beneath that cold expression, there was only a cruel, taunting child.

"Master Gel, sir," said Fentin, noticing the visitor. He got to his feet, nervously.

"Would you disconnect the translator?" asked Gel, nodding to the device.

"Oh, certainly," said Fentin. He touched the machine and it powered off.

"Very good," said Gel, but this time the words came in the native language. Mei would have to pay close attention, but her understanding had improved. She wasn't fluent, but close enough.

"What can I do for you, Master?" asked Fentin.

"Did you have a chance to analyze the blood I sent you?" asked Gel.

"From Titus Vin? Yes, sir. Everything is as you described. Quite remarkable, truly."

"I see, so he shows no abnormalities?" asked Gel.

"Not at all, sir."

"Interesting. Can you use the sample to assist you in your current project?"

"I believe so. Our analysis shows some similarities between the two. It should save us months of research."

"Months, you say?"

"Yes, sir. Perhaps even longer. Whoever discovered this cure, they've saved us an enormous amount of time. It is truly remarkable!"

Gel glanced briefly at Mei. "It was one of the human scientists, but it hardly matters. I need you to work diligently to find the link between this one's sequence and Titus Vin's. The safety of our people requires it."

"Yes, sir," said Fentin.

"Very good," said Gel. He started to leave, but paused as he was passing Mei's chair, looking her over.

"Something I can help you with?" she asked.

"I wonder, do you know what is going on right now?" he asked in English.

"You're bored and needed someone to talk to, now that all your friends are dead," she answered. "Oh, I mean because you killed them."

"What I did to the Leadership, I did—"

"For the good of Everlasting," she finished. "Yes, thank you."

"You say the words, but I suspect you do not understand them."

"Sure, I do. It means the ends always justify the means for you. It means you can do whatever you want if you can rationalize that it's for your city."

"You talk a great deal for a prisoner." He glanced at Fentin, switching to his native language. "Put her to sleep when I leave. In fact, until we need her again, I'd like her kept in stasis. Is that understood?"

"Yes, sir, but the samples we take will be less—"

He raised his hand to quiet him. "We have more than enough to finish the work, but if need be, we can always wake her up. Isn't that right?"

Fentin nodded. "Certainly."

"Proceed, then," said Gel, observing Mei, smiling just enough so she could see it.

Oh no. If Fentin did as he was told, she'd be finished. She had to say something, anything.

"Doctor Curie, you look concerned," said Master Gel in English.

"What?" she asked, playing dumb. "I was just wondering what's going on out there since you have me trapped in here."

"Nothing you need concern yourself with," he answered, opening the door.

She watched him leave.

Fentin stood at the counter, fixing what could only be her medicine. It looked the same as all the other doses she'd received, except this time when he injected her, she wouldn't wake up. She'd fall asleep forever and that would be the end of everything. She had to do something *now*.

Fentin brought the injection to her, sterilizing her neck with a piece of cloth. "There we are," he said, softly.

Her heart began to race. "Fentin, wait," she said, quickly, trying to think of a way out of this, anything to stop the needle from putting her to sleep.

She remembered the vial under her pillow. If she could just get to it, maybe then—

"What is it?" asked the doctor.

She swallowed. "Can you let me lie down first? Could you finish doing this once I'm in the cell?"

He tilted his head. "Inside?"

"Just let me lie down first. You don't want to carry me in there, do you? Wouldn't that be better for both of us?"

Fentin considered this for a moment. "I do get tired of dragging you in there. This is true."

"I won't do anything. I promise. I just don't want to fall asleep in this chair. Every time I do, it gives me such a pain in my neck, and then I feel sick to my stomach. Could you do this for me, Fentin? Please?"

"I suppose you could lie down first, yes," he said, nodding, and took a step back. "But, if you attempt to do anything, you will be punished. Do you understand?"

"Yes, of course," she said. "I wouldn't do that. Not after last time."

"Yes, yes. That would be bad for you." He took a pistol from the counter and aimed it at her.

"I promise, I won't," she said, staring at the barrel.

He unstrapped her wrists, giving her some space to stand. She walked into the cell and sat on the bed. He followed her with the gun still on her. "Lie down now."

She slipped her hand beneath the pillow, touching the vial. "Yes, of course," she said, beaming a soft smile at him.

She stretched her legs out on the bed, leaning back, the vial in her hand.

Fentin leaned over her with the injector, studying her neck and skin. She glanced at the gun in his other hand, which was no longer aimed at her. His attention was more focused on the medication than whether she would try to run.

"Do not move or the injection will hurt," said Fentin, the same as he always did.

"Yes, Fentin," she said, closing her eyes.

Focusing on his movement, clearing her mind, she could sense him there beside her, breathing.

The liquid in the injector sloshed as it neared her throat. As soon as it pierced her skin, that would be it. She'd have to be fast.

Fentin's hand drew close, the needle mere centimeters from her flesh.

She pressed her thumb into the crack along the vial, snapping it in half and cutting herself. Fentin paused at the sudden sound, glancing at her hand. "What—"

But before he could continue, Mei brought the vial from behind her waist, eyes still shut, and slammed it into Fentin's shoulder.

He screamed, falling back and dropping the pistol. Leaping from the bed, Mei dashed at the scientist, picking up the weapon as she went.

Fentin had tears in his eyes as he held his bleeding shoulder, whimpering like a child. As Mei neared him, he tried to strike her with the injector, but she aimed the gun at him. "Drop it!"

He let go of the needle, raising his shaking hands. "P-Please!"

"Inject yourself with whatever that is," she told him.

"W-What?"

"Do it!" she snapped.

He looked at the needle, then again at her. "But—"

"She squeezed the grip and furrowed her brow. "Would you rather I use this and then the needle? I know *this* one will only paralyze, but I wonder what would happen if we used both…"

"No, wait!" he begged.

She nudged the needle toward him with her foot. He swallowed, but then picked it up. A second of hesitation later and he had it on his arm.

"In the neck," she muttered.

He nodded, then did as she ordered. She watched as the liquid entered him and began its work.

"Good," she said, lowering the pistol, but not entirely.

"You…you…" His voice was already fading.

"Go to sleep, Fentin," she said.

"But…but…you…" His eyelids drooped, and his words began to slur. "Ish…no…"

Mei could feel his heart slowing as he faded into a tranquil coma. "I'm sorry, but I had to do it. I know you were just doing what he told you to do."

Fentin's eyes closed and, in seconds, he fell into a deep sleep.

She squeezed the pistol's grip. There were likely too many people to count in this building who believed as Fentin did, that Master Gel was looking out for them, that he would lead them to prosperity. Maybe they were right. Maybe he would.

But it couldn't come at the cost of humanity or the people outside of this city.

She backed away from Fentin, stepping out of the cell and into the lab, shutting the door behind her and locking him inside.

The hall door slid open as she neared it, startling her. Peering out, she saw the hallway was clear and empty, not a soul to be found. She glanced at the weapon in her hand. With any luck, she wouldn't have to use this, but based on past experiences, she had an idea of what to expect.

She'd do what she had to, no matter what it took. She wouldn't die in a place like this.

Mei stepped into the hall, leaving the prison behind, and started running.

Outside Ashby Harbor, Tharosa
April 3, 2351

"Are you okay to go?" asked Terry, concerned for his friend's condition. John still had blood all over his face from their fight.

"I'm good. Let's go talk to Jinel," he said, pushing himself up with the help of the nearby stump.

"Stay right there!" yelled a muffled voice.

"Speak of the devil," said Terry.

Jinel appeared from between the trees, her rifle aimed directly at John. "Terry, what happened?"

"He's okay, Jinel. Put the gun down," he said.

"He tried to kill me. I'm not—"

"John thought you kidnapped our friend. He's willing to hear you out now."

John raised his hands. "Sorry about that. I've been under a lot of stress."

"What friend are you talking about?" she asked.

"Mei Curie," he answered. "Gel said Garden kidnapped her. That's why I'm here, to find you and bring you back. He said you know where—"

"Garden wouldn't do that. We don't take hostages. That's what a coward does. Even if we did, we wouldn't involve an outsider like your friend."

"Maybe not, but you did blow up buildings and kill people," said John.

"I didn't say there weren't casualties. It's a war."

"If you didn't take Mei, then where is she?" asked John. "I'm tired of this nonsense."

"They rescued me from the Leadership," Terry explained.

"Rescued you?" asked John.

"The Leadership was going to experiment on me. They wanted to know what made me immune to Variant."

John's eyes grew distant, and for a second he looked lost in thought. "They told me they couldn't find you."

"What do you mean?"

"Gel said he looked everywhere, but their satellite couldn't track you. They said they were still looking. What the hell is going on?"

"Isn't it obvious?" asked Jinel. "The Leadership has been using you."

"No, I would've seen that," muttered John. "I would have—"

"Terry!" called a voice. Lena Sol came running from the field.

"Over here!" he returned.

"Who is that?" asked John.

"The soldiers are preparing to leave!" she yelled.

"Is that…" John stared into the woods at the woman running toward him. "Lena?"

"Yeah, you know her, don't you?" asked Terry.

"John, is that you?" asked Lena, once she was close enough to see him.

"What are you doing here, Lena? I heard you took a job on some island or something."

She shook her head. "No, I was—"

"Save your reunion!" snapped Jinel. "Did you not hear her? The troops are preparing to leave. We need to stop them before they reform!"

Terry grabbed John by the shoulder. "You with us?"

John looked at Jinel. "Are you telling me the truth about Gel? You think he has Mei?"

"Of course, I am! Only the Leadership is capable of such an act."

"Okay, but if you're lying to me—"

"Enough of your doubts," said the soldier. "We'll kill each other later if I'm wrong. Now, come!"

"Wait!" yelled Lena, running over to Terry. She handed him his sword. "You dropped this."

They ran through the forest and into the open field. John spotted the soldiers as they gathered near the aircraft.

He lifted his rifle, taking aim, but then lowered it. "We need to get to the ship before it takes off. The pilot will leave if we make a scene!"

"Then we'd better be quick," said Terry.

THEIR ASSAULT on the soldiers was haphazard, but it was easy work. Most were either injured or disoriented, trying to climb aboard the ship.

In moments, the Red Door was in the air, lifting from the field in an attempt to escape.

John dove through the open hatch and made his way to the pilot. "Set it down!" he ordered, pressing the barrel to the man's neck.

"Sergeant Finn!" yelled Emile Res from the back of the aircraft.

"Stay where you are, Emile!" answered John. He dug the weapon into the pilot's skin. "This'll only take a second."

The Red Door returned to the ground right as Jinel began giving orders to her new prisoners. "Everyone on the ground!" she demanded of the soldiers.

Terry had several of their weapons in his arms, dropping them in a small pile near the edge of the woods.

"If I see anyone move, I'll shoot your head clear off!" barked the Garden commander.

John emerged from the ship with the pilot still at the end of his gun. "Join your friends over there," he told him, then waved for Emile Res to come out.

"What is going on?" asked the scientist.

"Who's that?" asked Terry.

"She's a noncombatant," said John.

"Another tool for the Leadership," said Jinel.

Emile stepped out of the aircraft and looked around. "Will someone please tell me what is—"

"Turns out Garden didn't take Mei," said John. "Your boss did."

Emile cocked her head. "What are you talking about?"

"Where's Lena?" asked John. "You two know each other, don't you? She'll explain it."

"Lena Sol?" asked Emile.

"Is there a way to wake up someone after they've been hit by the toxin?" Terry asked.

"Emile, do you know?" asked John.

"The toxin? It doesn't take long to wear off. Do you remember when we used it on your team?"

John thought back to the day he first met Emile and Lena. They knocked out most of his squad with the stuff, but it wore off after an hour or so. "Is there anything you can do to speed it up?"

"We have some medicine on the ship, but…"

"What?" asked John.

"What you're asking is treason, you must realize," said Emile. "You're requesting I help the enemy."

"Not the enemy," yelled Lena, finally arriving.

"Who is that?" asked Emile, trying to see.

Lena approached the scientist. "Hello, Emile Res," she told her. "It's good to see you again. I think it might do you well to listen now."

"Listen?" asked Emile.

"Oh, yes," said the analyst. "There is much you do not know."

Hux, Ludo, and Ysa came out of their temporary stasis after a short while. Thanks to Emile and Lena, their punishment was severely reduced. With everyone recovered and back on their feet, it was time to decide what to do with the Everlastian soldiers.

"What about Emile Res?" asked Jinel.

"She's good," said John. "Aren't you, Emile?"

"If what you're saying is true, then it would certainly explain a great deal of things," said the scientist. "But I must admit, I remain skeptical."

"Of what?" asked Terry.

"Everything," said Emile.

"A reasonable position," remarked Lena.

"The loss of the Leadership has left a power vacuum, requiring Master Gel to temporary take control. Garden's actions left Everlasting in a state of panic, so you will forgive me if I am not inclined to believe your words."

"The truth is the truth, regardless of what you believe," said Jinel.

"Perhaps so, but until I have seen more, then I must keep my objectivity intact. Until then, I can only agree to cause you no trouble. I'm no soldier, nor do I wish to get involved any further than I already am."

"A coward's sentiment," said Jinel.

"A pragmatist," returned Emile.

"Nonetheless, if you cause us any problems—"

"Will you two drop it?" asked Terry. "We need to figure out what to do with these soldiers."

Jinel raised her rifle, taking aim at one of the soldiers' heads. "A thought occurs to me, now that you mention it."

"Hey, come on," said John. "I thought you said you weren't about that."

"We don't slaughter innocents. There are exceptions with dogs of the Leadership," said Jinel.

"No, John's right," said Terry, motioning for her to lower the gun. He'd had enough violence for one day. "There's no reason to—"

A hard rumble coursed through the ground beneath them, vibrating his feet.

He and John both looked at each other. "What was that?" asked Terry.

"Maybe an earthquake," answered John. Another tremor, this time stronger, followed shortly by another. "The hell is this? Emile, do you know?"

"Why are you asking me?" she asked, almost insulted.

"You're supposed to know about this continent," he said.

"There hasn't been an earthquake here for a century, so I'm—"

"Everyone be quiet," said Jinel.

The rumblings grew with each occurrence, repeating every few seconds.

Baroom.

Baroom.

Baroom.

"No!" screamed Lena, stumbling as the tremor hit. She fell to the ground on her hands and knees. "No! I know that sound! I know what's coming!"

"What is she rambling about?" yelled John.

"Sentries!" shouted Lena, pointing to the harbor.

Terry looked with his hybrid eyes to see a massive wave rise up, pushing boats into the docks, grounding some of them. The people screamed, dispersing through the streets, heading for the gates.

A thing emerged, tall as a building, with a body like a serpent deity. It looked like the Leviathan monster from the stories made real.

"What is it?" asked John.

"A Guardian," answered Terry. "Or sentry. Whatever you want to call it. They protect Everlasting."

"Then what's it doing here?" asked John.

"The Leadership must have sent it," said Jinel.

Another sound caught Terry's ear. A hovering, whirling

noise, coming from the other direction. He turned and stared to the horizon, but saw nothing yet.

"What's wrong?" asked Jinel.

"There's more," said Terry.

"I hear it, too," said John. "It's coming from—"

"There!" yelled Terry, pointing to the horizon's edge, high above the trees.

An object appeared, far into the distance beyond the mountains and clouds. Was it a ship like the one in the field? Perhaps, although it was a different design, and many times larger.

It boomed through the heavens, heading towards them. "It's coming this way!" yelled Terry. He turned toward the harbor. "We're surrounded!"

The Guardian emerged from the water and moved around the village, avoiding the crowds. Its tail slid along the earth, splitting the field like a plow.

The aircraft, if that's what it was, came to a stop above the mountain city, hovering there for several seconds.

"What is it?" asked John. "More soldiers? Another ship?"

"Both are sentries!" explained Jinel.

"Those?" asked John.

"This could be a problem," remarked Terry.

Ludo raised his hands above his head. "What reason have the Guardians to come here?"

"If those two have arrived, Master Gel must have sent them earlier this morning," said Emile. "He must really want you people dead."

John looked at Terry. "Any ideas?"

"We fight or run," he answered.

"How do you fight that?"

"I've done it before," he said, glancing down at his sword.

"How hard was it?" asked John.

"Toughest thing I've ever had to do." He swallowed hard.

The flying Guardian left the top of the mountain and flew down to the valley's edge. It grew several tentacles from its central body, extending them in multiple directions. In only a few seconds, it went from resembling a floating boulder to something closer to an octopus.

At the same time, the snake-like Guardian arrived from the ocean, taking up position next to the other.

"If we must die, then let it be with honor," said Ludo, glancing at his wife.

"You speak truly, dear Ludo," said Hux, and he smacked his chest. "But let us try to live through the day. Shall we?"

Ludo nodded. "Right you are."

"Let them come!" shouted Ysa, taking her stance.

"I'm ready," muttered Terry.

John nodded, lifting his rifle. "Time to go to work. Let's show these things what a couple of kids from Central can do."

"PLAN?" asked Terry.

"Take them on separately. Divide up into teams," said John.

"Right. Jinel and Hux, you two are with me," said Terry.

"What about us?" asked Ludo.

"You and Ysa back John up."

"Did you forget I'm occupied?" asked Jinel, referring to the fact that she had her weapon aimed at the dozen prisoners on the ground.

"Lena can take over," said John. "Right?"

She nodded. "I can handle it."

"Remember, if they move, you have to shoot them," said Jinel.

"I can do this," said the analyst.

Jinel placed her hand on the girl's shoulder. "Right. I think maybe you can now, at long last."

"If everyone's ready, I think those two things are headed our way," said John.

Terry watched as the Guardians began their approach. They moved along the field toward the crowd with fierce intent. "I'll take the water one."

"Then I've got the flying octopus!" barked John, and he exploded into a sprint.

Terry followed suit, with the group dividing as they'd been assigned.

John unloaded his rifle, spraying ammunition on the monster as it neared. Ysa and Ludo followed after him.

The priestess dashed forward, spear-in-hand. She dove beneath the tentacles, slicing a piece of its metallic skin clean off.

Ludo followed soon, his knives flying, hitting the monster in its chest. The orinchalium daggers pierced the creature's metal, but didn't slow it.

The Guardian's body morphed and twisted, its skin shuddering as the micromachines inside it transformed and reimagined its shape. John fired wildly into it, but the bullets bounced off the surface.

With its tentacles extended, it dropped itself and rolled along the ground toward him. He dodged out of the way, barely avoiding the attack.

Meanwhile, Terry was already on the other Guardian, his sword extended and ready to strike. He leapt high into the air, digging his blade into the serpent's side and slicing, cutting off a large chunk of its flesh in the process.

A lifeless piece of metal fell from its body and hit the ground with a massive thud, but it was already reforming itself, just like the spider in the mines.

Hux raised his spear and lobbed it at the goliath's center, piercing it straight through. The micromachines reformed, pushing the weapon through itself.

Jinel fired her weapon at its face, trying to draw attention so that Terry and Hux could continue their assault. "Wear it down!" she told them. "Piece-by-piece, wear it down!"

The Guardian snapped its tail around, hitting several trees, shattering them into thousands of pieces. The explosion sent a thunderous echo through the valley. Terry could only imagine what fear the villagers of Ashby must think, to see beasts like these battling so close by. It must have felt like the end of the world, and perhaps it would be, should he and his friends fail. Who knew what these Guardians would do to the people here, once the job was done.

Ysa ran to Ludo's side, avoiding another blow. "Throw me!" she told him.

With all his strength, Ludo lifted his wife and propelled her towards the Guardian.

She hit it dead-on, cutting into it with her spear, ripping a hole and punching through to the other side.

Another chunk of dead machine fell away as Ysa twisted around and landed in the snow, unharmed.

In response, the Guardian lashed out at once, its tentacle beating against the earth like a drum. "Out of the way!" cried Lena, who stood near the Everlastian soldiers.

The enemy combatants scattered, attempting to flee the chaos, but the monster's attack was quick and deadly, landing on several of the men at once, crushing them into the ground. Screams erupted from the panicked crowd as they died.

Terry ran to help the remaining soldiers, arriving in a moment, cutting the beast with several quick, but deep swipes.

The Guardian's tendril hit him on the back, lifting him off the ground, sending him into the forest. Before hitting one of the trees, he braced himself, shielding his face with his arms, and focusing.

He hit the trunk, breaking it in half, and went spiraling to the ground, mostly unharmed.

"Terry!" yelled Ludo.

"Focus!" ordered John. "Terry's not dying that easily! Don't let your guard down!"

The Leviathan Guardian unleashed another strike, sweeping dirt and snow as it dragged its massive tail towards

Jinel. She screamed, firing a barrage of bullets into the oncoming metal, chipping bits of its body off with each shot.

Terry came running out of the woods, covered in dirt. He was shaken, but present.

The tail slammed into Jinel, throwing her from her feet and sending the woman to the ground, burying her in a pile of mud and snow.

Hux beat his chest with his sword, then charged. He threw his spear into the side of the monster, ripping into it with the entirety of his blade, pulling pieces of its body clean off.

The serpent withdrew nearly a hundred meters, slithering its way towards its sister Guardian. "We have it on the run!" yelled Hux.

"No, wait!" ordered John.

Terry arrived at his side. He watched as the two monolithic entities began to morph, their bodies shaking as the micromachines inside of them reorganized and reformed. "What's going on?" he asked his friend.

"Something's happening," said John.

The Guardians came together, their metallic bodies merging. Pieces rolled over pieces, fusing one mass with the other, transforming into—

Into a single monstrous thing.

"They're merging together!" yelled John. "Everyone attack! Quick, before it has a chance to finish!"

Terry watched as the two goliaths became one. Layers of metal intertwined as the Guardians grew double in size. The new creature stood taller and wider, with multiple tendrils, ready to fight. Ready to kill.

Ysa, Ludo, Hux, John, and Terry attacked at once and in tandem from all angles, but in a single, wide sweep, the Guardian cast them all aside, pushing them away like dolls.

Terry got to his feet, wiping mud and snow from his face.

John lifted his rifle and shot wildly into the Guardian's chest, but the ammunition had no effect. "It's useless!" he cried.

But in that moment, a sound came from the mountain. A horn that blew through the valley and echoed in the hills. The sound of soldiers running. The anthem of a nation.

Barniby appeared with two dozen men at his back, each clad in armor, with orinchalium swords in hand.

"Barniby!" yelled Hux, from amid the chaos. "What kept you?"

"Apologies, cousin!" returned the prince, and he readied his blade, raising it high into the air.

The Guardian slammed a tendril on the ground, shaking the earth.

"It seems the gods would like a word," said Barniby to his fellow countrymen. "What say we show them how we scream in Tharosa?"

The soldiers beat their armored chests, bellowing loud taunts. The Guardian took notice, turning its attention to them.

Barniby pointed his sword toward the monster. "Attack!" he yelled, a mad grin upon his weathered face. "Kill the god!"

The men ran with weapons high, charging into chaos.

But none gave any sign of fear, for these were men of Tharosa, and they would not be so easily moved.

The soldiers attacked the lower tendrils first. The monster reacted fast, casting several aside, but not killing them. They rolled and righted themselves, doubling their efforts and attacking once again.

Terry joined them soon, taking position near Ysa and Ludo on the the Guardian's left side.

Another tentacle came down on them, but before it could hit, Ysa raised her arms to block. She made her skin like stone, holding the tendril back. At the same time, Ludo dug a knife into the metal and slid the blade across the metal flesh, spattering black liquid.

Terry leapt over them, his sword outstretched, and ran along the tendril towards the head.

He passed over John, busy firing his rifle into the beast's underbelly.

He passed over Barniby and the two dozen Tharosian soldiers as they cut away at the monster's base.

He passed over the pirate Hux, who stood with his spear, piercing the center of monster's chest, driving the blade as deep as his hulking arms would allow.

Terry reached the top of the morphing blob of metal, stopping at the highest point of its mass. He raised his sword with both hands, then pierced the monster at its highest point, and held on for all his life.

The Guardian flailed, attempting to knock them all away.

Terry fell forward, still holding on to the hilt of his sword, and he dragged the blade down the monster's front, splitting it apart.

The beast's skin rippled and morphed, attempting to repair itself, but it was no good. Too much of its body had fallen away. Instead, it collapsed onto the ground, stumbling over itself, rolling in the bloodied snow.

It stopped attacking, but Terry and his allies did not relent. They pressed it, piercing and stabbing the corpse without pause, without hesitation.

"The beast is felled!" cried Barniby. "Do not give it time to breathe!"

Like ants upon a dying animal, the soldiers of Tharosa climbed and covered the Guardian's body. They dug their many blades into the monster's flesh…and then ripped the "god" to pieces.

WITH THE GUARDIAN INCAPACITATED, the remaining soldiers secured the field and surrounding area. Barniby had them take stations along Ashby's streets to assist civilians in whatever way they could.

"I'm sorry you lost so many men," said Terry.

"So am I," said Barniby. "But we had no other choice. That beast destroyed two dozen buildings near the harbor, along with half the docks. We'll need to recall our other soldiers from the islands to help us rebuild what was lost."

"What about the war?"

"Nothing is as important as our own people."

"We found them!" yelled John from the edge of the field. He emerged from the woods with Jinel Din's arm around his neck, and Lena Sol beside them.

Terry smacked Barniby's shoulder, then ran to help his friends. "Are you guys okay?"

"I am, but Jinel needs to lie down," remarked Lena.

"I'm fine," said the soldier. "Mind your own business, analyst."

Lena smiled. "I was mistaken, it seems."

"We had no idea where you both went," said Terry.

"I found Jinel buried under some snow. Lena here was trying to dig her out," explained John.

"Glad you're both okay," said Terry, and he was truly relieved.

Jinel coughed. "It'll take more than that to stop me. I still have a mission to accomplish."

"Not in your state, you don't," remarked Lena.

"Don't tell me what to—"

"Hey, hey, let's just get you both to a doctor. You can argue later," said John.

Terry watched them limp off towards the city. It was good to see everyone coming together, especially John and Jinel. Hard to believe only a few hours ago, they were trying to kill each other. There was nothing like almost dying to bring people together.

Hux found him after a bit, having gone to check on his boat with Ysa and Ludo. "Our crew is alive!" he boasted, heartily.

"Any casualties in the town?" asked Terry.

"A few, but it could have been worse," said Ludo.

Terry knew he was right. Multiple buildings had collapsed. It was a wonder more people hadn't been killed in the chaos. Despite everything, they'd been lucky today.

"The *Waveguard* is safe, too," said Hux. "As well as the cargo."

"We'll need to leave before long. My guess is that if we don't, we'll have to deal with more of whatever that was," said Terry, motioning to the giant pile of dead Guardian behind them.

"Whatever the gods send, we'll smite them down," said Hux.

"Maybe so, but I'd rather get to them first, if we can."

"Did you have something in mind?" asked Ysa.

Terry looked at the airship, which still sat near the back of the field, untouched. "I might have an idea or two, but let's go meet up with John and the others first. It could get complicated."

"Let me see if I follow," said Emile Res. "You want to pilot the Red Door back to Everlasting, seize control of the Citadel, and take Master Gel prisoner. Is that right?"

"When you say it like that, I guess it does sound a bit out there," said Terry.

"It's insane," she said.

"Maybe not," interjected Lena. "The ship is coded to enter the domeguard. We could slip through without notice."

"Yes, but that doesn't account for the hundreds of enemy soldiers ready to kill you on sight," said Emile.

"Simple work," said Jinel, fanning her hand.

"She's right. I've seen those guys in action. They're a joke," said John.

"Perhaps so, but the toxin in their weapons can subdue you, nonetheless," said Lena.

"I can avoid them," said Terry.

"You're not fast enough to dodge several hundred of them."

"We may not have to," said Jinel.

"Got an idea?" asked John.

"If we can get a signal to Garden, I might," she said.

John cocked a brow. "What for?"

"Isn't it obvious?" she asked, looking at each of them.

"Oh!" exclaimed Lena, who had apparently figured out the riddle. "You're talking about a distraction."

She nodded. "Right you are, analyst. Draw the would-be king's attention to the streets."

"Meanwhile, we assault the castle," said Terry.

"And we'll get Mei back," added John, letting out his hand.

Terry took it. "Whatever it takes."

17

S.O.F.T. Mission Report
Play Audio File 335
Recorded: April 3, 2351

FINN: *Brooks, do you read me? Anyone at Bravo Point picking this up?*

BROOKS*: I have you, sir! What's going on?*

FINN*: Listen up! I need you to prep the team. Have them ready to go on my signal.*

BROOKS*: For an assault, sir?*

FINN*: No, I'm talking about going home. I need you to get ready to blow the bridge.*

BROOKS*: Are you talking about the Exodus Protocol, sir?*

FINN*: If that's the one where we evacuate and blow up the portal, then yes. Sorry, but you know I suck with mission names.*

BROOKS*: Yes, sir. That's the one. Are you sure?*

***FINN**: Positive, but wait for my signal. I'm not sure what'll happen, so if you don't hear from me in an hour, you go ahead and do it.*

***BROOKS**: But, boss—*

***FINN**: Don't argue, Brooks! Just do what I told you and get our boys home. That's your only concern.*

***BROOKS**: Right, but what about you? What are you doing?*

***FINN**: I've got business to deal with, but I'm right behind you. Terry and I gotta see a man about a girl.*

***BROOKS**: Sir? Did you just say Terry?*

***FINN**: That I did, Brooks, and we aim to bring a reckoning, but it could get messy. You know what they say about vengeance, don't you?*

***BROOKS**: That it's a dish best served cold?*

***FINN**: Hell no, Brooks! They say it's better than mourning, and I'll be damned if I'm giving up on Mei. You hear me? I'll rip this godforsaken planet in half before I quit.*

End Audio File

Everlasting
April 3, 2351

MEI HID behind a wall as several scientists passed by, pushing carts and talking amongst themselves. She'd made it down several corridors without being spotted, but she couldn't keep this up forever. She had to get out of here soon before somebody spotted her.

She listened from her hiding spot as the scientists continued along the corridor, entering a distant room. She waited for the door to close before allowing herself to move or relax. She waited a moment and, staying low, ran quickly through the hall to the nearest corner.

She could feel her adrenaline as it coursed through her, heightening her senses. Having rarely used her abilities, she had little experience to draw from, but here in this moment, surrounded by the possibility of death, her body knew what to do. She could hear everything happening around her, in nearly every room, and she moved like a ghost, quickly and quietly.

John must have known this feeling all too well.

No time to dwell on that, she thought. *John's not here, and you are. Get with it, Mei.*

She sped through the next hall, listening to whatever commotion lay ahead. Several men were talking in a side corridor, discussing a recent attack.

"Master Kai is dead, I heard," said one of them.

"Troubling news for all of us," said another.

"Master Gel is all that remains. Do you think they'll come for him, too?"

"Not if we do our jobs. We must protect him."

"For the good of Everlasting," said the soldier.

"Yes, for the good of Everlasting," repeated the other.

They didn't appear to be moving anywhere, these idiot soldiers. She might have to take them on and risk exposure. Mei might be a hybrid, but she wasn't John. She didn't know if she could take on a group of armed—

"We should report," said one of the men.

"Now? I wanted to get some food before the changeover."

"There's no time for that today. With everything that's happening, we have to do a good job."

"Yes, of course. The city needs us to be vigilant."

Mei watched as the two guards started to leave in the opposite direction. Now was her chance. She just had to—

A gasp came from behind her. "You…you're…"

She turned to see a scientist standing with the lab door open, staring at her, his mouth agape. Great, just what she needed. "Don't move!" she told him, lifting the gun.

"You're not supposed to—"

"Shut up!" she demanded, aiming the pistol at him. "You want me to shoot you?"

The scientist looked terrified, almost shaking where he stood. "Th-This is unacceptable! Master Gel will—"

She shot him and he fell to the floor, completely immobilized, but still breathing. Still awake, too. "I told you to shut it," she said.

He blinked, but was otherwise motionless.

At that exact moment, two more appeared from the same room. Seeing Mei, one of them panicked, screaming. "Someone help!"

Mei shot them both, but it was too late. She could hear several heavy footsteps running through the halls to her location.

Soldiers, for sure, with weapons clanging against their sides. There was no getting around it. If they caught her, she'd be put to sleep or killed…and she wasn't going back to that cell.

She clenched the pistol grip. No, she wouldn't go back. She couldn't. Not today or ever again.

She'd have to fight them, make her stand in this stupid hallway with nothing but her bare feet and this little gun. One way or the other, it was going to end today.

The only question was how.

Two soldiers came running down the corridor from each side, trapping her between them. Standing between the four of them, she had nowhere to go.

"Don't move!" ordered one.

This again, she thought. The last time she was in the position, they had shot her. She couldn't let that happen again. If she was going to escape this awful place, it was now or never.

She ran toward the nearest pair, shooting at them with her pistol. A dart hit one in the shoulder, while the other returned fire.

The shot barely missed her ear, hitting the floor behind her, near the other two guards. Mei leapt to the side, jumping off the wall with her bare feet and hitting the man in the chest with her knee, digging the barrel of the pistol into his neck. She fired immediately, instantly immobilizing him, making him go limp.

The other two guards came from the rear, but she fired her weapon before they could fully engage, and they dove to the floor to avoid the shots. She took the opportunity to run, but continued to fire behind her as she did. She slid into the corner, moving too quickly to stop, and slamming her knee into the wall, leaving a small dent. In a second, she was on the move again, running quickly.

She slipped into a nearby room, waiting for them to round the corner. As they did, she shoved the door with her shoulder into one and sent him careening into the wall. He let out a yelp as his head smashed into the metal.

The other soldier turned to see her. Too late. She fired her weapon into the side of his cheek, and he dropped to the floor.

Mei went for the other one who was struggling to reach his gun. She kicked him in the nose, feeling the cartilage as it broke under the heel of her foot.

He screamed as blood poured from his face.

She grabbed his own weapon and fired it into his leg, point-blank. The toxin took hold of him instantaneously, the same as it had the others, and he stopped moving.

Need to go, thought Mei, looking around. *Need to go, need to go!*

She fled through the halls as people started coming out of their labs and offices, quickly shutting the doors once they saw what was going on.

Finally, she came to an area she recognized. She'd been here before, hadn't she? *Wait a second,* she thought. *This is the central access hall near one of the analytics departments.*

Yes, she'd come here a few times before. First, with Lena Sol, and then with Gel. If this was right, she wasn't underground or in the city. She was inside the Tower of the Cartographers.

A swell of fear washed over her as she realized what this

meant. The Tower floated high above the city, inaccessible by foot. The only way out was on an aircraft. Without that, there was simply no way she could get to the ground. Not unless she decided to go skydiving.

The only solution was to steal a ship, but that was impossible unless she had an implant. Too bad she never took Lena's offer to get one. *What am I supposed to do?*

Several of the analysts had noticed her by now, and they gathered near the window to gawk. She must look ridiculous standing here, half-clothed and covered in Fentin's blood.

Someone yelled from the other side of the area. "Call security! Help! She has a weapon!"

She fired, instinctively, hitting the analyst in the chest and knocking him out. He moaned as he hit the floor. Mei glanced at the pistol in her hand. "Oops."

More screams from inside the analytics room. She couldn't stun them all, and even if she could, what would the point be? The only solution was to run, to keep going until she found a way out.

She bolted through the halls, trying to find the exit. The docking area wasn't far, but she'd have to pass through several areas before—

An explosion echoed in the distance, somewhere beyond the walls of this place. Her heightened senses told her it came from the city beneath this floating tower. She listened intently, picking up the sound of breaking metal and crumbling stone.

"What do we do?!" screamed someone from beyond the hall.

"Calm yourselves!" ordered another. "Master Gel is sending reinforcements. The city will be secured soon enough."

"What about us?"

"Those terrorists can't reach us here. Don't worry."

With the city under attack, the remaining soldiers in the tower would be scattered and distracted. Better to be quick and move while she could.

She'd need to force someone to fly her out of here, but who? Gel would never allow a ship to leave the hangar with her on board, even at the cost of someone else's life. He'd either seize them or shoot the aircraft down. Master Gel would never allow his precious genetic specimen to leave the tower. Not unless—

Unless he was standing next to her.

Yes, of course. The bastard couldn't order a strike on the ship if he was sitting in it, not without killing himself. He might spout all that nonsense about protecting his city, but Mei was willing to bet he'd never endanger his own life. He was too arrogant to be that selfless.

She glanced around the Analytics department. Gel's office wasn't far from this location. Given the danger in the city, he'd never leave the safety of this floating sanctuary.

Mei took a breath, bolting through the corridors. *Here I come,* she thought.

Gel's office was in a panic. Multiple analysts ran in and out. There seemed to be no order to the chaos in this usually tranquil place.

Two soldiers stood in the hall, trying to direct a crowd. As Mei arrived, several in the mob panicked, screaming and pointing. "They're here!" yelled one of them.

One of the four soldiers raised his weapons at her. "Stop right—"

Before the man could finish, he collapsed on the floor, struck in the leg by a shot from Mei's pistol. She'd been aiming for his chest, but oh well. She'd take what she could get.

The other soldier's eyes widened at the sight of this. "You—"

Mei fired several times, grazing his arm before finally landing a good shot on his neck. He joined his comrade on the floor.

Another soldier fired at her, ignoring the scattering crowd, and managed to nearly hit her. She ran at him, but was suddenly accosted by both guards. One of them tried to hit her with the butt of his weapon, but missed, only tearing her shirt. The other grabbed her pistol, trying to pry it free. She struggled to maintain her grip, but couldn't push him away. The man pressed a small button on the weapon and freed the ammunition clip, which fell to the floor.

Mei let go of the pistol and ducked to catch the clip. Inside were tiny gel capsules.

A hand clenched her neck, squeezing, lifting her up. She felt the pain and suffocating pressure as the stranger brought her to her feet. "Enough of that!" said the soldier. "Shoot her now, while I have her!"

Mei shoved a piece of her torn shirt, which she'd filled with a toxic gel capsule, into the guard's mouth. He spit it out, but suddenly went limp and collapsed. The toxin was fast-acting, so the moment it broke and touched his flesh, he stood little chance.

Mei sensed the second soldier's pulse quicken as he took a breath, squeezing the trigger.

She rolled, dodging the shot, which struck the floor.

He fired again, but only grazed her clothes.

Mei leapt up, then came in close and struck the man in the jaw, staggering him. Before he could react, she forced the cloth into his face, holding it there until he was incapacitated.

She left him there, but made certain to retrieve one of the soldiers' rifles, and headed straight into the Master Analyst's office.

The secretary stood behind his desk, throwing his hands up when he saw her. "Please don't!"

"Where is he?" snapped Mei.

The man's eyes glanced at the blacked-out office wall, then at Mei. "I don't know!"

"Is he in there?" she asked.

"Please, I—"

"Open it," she said.

"If I do that, I'll—"

"Do it or I'll shoot you."

His eyes dilated briefly as he commanded the door to unlock. "Done."

"Get out," she said.

He nodded and ran into the hall as fast as his feet could carry him.

Mei went to the side of the blacked-out wall, peering in through the cracked door. She could hear someone inside breathing calmly. "Gel!" she snapped. "I know you're there."

"Indeed, I am, Doctor Curie," said Gel from inside. "Come into my office so we might discuss your present situation."

She aimed her weapon through the opening. There was an empty desk and no one around it. "Show yourself, Gel!"

No answer.

She took a step forward, studying the room, trying to sense his location. Mei could hear him, his heartbeat and breathing, standing slightly to the right of the doorway, waiting, no doubt, to surprise her.

I don't think so, she thought, and swept the rifle around to greet him.

Gel stood motionless, unthreatened. "Hello, Doctor."

"I swear I'll shoot you where you stand if—"

He raised a hand and revealed a small blade, nearly striking her shoulder in the process. She dodged, barely avoiding it. "If what?" he asked, gripping the barrel of the rifle and stabbing at her stomach. "Fire away!"

She squeezed the trigger, but the weapon didn't fire. "What the—"

"Having trouble?" He sliced her arm, splitting the skin.

She screamed.

He stepped at her, holding out the small blade. "I've disabled that weapon, my dear doctor." He grinned. "Remember where you are!"

The knife came at her again, but she backed away before it could touch her, deflecting it with the barrel of the rifle.

"Bastard!" cried Mei, hitting him in the wrist with the gun.

He nearly dropped the knife, but managed to hold onto it. "You think you can do what you want. You forget yourself, Doctor. You forget where you are! You forget who I am!"

She ran behind the desk. "Back off!"

He charged, snatching her wrist and pinning her to the wall, holding the knife to her throat. "Quiet down, little girl," he said. "Drop the gun now."

She could feel the cold metal as the edge of the blade broke skin, releasing a thin line of blood.

The rifle fell to the floor as she released it.

"Are you afraid?" asked Gel, pulling her hair back so their eyes met. "I can feel you shaking, doctor. Trembling like an infant."

An explosion rang from beyond the building, coming from the city below. The lights flickered overhead. "Your city is dying," muttered Mei.

"Perhaps so," answered Gel. "Shall we go and have a look?"

She tried to move, but the knife dug into her. "Ungh!"

"Mind yourself," he told her.

Gel dragged her out of the office and through the now empty halls. He pushed her along, one step at a time. The pain from Mei's cuts burned as she walked. Her whole body ached, and for what? She had accomplished nothing.

Gel led her to a set of doors. "Here we are," he said.

Light pierced through as the metal slid open, revealing a gray sky. The landing platform was there before them, several ships docked and ready, a few more lifting off. "Garden thinks it can seize this city," said Gel. "But they're fools, just like you. Every soldier under my command is headed there to kill every last one of them, and I have a strike team ready to penetrate their command center. I was planning to give the order this evening, but it seems they're all rather eager to die."

He shuffled Mei to the edge of the platform overlooking the cityscape. The Hall of the Leadership, the largest building in Everlasting, blazed in fire as pieces of it lay scattered through the streets. Was Gel so blind that he couldn't see it?

She felt him stiffen, then relax. He cleared his throat. "It would seem my army has engaged the terrorists. Very good. Very good. Ah, yes, and now the invasion of their stronghold begins."

He must be receiving messages, thought Mei. *Maybe if I can—*

"If only you could live long enough to see the empire I will forge, perhaps you would understand, little doctor."

"There won't be anything left. Look at the smoke," she told him.

"From the rubble I shall build an empire like none other, and I shall use its strength to subdue both our worlds. Oh, if you could only see it, Doctor. If only you—"

She felt his body go rigid as another message came in. Something was happening.

I need to be ready, she thought, trying to focus. It was difficult with the knife at her throat. The adrenaline drove her to run, to flee, to do something—anything but stand there and be quiet—but she had to do it. She had to relax her mind.

She concentrated, pushing what she could manage, though it wasn't much, and a second later she heard the flutter of wings from far away, followed by shouts amid the madness underfoot. Screams echoed in the streets, followed by a spray of ammunition as the two factions engaged one another. Chaos was all around her, and she tried to close it out…shut it down the way John had…the way Terry did when he rescued her all those years ago, there in the Ortego facility, moments before she struck Alex in the chest and sent him tumbling into darkness… into death…

No, away with that. Away with anger. Away with fear.

Away with old regrets.

Away with all the weight.

That was when she felt it, a gentle relief, like weights lifting from her chest…and Mei Curie opened her eyes.

She took a long breath, filling her lungs, embracing the silence of a world under siege.

The air around her ceased to blow, and the smoke across the city no longer rose. There was only stillness left.

Only the moment.

She slid her neck along the knife, but the blade no longer cut.

In a fluid, single motion, she grasped his wrist and twisted it to aim the blade it at her captor's shoulder before pressing it into him, stabbing his flesh.

Gel fell to the ground, screaming. He tried to take the blade out, but Mei was already there, knees on his chest, hand around the knife.

She pushed against him, and though he tried with all his strength to move her, it was impossible.

Mei would not be shaken. Not anymore.

She gripped the Master Analyst by the throat, and with her other hand, yanked the dagger free.

His eyes went wide with terror as the blade came down again, plunging into his chest. He screamed.

"No!" cried Gel. "No, no, no!"

He tried to get up, but she continued to stab him. "Just die!" she yelled.

Blood filled his stomach and poured onto the platform, pooling around them. Mei looked down at her hands and was shocked at how red they were.

She backed off of him, leaving the blade inside him, watching as the self-proclaimed king of Everlasting dug the knife out with trembling hands.

He tried to stand, but collapsed on himself, screaming as he struck the ground. With one outstretched arm, he pulled his way to the side of the platform.

She ran to retrieve the knife, taking it for whatever came next.

But instead of getting up, Gel only turned to look at the city, lying motionless. She watched him from a distance, thinking he might be dead. After a long moment, the analyst stirred, licking his lips and blinking.

"Pitiful," he whispered.

She stared at him, saying nothing.

He shook his head. "Do you see them there? The people… like insects in the dirt…scurrying to live." He coughed and blood spewed out. "The walls are failing…soon the gas will come."

"What?" she asked.

"The gas, Doctor. It arrives to kill us all…to punish us for living. We don't belong here…we never did."

"The domeguard is failing?" she asked, but a second later, she felt it. The cold touch of a raindrop on her nose, followed by another.

He laughed, choking on his own fluids. "Everything is ending! Everything is done!" he cried as the shower fell.

Mei felt a panic in her chest. The people would die. All of them now. What could she hope to do?

Gel's eyes darted around, no longer focused. With a sudden gasp, he cried, and he reached with his hand toward the sky, grasping at the falling rain. "I did everything for them. I was good. I was—"

"You did it for yourself!" shouted Mei, dropping the knife from her hand. It clanged against the platform before tumbling off the side toward the blazing city below.

Gel watched it go. "I only wanted them to live," he whispered, staring out into the dying metropolis. "It was all for…"

He wheezed and gasped. "…It was all for the good of Everlasting."

As he spoke the words, his arm collapsed, and suddenly his face was cold and empty. It was done. Gel, the Master Analyst of Everlasting, was gone at last.

WHEN THE RED Door arrived at the Tower of the Cartographers, Johnathan Finn and his allies, old and new alike, unloaded from the side of the aircraft.

He had come seeking answers from Master Gel, the manipulator behind all of his problems, but it became evidently clear that there was no longer a need. The girl he was looking for was sitting on her knees at the edge of the platform, covered in blood next to the body of the one responsible.

John ran to her, grasping her whole body with both of his wide arms, kissing her soaking wet hair.

She threw herself into him.

"Oh my God! I'm so sorry, Mei! I'm so sorry! I didn't know what to do!"

Her fingers dug into his back, but she said nothing. She couldn't. Her entire body was trembling.

"Forgive me," he muttered, and suddenly he was crying, unable to stop. Unable to breathe.

They wept together, his tears covering hers, surrounded by a dying city, there in the freezing rain.

Terry left the Red Door with Jinel, noticing the downpour of rain. "This can't be good," he told her.

"The domeguard has fallen. We need to do something!" she said.

"Do what?" asked Terry.

"Evacuate," said Lena, stepping off the ship.

"To where?" asked Jinel.

"We have outposts," said Emile Res. "Are there any ships?"

"Not enough to carry a civilization," answered Jinel.

"Fair point," she answered. "There's not enough room for everyone, anyway. Each outpost can hold a few hundred at most."

"Then we shall need an alternate solution," remarked Lena.

"For now, I think getting everyone to safety is—"

The ground shook as another explosion erupted somewhere in the distance. "That can't be good," said Terry.

"The Citadel is held aloft using the city's power grid. If the shield is down, there's a chance this tower will fall," explained Lena.

"You mean this floating skyscraper is about to crash into the city?" asked Terry.

"Exactly that," responded Lena.

"How do we stop it?" asked Emile Res.

Lena looked at the building and then the sky. "There are multiple backup generators in place to prevent this exact scenario from unfolding. I don't understand why they haven't taken control, unless…"

"What?" asked Terry.

"They may have malfunctioned, but that's extremely unlikely," said Lena.

"Not when they've been sabotaged," said Jinel.

"What was that?" asked Terry.

"We had one of our people do it a few weeks ago. It was part of a plan to take out Master Gel. Our man was captured shortly afterwards, so we assumed the generators had been restored. It seems there was an oversight."

"To say the least," remarked Emile.

Lena bit her lip. "If this tower crashes into the city—"

"A lot of people would die," finished Terry. "We need to do something."

"I don't think we can," said Lena. She looked at Jinel. "How could your people do this?"

"I'm sorry," said the soldier, staring out into the cityscape. "I…"

"There's no time for your regrets," said Emile. "We need solutions!"

"Even if we could restore the generators, there's little time to do it. We need to evacuate the city. Get them to the shoreline. Can we do that?" asked Terry.

Lena thought for a moment. "Maybe. We would need access to the network. I could access it, given some time, but—"

"No need for that," said Emile. "I have administration rights. You can use my account."

"Great. Send it to each of us, please," said Jinel.

Emile's eyes dilated as she accessed the network. "I'm restoring your terminal access. One moment." She swiped her hands across the air in front of her. "There. I couldn't give you much, but you can now bypass level four protocols. That will give you access to the city's sound system."

"Perfect," said Jinel.

"We'll need a proper terminal," said Lena. "There are several inside. Let us go, quickly."

"How long before this thing collapses?" asked Terry.

"We have some time. It's enough to send a message to the rest of the city to leave," said Lena.

"Fine, but don't stay for too long. We'll be here waiting for you."

"I'll have the Red Door ready to go," said Emile.

Lena Sol and Jinel Din both ran into the Citadel. With any luck, they'd be able to get a message to the rest of Everlasting before it was too late.

Before this tower fell.

"Terry!" Mei came running from the end of the platform, barefoot with John's coat around her shoulders. "Oh, my God!"

They embraced. "Mei!" Terry answered.

"I can't believe it's you," she said.

"It is, believe it or not," he said, smiling. The platform shook, suddenly.

"We should probably get out of here soon!" yelled Emile, already on board the ship.

Terry sighed. "She's right. Looks like the reunion will have to wait."

"That's fine with me," said Mei. "I've had about as much as I can take of this place."

Lena made her way with Jinel to the second Analytics bay. "Here!" she told her. "Find a terminal and begin broadcasting."

"Right," she answered.

The network was chaotic, with multiple channels down and an array of panicked departments trying to comprehend the situation. With all of the Leadership wiped out, there was no one to give direction, no voice to tell the people what to do or where to go.

No matter. Lena Sol would have to be the voice in their ear. The last voice of a fallen city.

After only a few seconds, Lena had access to Everlasting's control system. "Are you in?" she asked her accomplice.

"I am," said Jinel.

"Begin instructing all occupants to evacuate through the seventh precinct's tunnel. Send the following coordinates."

"I have it," she said. "Sending now."

Lena sent commands to multiple offices at once all across Everlasting. Never before had she worked so quickly and with such fervor, but if ever there was a time for such a thing, it was now, here in this awful place.

The building shook. "We must hurry!" snapped Lena.

“Districts five through seventeen are evacuating,” followed Jinel.

“Eighteen through twenty-seven are as well,” said the analyst.

They continued, accessing each and every channel, sending orders to every citizen who could hear them.

The floor beneath them shuddered, tilting slightly. “It’s happening!” shouted Jinel.

“I haven’t finished!”

Jinel took her by the wrist. “There’s no time, Lena Sol! If we don’t go now, the Citadel will crash with us inside.”

“But—”

“Now!” shouted Jinel, pulling her away from the console.

They ran through the hall together, passing empty corridors and bays where there had once been hundreds of workers and analysts. Lena’s entire life of service.

The structure shook violently, like it was alive, knocking them both to the floor.

A nearby wall shook, dislodging a light fixture from the ceiling. It fell, landing slightly beside Lena. Her eyes went wide with fear.

“Get up!” ordered Jinel, snapping her out of it.

“Right,” muttered Lena, staring at the object that had nearly crushed her.

They kept moving to the exit, their progress made difficult by the shaking tower.

The light from outside shone through the outer doors as

they rounded the final corridor. "We're nearly there!" yelled Jinel.

Right as they neared the final stretch, another tremor overtook them, sending Lena to the floor.

Jinel hit the wall, still on her feet. As Lena struggled to stand, she heard her friend scream. "Move!"

The soldier knocked her forward, sending her out of the way of a falling piece of debris—a series of blocks used to separate the floors. "Jinel!"

"I'm okay!" she said, but the debris had filled the space between them, separating one from the other.

"Can you get through?" asked Lena.

"No, there's too much," she answered. "I'll have to find another way out."

"But the Citadel could fall before you make it!"

"I'll be fine. Get to the ship, quickly! You must not delay!"

"But—"

"Do as I say, Analyst!" ordered Jinel.

"Keep your implant open and let me know when you're out. We'll retrieve you."

"Go now!" she demanded.

Reluctantly, Lena fled, leaving the facility the way she had arrived. When she found the landing platform, everyone was already waiting inside the Red Door. "Where's Jinel?" asked Terry.

"She's inside," explained Lena. "She couldn't get out, but she's going to another exit. We have to wait for her."

"I don't know if there's time," said Emile from the cockpit.

The tower trembled, tilting slowly as its power continued to fail. The Citadel was going down, and there was nothing anyone could do to stop it.

JINEL DIN SAT inside the crumbling tower, her back against the wall, waiting for the inevitable. She had no intention of getting out of here. If Lena Sol had taken a moment to consider the situation, she would have realized that the nearest exit was too far removed from this location to be of any use.

Jinel let out a long sigh behind her breathing mask. *Pity it had to turn out this way,* she thought.

"Jinel, can you hear me?" came a voice. It was the analyst, by the sound of it.

"I'm here," said Jinel Din.

"We are in the air. Did you find a way out?"

"Not quite, no," she answered, staring at the fallen chunks of ceiling beside her. "I'm afraid there'll be no escape for me this time."

"What are you talking about? I thought you had a way out of there?"

"I only told you that to get rid of you," said Jinel.

"But—"

"There's no time for arguments," she told her. "Go with your friends. It's okay."

"No, it's not!" shouted Lena Sol. "You can't give up so easily! What kind of woman would that make you?"

The tower drifted, beginning its descent. She could feel the momentum. "A practical one, I'm afraid."

"What about your people? What about Garden? Without you, they'll—"

"Need someone else," she finished. "You'll do a fine job of that, Lena Sol. I have confidence in you."

"I'm no commander! Jinel Din, you mustn't do this!"

"It is already done, Analyst."

On the other end of the line, she could hear the girl choking on her words, trying to solve the situation with syllables and sentences, but there was no getting out of this. Not anymore. "You listen to me now, Lena Sol, and you listen with intent."

"I-I am," stuttered Lena.

Jinel took a long breath. "You must be strong now, do you understand? Stronger than you ever have been, for our people will need your experience and intelligence. They will need your strength to show them the way."

"I'm not that person. I—"

"You are, Lena Sol. I have seen it. Whatever you were when I met you, back when you were nothing but a junior analyst—that's not you, anymore. Do you understand?"

"Yes...yes," said Lena.

"Goodbye, Lena Sol," said Jinel Din, and she switched off the signal from her implant.

The tower broke, cracking at its core, knocking Jinel against the wall. Through the nearest window, which overlooked the cityscape, she could see the fires rising high.

"Better to die on your feet," the soldier told herself, and she struggled to stand. She gripped her rifle, holding it close to her chest, watching as the buildings came rapidly upon her, growing larger as the tower fell.

Jinel Din removed her mask, tossing it to the floor, and she took a breath of the toxic gas that now consumed everything. It burned like fire in her lungs.

She stared out at the oncoming sight before her, at the imminent doom that was fast approaching, riding the Citadel itself into perfect oblivion.

A full smile spread across her face.

Despite everything, she had to admit, this was one hell of a way to die.

18

Documents of Historical, Scientific, and Cultural Significance

Open Transcript 616

Subtitled: The Memoires of S. E. Pepper – Epilogue, added posthumously

March 19, 2268

PEPPER: *There is no greater joy in the history of the world, no better moment in a person's life, than when they hold their child for the first time. If it isn't already known, let me say now that such a feeling is doubled when it is your grandchild.*

My daughter Julia likes to say I've entered my golden years, as though this is something new for me. I've had grey hair now for two decades, I tell her, but she insists that no, I'm only getting there now because I'm finally a grandparent. Maybe she's right. I must admit I have a newfound sense of comfort, staring in the eyes of our little Ava.

She is, without a doubt, the most beautiful thing I've ever seen. How happy I am that I could live long enough to see her.

And I've been lucky. Much more than most.

To survive the end of the world and still live long enough to meet this tiny, little thing with arms and toes and eyes. To see that even after Armageddon, life can still go on. Humanity can survive.

My Julia and her darling Ava are part of that, I know. They are, not what the world is, but what it has the potential to become. They're all my hopes and fears, my intimate desires, my waking dreams.

In all my days, I have loved only a few as fully as I do them, and I have enjoyed these moments. Despite everything else, I am happy with what I was given. Somehow, here in this city, so far below the surface, nearly a century after the world was killed, I can say with all my heart that I lived a full and brilliant life.

And it was enough. It was good.

So, I think…I think I'm ready to see my father again, if all the fairy tales are true.

And I hope that they are, despite my doubts, because I'd like to tell him about all of this…about my sweet, beautiful girls and the joy they've given me. I want to tell him that everything turned out okay, after all.

Whatever place he's in…if it's really there like they say…then, it must be something beautiful, don't you think?

It must be something wonderful.

End Audio File

The Red Door
April 3, 2351

Terry watched the Citadel fall into the city, slamming into several buildings, creating a massive explosion of fire and dust. The entire center of Everlasting was engulfed in it, consumed by the tower's destruction. The sheer magnitude of it sent a shockwave so strong it nearly knocked him back.

He could only hope the civilians had escaped in time.

"I'm taking us out of the city!" shouted Emile, dipping the aircraft to the east.

They flew across the burning landscape. Terry watched through the window as smoke and rain filled most of the sky.

As they reached the evacuation area, he saw thousands of people running to get away from the city. Each wore a filtration mask to guard against Variant. Would they have to wear those things for the rest of their lives now? Without the protection of the domeguard to shield them from the gas, they might have no other choice.

Ludo, Ysa, Lena, John, and Mei each sat in the cabin beside him, with Emile Res in the forward pilot seat. They had come so far, each of them. So far alone and then together—half a dozen paths converging into this one moment.

But Jinel was gone, and so were many others, lost along the great path, never to walk beside him again. Their loss would eat at him, he knew. He would never be rid of it. But that was okay, because he didn't want to lose them. He didn't want to give up his grief.

The Red Door landed in the field outside Everlasting, not far from where the surviving citizens had gathered. Lena disembarked from the ship first, followed by the others. She ran to the crowd, telling them to head to the shore.

Ludo and Ysa helped, and while many Everlastians were surprised to see the two natives, all sense of discomfort and bigotry they might have felt quickly melted away. The husband and wife led the crowd forward, guiding them through the wilderness.

John remained in the aircraft with Mei, tending to her as best he could.

Over the next few hours, the crowds migrated to the beach, slowly moving through the rocky hills and woods outside the city. These people were unaccustomed to traversing rough terrain, having spent their entire lives comfortably inside Everlasting. It made them slow and clumsy.

A few hours after most of the civilians arrived at the shoreline, John and Mei departed on the ship to return to their camp in an effort to gather supplies. With any luck, Central would be able to deliver some relief to the now homeless Everlastians.

Still, there was the issue of survival. In a world as violent as Kant, Terry couldn't help but wonder how such an out-of-touch people could ever hope to endure. Not without some serious adjustment on their part.

Perhaps with a little help, they could do it. *We'll see*, thought Terry, but he tried to stay optimistic.

The Red Door lifted off the ground, and he waved farewell to John and Mei as they left the crowded beach behind. Hux would not arrive for a few days, but once he did, they'd have a little more help.

Everyone would have to come together if they hoped to save these people. Even then, it might not be enough.

Bravo Gate Point
April 3, 2351

Mei arrived, disembarking as fast as her feet would let her. She ran straight from the Red Door to her CHU, ready to change out of these awful clothes and shower. As much as the rain had washed away, she could still feel the blood on her.

John gave her some space while she took care of herself. Somehow, he seemed to know she needed it. And she did.

The image of Gel's body was still fresh in her mind, and while she wanted nothing more than to be with John right now, she also wanted to get this stench off her body. The scent of that room, the scent of the blood.

After scrubbing herself down for what must have been an hour, she emerged in new clothes and damp hair to find John waiting patiently with Sophie.

The assistant leapt to her feet, running to embrace her. The action surprised Mei, but she wrapped her arms around the girl and returned the hug. "Welcome back, Doctor Curie," said Sophie.

"Thank you," she answered.

"Sergeant Finn just told me everything. I knew you were alive. I just knew it." The girl's smile was bigger than Mei had ever seen it.

"I'm just glad to be back," said Mei.

"Shall I call the rest of the team together?"

"Not yet," said Mei. She wasn't in the mood for the attention. In fact, she would have given anything to go and lie down in her bed right now, but that wasn't going to happen. Tired as she was, she knew where to put her priorities. "Tell me everything that's happened since I left."

"Yes, ma'am! Oh, you'll be happy to know I kept working after you left. On the inoculations, I mean to say."

"On Lanrix?" asked Mei.

Sophie nodded. "Yes, that's it. I wanted to have something to show you when you returned."

"Oh, Sophie. I'm sorry I wasn't here to help, but I heard about the work you did, and I'm proud of you."

"You already know?" asked Sophie, a little disappointed.

"Yes. They let it slip when I was there. How much have you synthesized?"

"Several hundred doses to date, but more are on their way from Central as we speak."

"That many?" asked John.

"An impressive amount, but not enough for what we need," said Mei. "That crowd numbered in the thousands. Maybe more."

"They have their masks. They can wait while you get more," he answered.

Mei nodded. "I'm sure you're right."

"Hux's ship should be there in three or four days. How much can you make by then?" asked John.

"Who is Hux?" asked Sophie.

"It's a complicated story, but he's some kind of pirate or ship captain. I'm not really sure," said John. "But he has a large crew who can help us with distribution."

"I see," said Sophie. "Well, in any case, you said three or four days? I believe we can make several hundred doses by that time."

"I'll be here to help," said Mei.

"You two do your thing. I'm off to regroup with the Blacks. We'll need to start lifting food and supplies to the survivors. Sophie, you think you can open a channel up to Central for me?" asked John.

"Indeed, I can, Sergeant Finn," said the assistant, smiling. "Anything for bringing Doctor Curie back to us."

"Alright, boys," said John. "Let's get this cargo on the ship and head out."

"You sure this is right, Boss?" asked Track, looking over a package of miracle fruit, which had originally been a gift from Everlasting to Central.

"Yep, we're sending it back. Accept it," he answered.

Track frowned. "But I like this stuff so much. Can we have a quick bite?"

"Are you trying to take food out of starving mouths?" asked Short. "I'm shocked, Track."

"Hey, they only just evacuated. They're not starving yet!"

John smacked the crate. "Even still, they'll need it. Get this package on the ship, ASAP."

Track sighed. "You got it, Boss."

They had to move supplies in shifts, with the Red Door constantly moving. Emile claimed not to mind the extra work. She took brief naps when she wasn't in the air. After nearly a full day of back-and-forth, the Blacks had dropped most of Bravo Point's food.

It was exhausting work for everyone, but no one complained when it came to saving lives.

John found Terry and Lena helping Ludo and the others in the field near the shore. "Sorry I couldn't join you guys sooner, but the day's been wearing on me," he told his friend.

"Not to worry," said Terry. "We've had our hands full, too."

"Do you have a headcount yet?" asked John.

Terry glanced at the crowds. "There's no way to know, but I'd say we're dealing with tens of thousands. More are showing up every hour, though. Who knows how many we'll have when it's all said and done."

"There were sixty thousand people in Everlasting," said Lena.

"With any luck, we'll have most of them here," said Terry.

John hoped so, but given the sheer destruction in the city, he had his doubts. Master Gel's tower had obliterated most of what remained of the bustling metropolis. No doubt, many had been killed in the blast. "Any sign of Garden or ranking city officials yet?"

Lena shook her head. "A few lower end military personnel, but no one of note," she said. "The Leadership is gone. I suspect most of Garden is, too."

"What makes you say that?" asked John.

"Gel attacked their last remaining stronghold. Most of them were killed."

"All those people," muttered John.

Lena handed a piece of fruit to a nearby woman and her child. "There you are," she told them, smiling warmly.

"We'll have the first batch of inoculations here tomorrow. Mei is getting them ready as we speak," said John.

"You're sure they'll work?" asked Terry.

"Sophie is, which means Mei is, which means I am," he said.

"Good," said Terry. "Then it means I am, too."

"Stay still," said Mei, holding the inoculation to Lena's arm. The good doctor had assured her that the medicine would allow her to breathe the air, but her fears were getting the best of her. "Take a second if you have to. Relax."

Lena Sol nodded, trying to calm herself. "I'm ready," she said, extending her arm.

Doctor Curie stuck the injector into Lena's arm. She felt the sting, but it lasted only a moment. "There."

Lena felt her heart racing. "How long until I can remove my mask?"

"Sophie will tell you," said Curie. "Go sit over there and wait a bit."

Lena did as she was told, resting on the ground as she waited. Would she really be able to breathe the atmosphere after this? The very idea of it seemed impossible.

"You okay?" asked Terry, walking over to her side.

"As soon as this is done, I will be," she answered.

He joined her in the grass. "Don't worry. Sophie said they did this to a few other people from Everlasting and it worked fine."

"Of course," said Lena. She knew what he said was true, but still, the anxiety persisted.

"Maybe you're worried you'll be like me," said Terry, a bit of humor in his voice. "It's scary, I know."

"No," she said, closing her eyes and taking a deep breath. "This is what I want. It's good."

"It is," he agreed.

She smiled, and felt herself relax a bit. "Thank you."

Sophia Mitchell joined them a moment later, a digital pad in her hand. "Are you ready?" she asked.

"I am," answered Lena.

"When you remove the mask, you may find it difficult to breathe for a few seconds, but don't worry. That is normal. Your airways will open and promptly adjust."

Lena nodded, then took her finger and hooked it behind the

back of her mask. She looked at Sophia Mitchell for confirmation.

"Go ahead," said the woman.

"You've got this," Terry told her. He placed his hand on her knee. "And I'm here with you."

"Okay," she said, and removed the mask at once, accidentally dropping it.

She felt the thickness of the air as it entered her nose and mouth, tasting the bittersweet aroma. She gasped, unintentionally, and took the air in, nearly choking.

The air caught in her throat, stuck for a fraction of a moment, and then it all opened.

She gasped, suddenly, and breathed a deep breath, as though for the first time.

The gas filled her lungs, burning only a little, and then not at all. She coughed, licking her lips and wiping her eyes. "Oh!" she exclaimed.

Sophia Mitchell regarded her, tapping her pad. "Another successful transition. Congratulations." She turned and went to her next patient, a young middle-aged man.

"Are you okay?" asked Terry.

"I…" Lena's voice trailed as she inhaled the unfamiliar air which only moments ago could have killed her. "I think I am."

He gave her a knowing smile. "How is it?"

She closed her eyes, breathing again. The air no longer tasted bitter, no longer smelled of poison. Now, it was different, almost sweet. How had it changed so quickly? "It feels…good," she said, happily. "I don't know why."

"It'll get better," he told her. "The more time you're in it, the more you live in it, it'll get better."

"Truly?" she asked.

"Wait and see for yourself," he told her.

"I think that I shall," she said, looking out across the crowd. "I think I would like that very much."

Hux arrived in the late morning with a cloudless sky. The winds were strong on the journey to Everlasting's shore, so he found his way faster than expected.

Terry was relieved at this, for he had missed his friend, and looked forward to seeing him again.

The wavemaster set his crew to helping where extra hands were needed. These were capable and strong sailors with a penchant for work, and a strength that only the sea could give.

"Where is Ludo?" asked Hux, after seeing the crowds of Everlastians. "What of Ysa? Has everyone survived?"

"The two of them are fine, but there were problems," explained Terry, and he went on to tell him of Jinel's sacrifice.

A long frown formed on the sailor's face. "I'm sorry, my friend. She was a good warrior."

"She was," he repeated. "We've lost too many."

"What of the cargo?" asked Hux.

"Leave it for now. We'll figure out what to do with it later."

They found Ludo a while later, giving instructions to several Everlastians. He was trying to explain how to build a fire, among other things. "Ah, Hux!" exclaimed the farmer, once had saw his friends approach.

Hux beat his chest and Ludo returned it. "Good to see you, kind Ludo."

"You as well!"

"What are you doing over here?" asked Terry.

"Tora Ken is asking about fire, while little Jora Zur wishes to know about the local animals, and Sidda Mes says—"

"I want to know about the plants," interjected a small girl. Her mask was off, which meant she'd already gone to see Mei and Sophie.

"Yes!" said Ludo, happily. He smacked his chest. "Everyone has questions, so I am trying to give answers."

"How is the farmer doing?" Hux asked the crowd.

"He's very knowledgeable," answered an older woman.

"Better than anyone else we've talked to," said a man.

Ludo laughed. "They flatter me, these kind people."

"I think, dear Ludo, you might have a talent for this," remarked Hux.

"What's that?" asked Ludo.

"He means teaching," explained Terry. "I agree, too. You seem pretty good at it."

The farmer laughed, waving them off. "You go too far, my friends, but thank you! I only wish to help."

Mei and her team worked for days, almost nonstop, in an effort to inoculate every surviving Everlastian citizen. As expected, there were a small handful of complications, but no fatalities or serious damage, much to her relief.

By the twelfth day, they'd dispensed doses to nearly everyone. It had taken the entire sum of her team's energy, including Zoe, Bartholomew, Sophie, Tabata, and the nearly three dozen personnel sent by Central to assist. Between everyone, including the Blacks and Hux's crew, they found a way of getting the job done, however clumsily, and somehow it worked.

The Everlastians who had already been dosed also pitched in, offering their assistance. Mei was reserved to take it, but she had little choice. The decision turned out to be a good one, as many of the former citizens showed some aptitude for regulated tasks.

Later, when she could step away, allowing herself to delegate the bulk of her work to Sophie and the others, she found John and Terry and stepped away with them, heading quietly to the beach for a much-needed break.

They sat in the sand, staring out into the waves. John wrapped his arm around her, pulling her close to his chest, and gently rubbing her back. It calmed her, and she smiled.

They lingered there together for a while, enjoying the quiet moment as only old friends can.

Behind them, a mighty fire had grown, blazing further down the beach. Ludo's doing, of course. They could hear his jolly laugh all the way down here.

"Should we join them?" asked Terry.

"Maybe in a bit," answered Mei. "Let's wait a bit."

"I'm with the squirt here," said John.

She punched him in the stomach. "Watch yourself, Giant."

Terry laughed. "We can stay as long as you guys want."

"Not that it matters," said John.

"What's that?" asked Mei.

"Well, when we're done, we can all go home. No more of this craziness. Not for a while, anyway."

"Oh, yes," said Mei, relieved to hear it. "I could use a vacation."

"Maybe we can spend some time in Central. It's been a long time since we had a good night at the plaza."

"Pepper Plaza? That's right. There's the café you like," said Mei.

"Virgil's Diner," John reminded her. "They've got the best soy burgers in the city."

Terry laughed. "Some things never change, I guess."

Mei sunk into John's arms. "Some things do."

"Yeah," said John, looking down at her with that innocent, but strong expression. Oh, how warm it made her feel to look into those eyes. How at home she felt, even on another world.

"I guess they do," said Terry, smiling at them both.

"What about you?" asked John.

"Me?" asked Terry.

"You must be excited to go home after all this time. Oh, man, wait until you see what's happened. We're not even in the city anymore. There's outposts all over the surface," said John.

"That's amazing," said Terry.

"Plus, you'll finally get to choose a last name," added John. "You must have something good picked out by now."

The notion surprised him. He hadn't given a surname much consideration since he was marooned on this world. Now that he thought about it, he wasn't even certain he wanted one. "Not really," he finally answered. "But I'm open to suggestions."

"How about Terry Finn?" asked John, chuckling. "We could be brothers."

Mei shook her head. "John, that's silly. He has to choose a name he likes. Something with meaning."

"How did you choose yours?" asked Terry.

"I named myself after a scientist," she explained. "Someone that inspired me."

"Boring," said John, faking a yawn.

Terry looked at him. "What about you?"

John grinned. "Huckleberry Finn is my favorite book."

"Here we go," said Mei.

"A book?" asked Terry, blinking. "Didn't we read that at the Academy?"

John nodded. "Sure did. It was the best."

"So, wait, does that mean you named yourself after—"

"A fictional character," finished Mei, rolling her eyes. "Don't get me started."

"Ignore her, Terry. She's just jealous, naming herself after some boring biologist."

"Chemist and physicist, actually," corrected Mei.

"Same thing," said John.

"Still, those are both great names," said Terry. He looked out into the ocean, staring at the flowing waves, quietly reflecting.

"What's wrong, Terry?" asked Mei.

"It's nothing important," he said.

"Hey, come on," she insisted, and sat up. "It's been a while, but I can still tell when something's bothering you. Tell me what it is."

Terry twisted his lip. "It's a lot to think about, that's all."

"What is?" asked John.

"Going home. Everything. I don't know what to think or how to feel about it. It's just—"

"You aren't sure?" asked John. "But you've been marooned here for years. Don't you wanna leave?"

"I used to. Believe me, I wanted to get back there more than anything. I hated it here. The animals, the forests, the lack of food, being totally alone, but—"

Ludo let a loud whoop loose, his voice echoing along the shore, and the whole crowd laughed around the fire. The massive farmer clapped his hands as Hux and the other sailors beat their chests.

Terry smiled at the sight. The farmer looked happier now than he had in months. It filled Terry with so much joy. "I guess what I mean is…I'm okay now."

"It's alright, Terry. We get it," said Mei.

John looked at each of them, confused. "Hey, speak for yourself. What are you talking about?"

Mei smacked his knee. "He's got friends here. Pay attention."

"What about us? We're your friends, too," said John.

Terry raised his hands, defensively. "Hey, hey, I'm not saying I won't come back. I just don't know if I'm ready to leave yet."

"What else would you do?" asked Mei.

"Hux offered me a post on his ship. I was thinking about getting out there. You know, seeing the world. There's a lot more here than there is back home."

"That's true," admitted John, sighing. "There's not much else back on Earth except monsters and rocks, although we haven't gone too far yet."

"I'm sure that'll change once Mei cures everyone," said Terry.

"Not me," she said, shaking her head. "That was all Sophie."

"The girl's got skills," said John.

"She learns from the best," said Mei, smiling.

They all laughed.

"You have to promise, if you do this adventuring thing or whatever it is, that you'll come home and visit," said John.

"I will," said Terry.

"That's right," said Mei. "Don't make us come find you again. It was hard enough the first time. I had to rip a hole in the universe, in case you two forgot."

"You gonna keep bragging about that for the rest of our lives?" asked John.

"I just might," warned Mei. "It was a pretty big deal."

After days of celebration, Hux agreed to return to Tharosa with several Everlastians, including Lena Sol. Together, they would meet with the queen to open official trade discussions and request additional provisions and assistance in establishing a new city.

Ludo agreed to stay with the survivors, who seemed in desperate need of his help. He offered his guidance on fishing, hunting, and planting crops, new skills that the Everlastians would have to know if they hoped to survive this new world.

Additionally, the orinchalium cargo was left behind in order to help establish a new colony. The survivors would need the precious metal to forge new weapons. There were still several other automated Guardians patrolling the border, and they would need to be destroyed in time.

As for Terry, he would act as an ambassador of Earth, joining Hux and Lena on a journey overseas. It was decided that the show of unity between their three countries would go a long way in laying the future groundwork of a treaty. Terry was just happy to be at sea with his friends.

John and Mei watched from the shore as the boat set sail, waving. "Make sure you call us when you get there!" yelled John.

Terry smiled, returning the motion.

He clicked a small device in his palm, something John had given him to help them stay in touch. It was of Everlastian design and used the only remaining satellite in orbit to communicate directly with the Red Door. This way, John had said, they could remain in constant contact. Terry was happy to have it, because it meant his friends would never be more than a phone call away. It was the greatest gift he could have asked for. "John, do you hear me?" he asked, speaking into the device.

"Loud and clear," responded his friend.

"Can you do me a favor whenever you get back to Central?" asked Terry.

"Sure thing. Whatcha need?"

"Get a message to my mother," said Terry. "My sister, too, if you can. Tell them I'm okay. Tell them I'm happy."

He could see John smile, far across the waves. "Of course I will. You got it."

"One more thing," said Terry. "If you don't mind."

"Anything," said John.

"I decided on a name last night. I stayed up late thinking about it, but you'll have to tell me if it's any good. You want to hear it?"

"Oh man, you know I do," said John.

Terry took a long breath, surprised at how nervous he was. He'd never given himself a name before. "It's Echols," he finally said. "You think that's okay?"

"After your mother?"

"That's right," he answered.

"I think it fits you," said John. "Terry Echols."

"Tell her for me, okay? Tell her I'm sorry I couldn't come home yet, but I hope to see her again soon. Tell her this name is for her and everything she did for me."

"I'm sure she'll appreciate it," said John.

"One last thing," said Terry. "I want you to find Janice, my sister, and check up on her. See how she's doing. You don't have to tell her about me or anything. I just want to know if she's okay."

"I will, Terry," said John. "You have my word. I promise you I will."

The ship left the bay, slipping through the opening in the great wall and entering the sea. Terry watched until he could no longer see the beach, until the figures faded into a distant haze and all that was left was the sea. "Goodbye," whispered Terry, but kept staring at the horizon.

"We'll see them soon enough," said the woman beside him.

He turned to look at Lena smiling at him in the Variant air. "I know we will," he answered. A hard wind blew, tossing his long hair. He glanced down at the device in his hand. "They're not so far away anymore."

"No, they're not," she said, placing her fingers on his. "But the road ahead will be long. There is much to do."

"Enough for a lifetime, I hope," Terry Echols answered, looking out across the sea, toward the rising suns.

Lena Sol smiled. "Maybe even for two."

EPILOGUE

THE AUDITORIUM WAS silent as the professor concluded her lecture. The middle-aged woman, the most respected and prominent figure in all of Central, stared out across the nearly two hundred graduate students, each of whom looked on with fascination.

"There you have it," she told them, flicking her nail as she glanced up at the holographic display—a transcript of an old journal entry. "The complete history of the Second Jolt and the early years of the subsequent Variant Expansion."

"Thank you very much, Professor Curie," said Professor Milton. "Does anyone have any questions? Please, students, it's not every day that you have the chance to talk with such a prominent figure."

Curie motioned at the man. "Enough of that."

A young girl a few rows back raised her hand. "Professor,

how long after that did you become the new director of the Science Division?"

"Five years," answered Curie. "Although I never asked for it. The board needed someone who spent time in Kant, so they asked me to fill the position. I nearly declined, but my husband pushed me into it."

A boy two rows from the front raised his hand. "Did you ever see Ludo and Hux again?"

"Oh, yes. Ludo and Ysa became well-respected members of the Everlastian council. I saw them at least once a year. As for Hux, he nearly became king of Tharosa, if you can believe it."

Everyone laughed.

"As I expected, the old pirate couldn't give up his sea legs, so Barniby took the crown instead. Hux is currently helping us chart our own oceans. Last I heard, he was somewhere in the Atlantic with Doctor Mitchell's team, cataloging new species along the coast of Africa. Very exciting."

"What about Terry?" asked someone in the front row. A young boy with black hair.

Curie smiled when she heard the name. "Oh, he stayed rather busy after that. I'm sure many of you heard about the events in the Cataclysm Vaults. It was quite the ordeal."

The door in the rear of the auditorium opened and a man walked in. He waved at her, pointing to his stomach and frowning.

Curie clicked a small handheld device and switched the display off. "The rest will have to wait for another time, I'm afraid. It seems my time with you has come to an end. I hope this lesson has proven valuable to your studies. Please, remember, the world needs minds like yours to keep us looking forward. It's been forty-three years since we first discovered Kant, and in that time we have done more than anyone ever dreamed, but the journey is not over yet, nor should it ever be. Many of your own ideas will lay the foundation of what comes next, so please don't keep them bottled up. That's not what we're about. I challenge you to bring those thoughts to the forefront. Don't be afraid to counter traditional thought and renew our collective sense of curiosity. Believe that a brighter future is coming, and then make it happen. That is my request."

As she left the podium, the auditorium exploded into thunderous applause, which continued until she closed the door behind her, joining the man, her husband, in the outer hall. "What a show," he said, raising his brow and grinning. "You really riled them up back there."

"Just trying to motivate the kids," she said, holding his hand.

"Not bad for an old lady," he said. It was a joke they often made, since neither had aged much in forty years. They were in their sixties, but each had the appearance of someone in their late thirties.

"Thank you," she said, winking. "Did you decide on dinner yet?"

"I was thinking Virgil's, if you're up for it. I've got a hankering for soy burgers. Maybe a chocolate shake." He grinned.

"Oh, John. You're such a child," she said, rolling her eyes.

"Maybe so, but you like it." He kissed her on the cheek. "Don't try to lie."

She giggled, squeezing his hand. "I do," she said as they made their way down the steps of the Central Institute of Technology. "God help me, I really do."

For more updates, join the Facebook group and become a Renegade Reader today.

-Read on for a special note from the author-

AUTHOR NOTES

You really never know where you're going to end up in life. I wrote the first sentence of the Amber Project when I was sitting behind a desk at Verizon Wireless, waiting to close the store for the night. I typed the words down thinking this would be a short story, probably something about a kid having a really lousy birthday (Maybe he'd wind up in a car accident. Maybe he'd experience some trauma). I had no idea, because it was just a thing I was writing to kill time before I could go home and play some PlayStation before bed.

I never dreamed it was going to take me this far. I think I probably would have laughed in your face if you tried to tell me otherwise.

But, that was seven years ago. I was in my mid-twenties, totally lost in life. I'd gone to college and graduated, and then I just sort of floated around for a bit. I told myself, you'll figure this out. Don't worry. All you need is some direction.

But nothing ever came, and while I'd like to tell you I had my lightbulb moment sitting in that store, that's not really how it goes. Not for most of us, anyway. Something happens, like a seed of an idea, an inkling of a notion, and then it just builds, maybe a little every day. One thing leads to another and eventually you're in another place, living another life, all thanks to a series of moments.

After writing fifty pages of that book, I set it aside for about a year. I went and joined the Air Force, which took me across the country and into a new career. It was a fantastic experience (mostly) and it allowed me to get my Master's Degree in Creative Writing while occasionally plugging away at the same old manuscript. I wrote and rewrote it, making rare, slow progress, often putting it away in a digital drawer and later returning. I didn't finish it until my military term was up, but once I did, it felt like a massive weight had been lifted.

That was two years ago and I've been writing ever since, determined to see this project through to the end. I never dreamed I'd be capable of an entire series, but somehow it happened, and I'm glad it did. I've written five books (to date), met a ton of interesting authors all over the country, and corresponded with readers from across the globe. It's allowed me to do the thing I love each and every day, and it's brought me into contact with an entire world I never believed was possible.

Those things only happened because people like you bought my books. You changed my life for the better, and you're the only reason any of this exists—the only reason I was able to keep going after I published that first book. Without an audience, I suspect I wouldn't have made it very far at all.

I didn't grow up reading books, not because they weren't available to me, but because my school didn't put much importance on the subject. It wasn't until I was older that I learned how a story could move me, sometimes even force me to think, to make me reevaluate my views.

It all started with Narnia when I was thirteen. I met Ender a few years later, and then I found Atticus Finch and Gatsby after that. I learned to value stories for what they were: portals to other worlds. Gateways to alternate realities made up of people I wanted to know, people I wanted to hate. Friends and enemies, acting out their lives on fallen trees, set in binding.

Somewhere along the way, I started writing my own. I never thought they would grow into a career, but life is funny like that.

We never see the path before us until we've taken it. Even then, we rarely stop to appreciate it.

I hope you'll come along with me as I continue to explore the wilderness and take new risks. There are still so many stories to tell, beginning with The Renegade Star Series, which you can find **exclusively on Amazon** right now.

As always, my dear friends, thanks for reading,

J. N. Chaney

PS. Amazon won't tell you when my next book will come out, but there are several ways you can stay informed.

1) **Fly on over to the Facebook group, JN Chaney's Renegade Readers**, and say hello. It's a great place to hang with other sarcastic sci-fi readers who don't mind a good laugh.

2) **Follow me directly on Amazon**. To do this, head to my Amazon author profile and click the Follow button beneath my picture. That will prompt Amazon to notify you when I release a new book. You'll just need to check your emails.

3) **You can join my mailing list by going to** https://www.jnchaney.com/variant-saga-subscribe. This will allow me to stay in touch with you directly, and you'll also receive a free copy of The Amber Project.

Doing one of these or **all three** (for best results) will ensure you know every time a new book is published. Please take a moment to do one of these so you'll be able to join me on the next adventure.

CONNECT WITH J.N. CHANEY

Join the conversation and get updates in the Facebook group called "JN Chaney's Renegade Readers." This is a hotspot where readers come together and share their lives and interests, discuss the series, and speak directly to J.N. Chaney and his co-authors.

https://www.facebook.com/groups/jnchaneyreaders/

He also post updates, official art, and other awesome stuff on his website and you can also follow him on Instagram, Facebook, and Twitter.

For email updates about new releases, as well as exclusive promotions, visit his website and enter your email address.

https://www.jnchaney.com/variant-saga-subscribe

Enjoying the series? Help others discover the *Variant Saga* by leaving a review on Amazon.

ABOUT THE AUTHOR

J. N. Chaney is a USA Today Bestselling author and has a Master's of Fine Arts in Creative Writing. He fancies himself quite the Super Mario Bros. fan. When he isn't writing or gaming, you can find him online at **www.jnchaney.com**.

He migrates often, but was last seen in Las Vegas, NV. Any sightings should be reported, as they are rare.

You can also actively engage with him on his Facebook group, **JN Chaney's Renegade Readers**.

Made in the USA
Coppell, TX
12 October 2021